THE HOLLY BIBBLE
OF BABBLE ON

Michael Paul Girard

Copyright © 1991 by Michael Paul Girard
United States Library of Congress
TXu000465820

All rights reserved. No part of this book may be reproduced by any
means without the prior consent of the Author, excepting brief quotes
in reviews.
For information email: mpg@michaelpaulgirard.com

A private, limited printing of 50 copies of this book was made by the
Author in July 1996 to share with family and friends.

First Published Printing: November 2014
RipRoRing pRess

ISBN: 978-0-692-27459-0

Cover Art & Book Design by the Author

For Chastity —
May you find again your youthful wonder
and aspire then to do great things.

"It's a cold,
and it's a broken Hallelujah."
—*Leonard Cohen*

~

"To be is to do."
—*Plato*
"To do is to be."
—*Aristotle*
"Do be do be do."
—*Sinatra*

From "The World's Best Loved Graffiti"
The Johnside Review, April 1999

Prelude

The turn of the millennium was being trumpeted by advertisers, Hell-holed by preachers and raving street-madmen. Some said the end of the world was near — Jesus would return to punish all sinners.

Others proclaimed it the best time to buy a new car.

Overture

In the waning weeks of 1999, Senator Bane's shriveled penis was a mournful reminder of his standing in the polls. Never had his popularity been so low. And he hadn't had an erection since early July.

With the U.S. Congress in winter recess, the 53-year-old lawmaker was back in his Birmingham office. Five empty boxes of doughnuts lay strewn on his desk (his morning breakfast!) Food had become a replacement for sex. The desire was there but the wangger unwilling. So the Senator now was in excess of 300 pounds.

Bane swung his hippo-sized haunches in the big swivel chair and turned toward the window. His view from nineteen floors up was blurred by the rain. For the umpteenth time since the trial ended last June, the Senator's brain replayed the events that led to the limpening of both cock and career:

The previous January, Senator Bane and his wife Dolores attended a premier at The New York Museum of Modern Art. *Crucifax*, the latest work by Jon LaRue was to be unveiled. At the time, the name Jon LaRue was not well known outside New York art circles. His most celebrated work during that era was *Book Burning Bush* — a performance art piece during which he set fire to his pubic hair on the steps of The New York Public Library.

The notoriety LaRue gained after the performance of *Book Burning Bush* secured him a quarter-million dollar grant from the Government to further the development of his budding artistic talents. Senator Bane wanted to witness first-hand what the taxpayers were getting for all that money.

The evening began inauspiciously enough: an art museum filled with high society types nibbling caviar on crackers and sipping red wine served by flamboyant homosexual waiters. In the center of the room stood a wooden outhouse with a crescent moon cut in the door. It reminded the Senator of his childhood days on a farm in rural Alabama. Sprinkled throughout the well-to-do crowd were the *artistes:* the pretentious poets, painters, and posers who longed to be government funded like LaRue. The *artistes* could be spotted not only by their offbeat hairdos and rummage sale clothing, but more by they way they gobbled and guzzled the free catered food and wine. Some even brought along doggie bags to maximize their quarry.

Fat Lucius Bane and his tubby wife Dolores made their way through the sophisticated crowd. At that time the Senator was a cottonseed shy of 280 pounds. His wife weighed in at a solid 220. Together they cut a swath through the tuxedoed minglers like two beached whales at a picnic for penguins. Moving unswervingly toward the table of food, making small talk along the way, Lucius and

Dolores's hillbilly accents left pockets of snickering whispers in their wake. But once the *artistes* in the crowd caught wind that the over-stuffed hayseed was Chairman of the Senate Arts Committee, they sucked up to him like flies on a two-day-old turd.

One of the *artistes* told the Senator he aspired to paint a circle around New York "...as a signal to extraterrestrials."

One wanted to start a Circus for Crickets. Another had written a One Woman Play that consisted of only two words. Each claimed their project would "...revolutionize Art," or "...change the course of Western Civilization." One even claimed he had written a musical "...that *must* be performed within the next two years to save the world from total annihilation."

Just as this particular grant-seeker began telling the Senator the storyline of his world-saving musical, the gallery suddenly went dark. A murmur of muttering spread through the room as a flurry of activity could be heard from the vicinity of the outhouse. Ear-splitting clanks of hammers against nails jarred the upper-crust crowd into silence. The hammering sounds ended abruptly. A crimson-red spotlight ripped across the room: revealing the featured artist Jon LaRue. Only his face was touched by the beam, creating the appearance that his head was suspended in mid-air. His dark beard and shoulder-length hair blended into the blackness that swam like an oil-spill around him. Two eyes the color of coal stared unflinchingly outward like taxidermy marbles. Lips pursed tightly as if enduring excruciating pain.

The spotlight began to widen, shifting from crimson to El Greco green. Gasps rippled through the shocked gala crowd when they saw LaRue's blood-dripping outstretched hands impaled to the outhouse door. A six-inch spike shish-ka-bobbed his feet. He hung there completely naked except for a small crown of thorns that encircled his scrotum. And to bottom it off, a .357 Magnum was hanging precariously out of his ass. The crowd *oohed* and *ahhed* at first sight of the impaled artist. Senator Bane was so aghast he farted.

The lighting changed from El Greco green to a vitamin-rich-urine-yellow as Jon LaRue twisted his agonized body, causing the outhouse door to creak open halfway. Inside, a fax machine was perched over the toilet hole. With a whir and a hum some fax-paper rolled from the machine like a tongue in slow motion. A woman, dressed as a nun, walked up and tore off the freshly spewed paper. "These messages," she announced to the mouth-agape crowd, "are being faxed here from all around the world!"

Small pockets of applause erupted in the room and spread like herpes in a hot tub.

"This one is from Oslo, Norway!" the nun yelled before reading aloud from the page: "It says: 'Follow me, I will make you fishers of men!'"

One of the swishy-bunned waiters was overheard commenting: "Mm, sounds yummy."

Again, the applause was sporadic at first. But when the socialites noticed the enthusiasm of the *artistes,* they clapped as if begging an encore from a pianist at Carnegie Hall.

The faux nun tore off another piece of fax paper and handed it to a mustachioed man in the crowd. "This one's from Berlin!" she called out, gesturing for the man to read it.

"'Blessed are the meek,'" recited the man with a thick Brooklyn accent, "'for they shall inherit the earth!'"

The applause became thunderous, led by the *artistes*. The socialites followed like lemmings. A voluptuous woman in a *Bob Mackey* gown, with cleavage busting out like spring all over, wiggled up to the outhouse and grabbed the next fax, eager to show off her new dress and liposuction.

"From Buenos Aires!" she proclaimed, then read with bravura: "Take no thought for your life, what ye shall eat; neither for the body, what ye shall put on!"

The museum crowd whistled and whooped, spilling wine from wildly clapping hands. *Crucifax*, by Jon LaRue was a hit. An esteemed art critic for *The New York Times* would later spume a gusher of praise from the bottomless well of an online thesaurus.

"Well I never—!" hissed Dolores, the Senator's wife, her eyes bulging *Beaujolais*-red.

Lucius stood next to her. Arms crossed. Scowling. Motionless as a wooden tobacco store Indian Chief. He didn't know much about art, by golly, but he damn well knew trash when he saw it!

Suddenly the pseudo-nun handed the Senator a fax message fresh from the crapper to which the artist was nailed: "It is easier to pass through the eye of a needle than it is to enter the Kingdom of God," Bane silently read. The message was sent from Colombo, Sri Lanka.

The Alabama Senator lost all control. Furiously, he crumpled the paper and tossed it at the naked man with skewered palms.

"Wait'll I git back to Washington, Young Man," Bane boomed in his deep Southern drawl, "I'll fix your squirrelly little wagon!"

He stormed for the exit with Dolores in tow. *Artistes* and socialites cleared a wide path.

"Let those without sin amongst you cast the first stone!" LaRue railed as the Banes made their exit toward the door.

Soon as the Senator got into the hallway, he up-chucked the crackers and caviar dip, coughing it into a round sandpit ashtray that stood by the elevator doors. Two or three gut wrenching volleys was all it took to fill the receptacle to the brim. With a monogrammed handkerchief she'd kept thirty years — since their wedding — Dolores bent down and wiped the drool from her husband's double chin.

The door leading into the gallery was open. The spittle-mouthed Bane and his Misses could see the crowd clapping inside, yelling "Bravo!" and "Brilliant!" and "More! Give us more!" The woman in the nun's habit took a theatrical bow. LaRue merely nodded his head in acknowledgement as blood dribbled down off his toes to the flowers the audience was throwing just beneath his carpentered feet.

"What's this world comin' to?" Bane wheezed as his wife wiped the slobber from both corners of his mouth. Then he heaved some more chunks from his stomach. They splashed in the chrome-rimmed ashtray swamp of puke and crumpled cigarette butts.

"Hey," quipped a stocky black security guard standing nearby the Banes, "Be sure you sign that ashtray before ya leave. It's better'n half the stuff that passes for art around here."

"What I saw last night," the Senator told the group of reporters assembled for a press conference the next day, "was an affront to decency and a crim'nal waste a' the taxpayer's money. I plan on findin' who's responsible and puttin' 'em in prison where they dang well belong!"

Polls showed public sentiment was firmly behind the Senator in his stand against "perverted art." His office was flooded with letters of support, not just from his constituents but from voters all over the country. Bane was getting national media attention that enhanced his stature on Capitol Hill. Best of all it brightened his prospects for a future run at the Presidency. As Chairman of the Senate Arts Committee, he convinced a Federal Prosecutor to file charges against LaRue for "misuse of public funds." The Prosecutor warned Bane that they were on shaky legal ground, but the Senator adamantly insisted. He felt confident that a jury of decent, hard-working American citizens would agree with him that La Rue's *Crucifax* was nothing more than sacrilegious smut. The government could then charge the overrated performance artist with misappropriating the money it gave him to create "a work of art." In Bane's mind, the case was ironclad.

In a matter of weeks, Lucius Arnold Bane went from obscure Alabama Senator to Household Name (a requisite for anyone with national political ambitions.) He became a sought after guest on TV talk shows and gave numerous interviews to newspapers and magazines. Reporters would be lying in wait at the Capitol steps every morning to register his comments. Cameras would flash as Bane stepped from his limo. Microphones would jab toward his flabby-jowled face. Suddenly the world became eager to hear what the Senator had to say about everything under the sun: be it depletion of the ozone layer or the latest War Over Oil.

It was February of 1999 when Senator Bane lunched with Republican Party leaders. The Chairman of the National Selection Committee spoke first:

"Lucius, we think you should run for office next year."

"Of course I'm gonna run, Gentlemen," the Senator replied in his congenial Southern manner, "You know I wouldn't go givin' up my seat to no Democrat."

"We're talking about the Presidency, Lucius."

Those words bounced around Bane's brain like two dice on a hot Vegas crap table. His career was on a roll. Nothing could stop him now. Every throw was coming up seven.

The movers and shakers of the Grand Old Party took turns citing reasons why Senator Bane could very well be the man to pave their way back into the White House:

"Recent polls show voter recognition of your name is running neck and neck with all the other candidates."

"We've had media analysts measure your 'likeability factor' from videos of your recent talk show appearances. All factors indicate you've got what it takes to mount a successful national campaign. Although most of the analysts agree you need to lose a few pounds."

"Why, Gentleman," the Senator blushed, "this whole thing's got me speechless. Abs'lutely speechless. Any a' you Boys ever heard of a politician bein' speechless?"

They all chuckled.

"You're our man, Lucius," said a Party stalwart, "all you have to do is say the word."

Bane said the word. And the race was on. As the table full of powerful men poured stiff drinks and puffed long Honduran cigars, the Alabama Senator remembered the very first report card he brought home from grade school. All A's.

"You keep this is up, Son," his Father beamed brightly, "and someday you'll be President of the Yoo-nited States."

Lucius Bane started laying the groundwork for his Presidential Campaign by late May. Around that same time the Crucifax Trial of Jon LaRue had begun in Washington.

The Trial lasted only three weeks into June. It was front-page news almost every single day. Senator Bane was a witness for the prosecution:

"Not only was it a crime against the people of the Yoo-nited States of Amer'ca, it was a crime against hyoo-manity. A crime against Nay-cha. A crime against Mutha-hood 'n apple pie 'n all we Amer'cans hold dear. An' worst of all, it was a crime against Gawd Almighty His-self!"

He played to the gallery like a master politician, delivering each statement like a campaign trail speech. His words would be printed in newspapers all around the country. Ten-second sound bites were plucked from his testimony and repeated on network newscasts.

Like a flawless pearl necklace, Senator Bane's career had been a constant string of successes. Elected to Student Council in the seventh grade. He won every election after that: one term in the U.S. House of Representatives and four consecutive terms in the Senate. Now he had finally set his sights on every American's ultimate dream house: the one with the fountains and wrought iron fence at 1600 Pennsylvania Avenue.

In the first few days of the summer of '99, the life of Lucius Arnold Bane was a classic American Success Story.

Until Jon LaRue took the stand.

The attorney for the defense was Sheila Norwood, a slick Jewish lawyer renown for representing high profile ACLU cases. *The United States Government v. Jon LaRue* was an emotionally charged case that polarized American society. There were those who supported LaRue and his inalienable artistic right to be nailed to an outhouse. And there were those who felt dregs like LaRue should be shot or at least locked up in jail. Ms. Sheila Norwood, Esquire, waved all applicable fees to defend the beleaguered artist. In her opening statement she quoted Salman Rushdie:

"What is freedom of expression? Without the freedom to offend, it ceases to exist."

Ms. Norwood introduced evidence refuting the allegations that her client had pocketed the grant money. She presented documented proof that LaRue gave ten thousand dollars to twenty-four different environmental groups: one in each of the cities from which the Biblical messages were faxed. This alone totaled $240,000. The ten thousand dollars left over from the quarter-million was used to finance construction of the outhouse, rental of the fax machine, the spotlight, and the wine and hors d'oeuvres that were served to the guests.

"The nails," Norwood added, "were donated by a friend of the artist who works in the construction industry."

Jon LaRue hobbled to the witness stand. Still on crutches, his feet were not yet fully healed from the nail wound administered five months before.

When he held up his right hand to take the oath, everyone in the courtroom, including the jury, could see the large purple scar in the center of his palm. Clearly, here was a man truly willing to suffer greatly to purvey his artistic vision.

"What is the significance of the twenty-four cities you had the fax messages sent from?" Ms. Norwood asked LaRue in front of the Court.

"They represent the twenty-four time zones around the world," the perforated performance artist replied. His voice sounded humble and gushed with sincerity. "With all due respect for Senator Bane, I'm afraid he's grossly misinterpreted my work. You see, *Crucifax* wasn't intended to be a religious statement at all, even though I did incorporate some popular religious imagery to make its message more universal. My intention was to make a purely ecological statement. The outhouse symbolized the planet Earth and what we've done to it. I'm sure everyone can see we've turned it into a toilet. The fax machine is a symbol of technology, the very same technology that has befouled our beautiful planet. Nailing myself to the outhouse was my way of showing that there's no escape from the mess we've made. Having fax messages sent from all over the world was my way of saying we're all in this toilet *together*. And together we must work to turn this polluted Hell we've created into a perfect Heaven on Earth."

Overnight the tide of public sentiment turned against Senator Bane. Suddenly the left-leaning media was comparing him to Hitler, calling him a book burner. A censor of the arts. A man turning America into a police state. Within days his popularity plummeted like the Dow Jones Industrials in October of 1929. And with knee-jerk precision, the Republicans scratched the name Lucius Bane from their list of Presidential contenders. His colleagues who'd been so eager to phone him during the early part of the trial would now not even return his calls. All he could do to ease the pain of being a political pariah was to hole up in his office and eat...and eat...and eat...

THE RAIN CONTINUED ITS incessant wash against the window of Bane's Birmingham office. The colorful Christmas decorations outside were not enough to elevate his mood. Shifting his enormous weight from one flabby buttock to the other — he released a flatulent stream that made the room smell like a horse's stall long left un-shoveled.

Loni, his shapely 28-year-old secretary walked into his office with the mail. She had grown quite accustomed to the foul-smelling air during her five years of gainful employment. Senator Bane broke wind around Loni often, even when he was having sex with her. Once he let go while they were entwined in a pretzel-like sixty-nine. Loni liked her high-paying job and never complained of the malodorous emissions. To her they were merely an occupational hazard — like lung cancer to a coal miner or asbestos worker.

As she walked toward him, her corn silk blond hair swept down onto the delicate nape of her neck. Bra-less, her pert little nipples protruded through her chartreuse sweater. Her ample, un-harnessed bosoms bounced en-ticingly as she laid down a thick stack of letters on his desk.

"Will there be anything else, Senator?" Loni asked, her crayon-red lipstick glistening as if she'd just eaten some-thing very sweet.

"No, that'll be all," her boss droned, watching her wistfully as she turned and walked away. He could only look longingly as she sashayed her sweet *derriere* toward the half-open office door. Her long slender thighs were sleek as a panther's. Shapely calves taut as a drum. Black high-heeled shoes that strapped up around the ankles. As a drought-stricken farmer prays for rain, Senator Bane wished his kingdom for an erection. Not even a prescrip-tion to Viagra could rouse the slumbering beast. His top desk drawer was full of folk remedies he had tried: ginseng, reindeer antler, vitamin E. Even endangered African rhinoceros horn he'd obtained on the black market.

The Senator resorted to these powders and potions after a urologist told him his problem was purely psychological. Bane knew he could never go to a psychiatrist as long as he still held hopes for the Presidency. The slightest hint of a psychiatric record could torpedo him during the heat of a campaign.

"Would you want this nutcase in the White House with his finger on the nuclear trigger?" his opponents would snipe.

Others might speculate he was a closet homosexual who underwent psychotherapy in an attempt to go straight. Then to prove he was neither nutcase nor fruitcake the Senator would have to go before the American Public and admit he could not get a hard-on. To the fragile, penis-centric male ego, it would be easier to confess being an axe murderer than to admit having erectile dysfunction.

But his hopes for a future Presidency would have to be put on the back burner. For now he had to fight to keep his incumbent Senate seat in next November's election, which was eleven months away.

The radio in his office was tuned to the local classical music station. The Senator hated classical music. Ordinarily, his radio would be set on country-western. But earlier that day he'd given an interview to a reporter from the *Birmingham Bijou*, a local arts publication that he and his cronies oft referred to as "that left-wing radical rag." The interview was set up by Charles Russell, a publicist Bane hired to rebuild his public image after it was decimated by the Crucifax Trial. The strategy Charlie Russell proposed was to win back some of the 'artsy-fartsy First Amendment types' without losing his voter base of religious fundamentalists. Bane had a lot of rebuilding to do since polls clearly showed he was trailing all possible opponents.

Part of Bane's problem was Jon LaRue. Instead of fading from the limelight after the trial, the palm-skewered huckster kept gaining in popularity. DVDs of his recent performances were selling like hotcakes in the stores. He was constantly being interviewed by magazines and appeared on talk shows as an advocate of free speech. The more Jon LaRue was in the public eye the more people remembered the Crucifax Trial and how Lucius Bane tried to tinker with their precious Bill of Rights.

Suddenly the Senator's thoughts were diverted by an almost imperceptible sensation between his thighs. It began as a slight twitch beneath the overhang of his belly where his wet-noodle prick clung like a bat from the roof of a cave. Like an accordion carefully pulled by a strolling Bar Mitzvah musician, the long dormant organ awoke. The Senator sat awestruck in his upholstered leather chair staring crotchward as if witnessing nothing less than a miracle.

Bane reached toward his zipper zone. Touched the uncurling creature through the fabric of his pants to make sure it was no figment of his mind. Slipping his right hand down the tops of his trousers he gripped the firm pole like a proud Papa embracing a long lost Prodigal Son. The indisputable proof of palm against penis confirmed his perception was firmly rooted in reality. There it was. Tall as timber. Standing steadfast and sure. Swaying from side to side with gearshift rigidity.

With his free hand Bane reached over and punched the intercom button on his desk: "Loni, get in here quick!"

Spurred by the urgency in her boss's amplified voice the secretary rushed in hoping she had done nothing to jeopardize her employment. She found her overweight boss standing next to his desk with his zipper undone. His penis was poised like a Patriot missile.

"Lock the door!" Bane commanded in the tone of a Field Marshal readying his troops to deploy.

As always, Loni did as she was told. The Senator turned up the volume on the radio. An orchestra was in the midst of Handel's *Messiah.* Bane grabbed his secretary, spun her around and pushed her face down on the desk. Her breasts were pressed down into one of the empty doughnut boxes, powdering the front of her sweater with confectioner's sugar in a way that resembled a light dusting of snow. The Congressional Record was under her chin. She felt her panties pulled to one side. The half-year hiatus from banging her boss was now history. Resigned once again to the unspoken requirements of her job, Loni faked the passionate moans she knew her boss liked to hear while he thrashed about within her. When she felt the familiar quiver of his pelvic thrusts that always foretold a climax was imminent, she cried out: "Oh, Arnie! You're King! You're King!" as the choir on the radio erupted with the Hallelujah Chorus:

> "HAL Lay-LOO-ya!
> HAL Lay-LOO-ya!
> Halla-LOO-ya. Halla-LOO-ya.
> Halla-LAY LOO YAAAAH!"

During that moment of orgasm a revelation struck Bane like the flick of a Bic during a gasoline enema. A plan that would not only ensure his re-election to the Senate, but could possibly pave his way to the White House in 2004. But he had to move quickly. Time was running out.

"And HE shall REIGN
For-EV-er and EHHH-ver!"

Bane stepped back from his bent over secretary and stuffed his spent pecker into his ruffled tidy-whiteys then zipped up his lightly moistened pants. Newly empowered by his vision of political salvation, the Senator barked at his semen-filled subordinate as she turned toward him revealing her doughnut-powdered snowcapped peaks:

"Loni, get Charlie Russell on the horn! I got sump'm big. Sump'm *really* big! If those goddamn Democrats think Jon LaRue can make art, wait'll they see the kinda art I can do! An' I won't have to shove nothin' up my ass to do it neither!"

Adagio

Matt tried his darnedest to make a pleasant sound come out of the trumpet. But when he blew into the horn it was all Holly could do to keep from plugging her ears.

"Maybe the trumpet isn't the right instrument for you," said the thirty-year-old teacher to the frustrated fourth grader. He'd been practicing the trumpet for a month — much to his parents and neighbors' dismay.

Holly walked Matt over to a snare drum. After showing him the proper way of holding the sticks, she taught him a few simple alternating strokes. The tenacious ten year old picked it up right away.

"Very good," she encouraged, flipping her shoulder-length brown hair away from her angelic face, "I think we've found your niche in the musical family of instruments."

Holly watched as he practiced the drumbeats. Each time he repeated them he improved his control. Occasionally she noticed Matt's eyes averting the snare drum and zeroing in on her breasts. Ever since Junior High, Holly considered her mammaries to be proportionally too big for her body. She was a petite five foot two with eyes that on most days were a deep shade of aquamarine. Sometimes her eyes would change color like a chameleon. One day they'd be hazel. Occasionally pale-blue. At times a translucent gray.

Even though Holly considered her eyes to be her most intriguing feature, during conversation Holly found that men always stared at her bosoms. Even when the topics were intellectual in nature the eye line was always the same. Holly surmised that most men grow up still wanting to be nursed by their mothers.

Every time the redheaded freckle-faced boy would stare at her tits he would miss a couple beats. Then he would immediately re-focus his attention on the drum and regain his precision. Holly noticed how boys reaching puberty would slowly start looking at her in this manner. The same way men stared when she worked as a cocktail waitress at the Bulldog Saloon.

Holly Bibble never planned on becoming a teacher. She only wanted to be a composer. She took Music Education on her father's advice to have "something to fall back on, just in case."

Matt kept playing the two-against-one strokes over and over like a machine-gun blast. Holly could see his face light up as he mastered the simple technique. She had grown to love teaching elementary school music. Helping young-sters discover the joy of music gave her a sense of ful-fillment not attainable any other way. Seeing that sparkle in the eyes of her students when they master their very first melody. Hearing their bursts of laughter echo in the halls after first performing in an ensemble. It kept her in touch with her own youthful dreams. Dreams that had long since been torn up and bulldozed by the unflinching demands of adulthood.

It was during her three days of teaching each week that Holly often thought of having children of her own. She had recently discussed it with Kim, her lesbian significant other.

Kim was reluctant. Fresh out of med school, she had just begun a two-year internship at Johns Hopkins University Medical Center. But Kim said she would be open to the idea of childrearing in the future. Although, she pointed out, there were several considerations that needed to be thoroughly thought through. Such as: where would the semen come from? A sperm bank? A friend? A stranger picked up in a bar? Should they ask the sperm donor to be genetically screened to detect any congenital abnormalities?

Matt kept ratta-tat-tatting on the drum until Holly finally made him stop. She reviewed quarter notes and eighth notes with him. Then gave him some assignments to practice on a drum pad at home during Christmas vacation.

On the way to her car at the end of the day Holly remembered the Principal wanted to see her. She walked back across the staff parking lot toward the cherry-brick buildings of the school.

Snow had begun to fall. Some of the weightless white flakes would settle on her earmuffs and layered winter clothes. One in particular caught her attention. It fell in the palm of her mitten. She studied it closely while walking toward the school. Holding it close to her face, she was awed by its symmetry. Its intricacy of design. Holly knew each snowflake was unique. One of a kind. Never before in the history of the world was there ever a snowflake shaped quite like this. And never again would there be one like it.

Walking along in the cold winter air she cupped it in her palm like a rare hand-cut diamond. In her heart she said silent thanks to God for creating a world so full of beauty and wonder.

She scraped off her boots before entering the building. The heater was turned up full blast. The snowflake quickly melted on her mitten, becoming a droplet that seeped through the wool.

"Miss Bibble is here," the fortysomething secretary spoke into the intercom to the Principal's office.

"Send her in," came the deep, friendly voice at the other end.

Mr. Adajian greeted Holly warmly, motioned for her to have a seat as he poured them both coffee. He was not much taller than she was. Only five foot four, which was usually considered short for a male. Like some men in their late thirties, he was going bald. What remained of his curly black hair was peppered with gray, mostly over the temples. He had on the same brown suit he wore almost every day. His tie hung to one side like a pendulum frozen in time. Shoes shined to Army boot camp perfection. Holly knew him to be a kind man, fair in his dealings with teachers and children alike.

"Any luck on the love front?" he asked, stirring his coffee with a badly mauled spoon.

Holly recalled their most recent conversation at the school Christmas party of a week before. He inquired why a woman as attractive as her did not have a husband or boyfriend. She shrugged it off, saying she had yet to find "Mr. Right." But the truth she kept hidden like a fine bottle of wine locked in the closet for her own personal use. No one in the school system knew she was gay. It was not something she liked to advertise.

"Personal ads," the caring Principal shot back. "I know you think I'm crazy — I did when someone first suggested it to me. But then I got so lonely I was willing to try anything. And it was the best thing I ever did. That's how I met my wife."

He plucked the gold-framed photo of himself and Mrs. Adajian from his cluttered desk and handed it to Holly. His wife was a very pretty Filipina in her late twenties. Judging by the size of their smiles they appeared to be quite happy.

"You're a lucky man," Holly congratulated, handing back the framed photo.

"Personal ads," he reiterated as he placed it back down amidst the jumble of papers.

Mr. Adajian took a long sip of coffee. Took a deep breath. Then dropped the H-bomb: "You know the Baltimore School System has been having money problems lately."

"So what else is new?" Holly replied.

"This time the budget cuts are deep. And you know music and art are always the first things to go."

"I know."

There was a long, uneasy silence marked by the sound of sipping coffees. Mr. Adajian stared at the photo of his wife. Holly looked out the window at the snowflakes falling outside.

"So when's my last day?" she finally asked, breaking the unbearable silence between sips.

"Today," he answered, handing her the pink slip that was buried in the clutter on his desk. "I'm sorry. I know how the kids are going to miss you. You're the best music teacher Fremont Elementary ever had."

*

SENATOR BANE HAD HIS public relations manager Charlie Russell on the phone: "Charlie, let me run this by ya."

"I'm all ears, Big Guy. Shoot."

"I just got this vision. This insp'ration," Bane sputtered, trying to put his idea into words for the first time, "Ya know how everythang on TV right now is geared toward it bein' the beginnin' of the twenty-first cent'ry an' all?"

"Yeah, uh-huh."

"Well, everybody's gettin' all built up for it, right? Well, what's gonna happen the day after New Year's after all the fireworks have gone off an' ev'rybody's got hangovers? They're gonna feel real let down, don't ya think, Charlie? 'Specially after such a big build-up."

"I suppose."

"One thang I know about people is: they gotta have sump'm to look forward to. I got sump'm they kin look forward to for a whole 'nother year. Charlie, it ain't the first a' January that starts the new millen-yum. It's Christmas! Think about it. They start the calendar on the birth a' Christ. But Jesus's two-thousandth birthday ain't till next Christmas. That's when the new millen-yum *really* starts."

"Could you get to the point, Senator, I've got four lines on hold."

"I'm gonna get some money appropriated through the Arts Committee to get a composer to write a big orchestra piece. Just like they got that Handel fella to write that Hallelujah thing way back when. You know, the one where the King stood up and now everybody does it? Think about it, Charlie, if you could work the Press the right way on it, I could git back some a' the art crowd vote and still keep the dyed-in-the-wool Christians too. Whadda ya think?"

"I think you might be on to something there, Senator. Let me call you right back."

Charlie Russell didn't actually have four callers on hold. What he did have on hold was his cock. On his desk was the latest edition of *Beaverboy*. The centerfold was a naked nineteen-year-old girl whose pink pubic lips were spread wide as the Missouri.

Charlie reached in his bottom desk drawer, took out a Love-Sandwich and tore off the wrapper. He remembered when the product first came on the market. People were appalled. The inventor in Menlo Park, New Jersey, who held the patent on the fake female organ, would receive death threats from religious fundamentalists from all over the country. But as the HIV virus kept worming its way through the populace, autoeroticism gained considerable strides in popularity. As someone once said: "There is nothing more powerful than an idea whose time has come."

The oblong vulva facsimile was about the size of a medium taco. Its inner sheath was latex, already lubricated for insertion. Padded with industrial foam rubber to give it bulk and a bit of pliancy. Around the rim was a pelt of artificial pubic hair. Love-Sandwiches came in three basic colors: Bimbo-Blond, Baddass-Brunette, and the hands-down top-seller — Ravishing-Redhead.

Disposability was part of the Love-Sandwich's appeal; they were used once and then thrown away. From vending machines they sold for three dollars. In a six-pack they came to about two bucks apiece. For a man who was horny, this was a bargain — considering the high cost of flowers, candy, dinner, wine, and a movie as prerequisites to sex.

Charlie Russell twitched in his chair, ejaculating into the Love-Sandwich he held in his grasp. Then he tossed the pseudo-muff receptacle into the wastebasket and called the Senator back.

"Brilliant idea!" Charlie complimented his client, "An oratorio for the two-thousandth Christmas. When do you want a press release on it?"

"I gotta work out the dee-tails with some people on my staff," the Senator responded.

"Such as?"

"You know, we gotta line up an orchestra."

"The New York Phil. Go for the best!"

"Yeah, but I don't want this thang to be in New Yawk. I hate New Yawk. Nothin' but a bunch a' perverts there stickin' things up their buttholes 'n callin' it Art."

"Get the Phil to come down to D.C." advised Charlie, "Get 'em to play at the Kennedy Center. Now you're talking *class!*"

"An' it's gotta have a chorus, too," Bane insisted, "just like the Hallelujah thing."

"Get the Mormon Tabernacle. And I take it you're planning on hiring an American composer?"

"Ain't nobody gonna be writin' this thing with a dang green card hanging out their ass. They gotta be red, white 'n blue through 'n through!"

"Lucius, the idea is brilliant!" cheered the publicist, "Absolutely brilliant! You're gonna go national on this one, Loosh. All the way to the White House!"

THE SNOW WAS NO longer coming down in gentle flakes. It was dumping like gruel from an angry orphan's bowl — covering Holly's car like a field of Robert Frost. Caught in rush-hour traffic, Holly slowly inched her rusted blue Jetta through the maze of crimson tail-lights. Her metronome wipers kept a constant beat, struggling to maintain an arch of visibility through the windshield. She bent over the steering wheel to better watch between wipes, hoping to catch a glimpse of the road. It was nose-icicle cold. Holly's breath billowed down toward the dashboard, enveloping it in thick white plumes. She had planned on getting her car heater fixed. But now, being unemployed, it moved further down the list of priorities.

Shivering as she drove. Teeth clattering. Crying profusely with no windshield wipers on her eyes. Tears rolled down her cheeks and dropped from her chin to her wool-covered lap — where they instantly froze into a chaotic array of tiny glass beads.

She pulled into her parking space in the underground garage. Her apartment was high up in the ten-story building overhead. The creaky old elevator squeaked and squealed, finally delivering her to the hall on the seventh floor. The carpeting in the hallway had a strong musty smell that seemed particularly acute that afternoon. Holly slid her key into the deadbolt of the door. The lock was old and worn. She had to jiggle it, as usual, to get it open. These things never bothered her before. Her attitude had always been *go with the flow.* But on this day there was no flow to go with. Holly felt like a trout struggling endlessly upstream.

Her lover Kim was still in bed asleep. Her long, thick, waist-length hair cascaded over the pillows like a horse's mane. Her skin was cocoa-colored. Kim was half black and half Asian. She worked the graveyard shift at Johns Hopkins: nine at night until 8 a.m. So she usually slept until five or six in the evening.

Holly didn't want to wake her. She didn't want to burden her with her depressed state of mind. Instead she chose to deal with it herself. Alone.

She walked out into the living room. It was getting dark outside. The wind howled, rattling the large windowpane. In the distance the lights of downtown Baltimore were peeping through the low gray clouds. Like Ravel's *Bolero*, the snowfall kept slowly increasing in intensity. Beat by beat.

Holly plugged in the Christmas tree and remembered herself as a child sneaking into the living room after her parents had gone to bed and staring at the festively adorned evergreen for hours. It never failed to give her a warm, secure feeling that everything was right in the world. She hoped that the sight of the Christmas tree lights would now give her that feeling once more.

Holly looked at the lights and baubles and tinsel that she and Kim had strung the night before. The silvery star at the top of the tree was the same as the one from her childhood. The symbol of the star that guided the Three Wise Men to Bethlehem. She prayed to God to lift her out of her depression. Her prayers went unanswered. She walked over to the window. Opened it. The cold wind and snow whooshed in, blanketing her clothes and the carpet with a layer of white. The beige curtains flapped like large flags on flagpoles. *I'm a failure*, Holly thought. *I took everyone's advice and got my teaching degree so I'd have "something to fall back on" if I failed as a composer. Not only did I fail as a composer but what I had to fall back on has just fallen through.*

Holly placed one foot on the ledge of the window. The bitter cold felt good against her skin. It took her mind off the pain within her. The pain of all hope being lost. All the dreams she had worked so hard to realize seemed as distant as the Wise Men's star out in space.

The lights of the city below reminded her of the Christmas tree lit up behind her. She remembered the conversation she and Kim had the night before while hanging the ornaments on its limbs:

They were discussing the origin of the Universe, of all things. Kim was championing the scientific view. The Big Bang. The chance positioning of Earth just far enough from the Sun for water to exist in liquid form. The billions of years of volcanic eruptions that filled the atmosphere with nitrogen and oxygen. Earth passing through the tail of a comet. The comet dust easing its way through the skies without burning up the amino acids it contained. The amino acids combined with carbon and other elements in the primordial ooze. Lightning strikes. A spark starts a chemical reaction. *Voila!* The genesis of life as we know it.

"But Life couldn't have gotten this far without some Guiding Intelligence," Holly argued that night. "It's much too intricate and incredible to just be accidental chemistry. Some cosmic fluke."

"Who knows?" Holly remembered Kim answering, shrugging her shoulders while hanging a smiling Rudolph the Red-Nose on a twig of the Douglas fir.

Holly lifted her other leg up onto the window ledge. She stood gripping the sides with both hands. The wind-driven snow whipped against her small body. Numbing it. Making her skin match the color of her eyes.

Peering down at the city below, it looked like an elaborate toy train set. Storefronts in miniature with pinhead sized lights. Little toy cars forming single file lines behind streetlights strung from toothpick telephone poles.

Holly knew that inside each car was a driver. Each one with a different destination in mind. Led by their joys and dreams and desires. Suffering in a way that no one will ever know.

The thought of killing herself made perfect sense. It seemed like the only logical way of ending her despair. She was just about to jump when something warm brushed against her ankle. Holly looked down. It was Toes. Their cat. The big shorthaired tabby was nudging her leg. Toes meowed and blinked his eyes and purred.

"Oh, Toes, you crazy kitty," Holly said, bending down to pet him. His warm fur felt good against the cold of her hand. Then he jumped down off the window and ran over to his bowl. And meowed, and meowed — demanding his dinner.

He doesn't want love, Holly thought, *Kim was right. We're only accidental organisms from the primordial ooze, searching for food, sex, and shelter. Love is a luxury we share when our stomachs are full and our sex organs sated.*

Holly stood back up on the windowsill. Her vision became blurred with the onslaught of snow. The miniature train set beckoned far below: *Come fly, come fly, like the bird you always longed to be!*

"Dee Dee! What are you doing?" Kim yelled from the bedroom doorway. "It's freezing in here!"

Holly turned around on the windowsill, facing her awakened lover. Tears frozen to her cheeks like elf-sized ornaments glistened with reflections of the Christmas tree lights.

"You're right, Boo Boo!" Holly screamed, "There isn't any God! We're all just cosmic flukes from a big comet dust bowl!"

"Oh, Dee Dee!" Kim gushed, rushing toward her distraught partner. She wrapped her arms around Holly's frozen hips and pulled her from her icy, precarious perch. After pushing the window shut she carried her girlfriend into the bedroom and brushed off the snow while helping her out of her schoolteacher clothes. Then tucked her in under the thick, down comforter.

"What's the matter, Dee Dee?" Kim asked, watching the last of the unthawed snowflakes melt into Holly's hair.

Over the course of their five-year relationship the two had adopted their own nicknames for each other. Early on, Holly would call Kim her "teddy bear." Eventually this evolved into "Boo Boo Bear." Finally it became just "Boo Boo." Kim started calling Holly "Baby," especially during the throes of lovemaking. This later permutated into "Bee Bee," and then somewhere along the line it became "Dee Dee." But whenever Holly and Kim were calling to each other, they never merely spoke their pet names. They always sang them like two notes of a melody — imitating the tones of a doorbell.

"Dee Dee," Kim sang again when Holly didn't answer, "tell me what is the matter?"

Burying her face into Kim's dark-skinned shoulder, Holly sobbed: "They laid me off today, Boo Boo."

"Why?" Kim asked, stroking Holly's brown hair, wet from the freshly melted snow.

"No money," Holly sniffled as she reached for a Kleenex on the nightstand. She blew her nose with a sound that rivaled Matt's fledgling attempts on the trumpet.

"Do you think that's reason enough to jump out the window?"

"It seemed like a good idea at the time," Holly replied, drying her eyes with another tissue, "I should have known something like this was going to happen this week with my Mercury in retrograde."

Holly was a Libra. She read her horoscope almost every day. Kim was a Leo. She never read her horoscope. She thought astrology was bullshit. According to a book Holly kept on her shelf, Libras and Leos weren't supposed to get along. Having been together for five years in a row, Holly and Kim were pushing the stars to their limit.

"How much do you think you'll be able to get from unemployment?" Kim asked, aware that her meager internship paycheck would barely cover the rent.

"Maybe two-twenty a week," Holly answered, "But don't worry, I'll find something to supplement it."

Holly had worked her way through college by cocktail waitressing. She hated it, dressing like a sex object for baseball-capped, bow-legged, beer-swilling men. Crude-talking yee-haws who drooled when they leered and wore Levis that always showed the cracks of their asses. But in spite of the affront to her feminist ideals it *was* at least a hundred dollars cash every night.

"Dee Dee?" Kim sighed, holding her slowly thawing lover in her arms, "promise me you won't be a cocktail waitress."

Holly and Kim met while both were students at George Washington University. Holly was finishing her Masters Degree. Kim was in her second year of med school. One night Kim came down to the Bulldog Saloon to see where her new lover worked. She was thoroughly disgusted. And told Holly so. Just as she was telling her now.

"But it's good money," Holly pleaded, "and it's *cash.*"

"So is prostitution," Kim replied.

"I love you, Boo Boo."

"Oh Dee Dee!"

Kim wrapped her arms around her, pressed her dark full lips against Holly's pink puckered thin ones. Their tongues darted and dashed into each other mouths like two mollusks wrestling on Venus's half-shell. Holly ran her fingers through Kim's black hair that draped to the top of her tailbone. Her hair was thick, yet straight as string — a genetic hybrid of being half black and half Vietnamese.

Kim's father was an African-American soldier in the Vietnam War. Her mother was a Saigon prostitute. He kept going back to her until she didn't charge him anymore. Then he married her and brought her to the United States.

During elementary school Kim's classmates often teased her about her mixed racial background. A joke that circulated back then went something like this:

"Did you hear about the kid who was half black and half Japanese? He was so confused every December 7th he'd try to bomb Pearl Bailey."

The jokes and teasing hurt young Kimberly Jackson. But she rarely showed her feelings in public. Her mother brought her up in the teachings of Buddhism:

Life is suffering. Suffering is caused by desire. The path to Enlightenment is through cessation of desire.

Both Kim's parents were killed in an automobile accident when she was twelve. Up to that point in her life, she had believed in a Buddha, or Supreme Being governing the world. She believed that everything that happened in life had a purpose. But after her parents died she didn't believe in anything. She just believed that 'shit happens.' A year after the tragedy, she even bought a T-shirt that said the same. Kim was placed with a foster family who treated her like a maid. She ran away from home at fifteen and never went back. Working her way through school, she got scholarships and loans to finish college and med school at the George Washington University School of Neuro-surgery.

Kim had wanted to become a doctor ever since she had a tumor removed when she was eleven. The idea of helping sick people get well gave her a good feeling inside. She felt the Universe was completely meaningless except for whatever meaning people create for themselves. She believed life had unlimited potential — but only if we take responsibility for it ourselves. No Knight in Shining Armor, no Big Man in the Sky was going to swoop down and do our work for us. It was up to each of us to make our lives the best they could possibly be.

"Promise me," Kim insisted as she pulled her mouth away from Holly's lips, "promise me you won't work in a place like the Bulldog Saloon."

"I promise," Holly whispered in her gay lover's ear. Then softly blew into it while touching her tongue to the tip of Kim's earlobe.

"I love you, Dee Dee," Kim quivered as she pulled Holly's white satin panties down her olive-skinned thighs. She tossed them like a horseshoe across the small room. They landed dead-ringer on the doorknob — a lucky shot. Pressing their naked anatomies together, they kissed at one end and played footsies at the other.

Kim's body was warm as a fireplace. Holly was still cold from the winter storm outside. That was changing as Kim rubbed her body against her. Soon Holly was hot as the seashore in Rio. And rising.

The African-Asian brain surgeon let her tongue drift below Holly's chin. Down the length of her neck. Over her collarbone. Slipping on down past her shoulders.

She reached Holly's breasts. They were mountainous, even when horizontal. Kim slowly ascended one of them, dragging her tongue like a slippery snail up a slope. Holly's skin was white and soft beneath the faint remnants of a tan line left over from summer. Upward her tongue went till reaching the top. Circling the dark areolae, she watched Holly's nipples become aroused and erect. Hovering just over the lust-hardened nipple, Kim flicked her tongue fast as a hummingbird's wings. Holly cooed like a mourning dove drenched in morning dew as Kim continued flutter-tonguing her nipple. Dancing wet circles 'round 'n 'round the rim then spiraling upward and engulfing it between her chocolate-colored lips.

Holly began breathing heavily, punctuated by occasional — almost inaudible — high-pitched squeaks. Kim carried her exploratory tongue into the valley. To her bellybutton. Past her waist. At first circumventing the entrance of Holly's garden of Earthly delights, knowing how easily she'd get lost if she lingered there.

Sojourning ever southward down her creamy-smooth thighs, Kim retraced her tongue's trail to where Holly's legs made their juncture. Her rapturously arousing tongue met with hair as soft as a kitten's. Holly purred with delight. The barely buried treasure of Holly's rosebud revealed itself as the petals of her flower unfolded. Kim suckled it, summoning the nectar from within.

Her tongue tickled Holly's treasure as softly as she possibly could. Sometimes not even touching it at all except with the wisp of her breath. Gingerly guiding it into her mouth like an oyster carefully coaxed from its shell — it was slippery and kept slip-sliding away from her. Playfully playing hard to get.

Finally, she trapped the elusive clitoris between her lips and held it as if trapped in a pillory. With a surgeon's precision Kim began drawing little circles around it with her tongue. Soon the circles turned into letters of the alphabet. She traced the letters

"I-L-O-V-E-Y-O-U"

over and over several times. Then spelled out many other words — licking one letter at a time. Twenty minutes of tongue crossing T 's and dotting small i 's with a well-moistened flick, Kim etched an epic love-poem on her sweet lover's clit that sent all thoughts of suicide sailing out the window.

Holly began to writhe and moan, arching upward into her darling's face. Her entire body began shaking from within. She met her lover's prolific tongue with one final uncontrollable pelvic thrust. A wave of unspeakable ecstasy surged through her cells like ten-thousand screaming butterflies on fire!

"OHHHHHHHHHH! GOD!" Holly cried into the night, causing some loose plaster to drop from the walls. She collapsed on a heap of pillows — Kim's face locked between her legs. For an instant she was at one with the Universe — whatever It was and however It came into being.

Many minutes passed before Holly was again able to speak.

"Boo Boo?"

"What, Love?"

"I wanna have a baby."

"You know we can't afford it right now."

"I don't mean now. In a couple years or so. After you're done with your internship. I really think we'll be missing out on one of life's great joys if we never raise any children."

"As soon as my practice is up and rolling," Kim said, "I've got a lot of student loans to pay off, you know."

"I know. I just figure it might take us a while to find the right donor."

"What's wrong with a sperm bank?"

"I don't know," Holly shrugged, "there's just something about it I don't like. If I'm going to have a baby I'd like to at least know who the Father is."

"The problem with that is you have to deal with a man," Kim countered, "and whether you like it or not, when there's a kid involved, you'll probably have to deal with him the rest of your life. And you know as well as I do that most men are assholes who always want to be in control."

"I know," Holly lamented, "but somewhere there's gotta be a man who's not your *typical-garden-variety-controlling-asshole alpha male.*"

"Good luck with that, " Kim chuckled, "And where are you gonna find this Prince Charming, hm? Fairy Tale Village?"

"No," Holly answered, softly petting the dark tuft of hair between her lover's long legs:

"Personal ads."

Allegro non troppo

The New Year rang in with much hoopla. Turn of the century parties were all the rage. Television spent countless hours recounting the milestones of the bygone millennium. Newspapers and magazines pressed reams to say the same. But most of the coverage was focused on the 20th Century.

The century that saw the first airplane fly and the first men land on the moon. Hitlers and Ghandhis and Gorbachevs and Elvises. Faces of the famous popped up everywhere. Everyone who was anyone was interviewed by the media. "What do you think the new millennium will bring?" was asked of every living Household Name. Some said the world would soon come to an end. Others were much more optimistic.

Soon after New Year's, when the last of the fireworks had faded into brown puffs of smoke in the sky, after all of the cheering and lipstick and liquor and off-keyed *Auld Lang Synes* — everyone went back to resuming their lives exactly where they left off back in 1999.

Back to their jobs and bills and insurance. Putting food on the table and gas in their cars. Keeping their credit cards from exceeding their limits. Everything was exactly the same except for the new date numbers printed on their checkbooks.

People had trouble adjusting at first. Whenever they had to write the date on anything they would instinctively start writing the year '19— ,' then stop, scratch it out, and write the year '2000' in its place.

And the Y2K computer bug that was supposed to bring civilization to a grinding halt turned out to be a dud. Senator Bane was right: to most people, after the second or third week in January, the fact that it was a new millennium was no big deal at all.

The 106th Congress was re-convened in mid-January. By that time, Lucius Bane had already laid the groundwork for Jesus' 2000th birthday celebration. Of course, he couldn't officially call it that or else the atheists and non-Christian religious groups would file lawsuits invoking the Constitutional separation of Church and State. Officially it was called: *National Endowment For The Arts Commissioned Musical Work In Celebration of the New Millennium.* But whenever Bane recited the long-winded title, he accompanied it with a wink — especially in front of the television cameras.

Bane booked the John F. Kennedy Center for the Performing Arts eleven months in advance for the next Christmas Eve. He secured The New York Philharmonic and the Mormon Tabernacle Choir. The four networks were bidding for live broadcast rights. Record companies sent legions of lawyers and lobbyists to try to secure exclusive distribution of the recordings.

Senator Bane's initiative was applauded in art circles as well as religious communities. His popularity in the polls took a sharp turn upward. Now all he had to do was pick the right composer for the job. Aware that he didn't know diddly-squat about orchestral music, the Senator retained a local music professor as a consultant.

Professor Sydney Bormstern was in the music department at George Washington University. He was bald on top with medium-length Santa-white hair slicked back on the sides. The two met at a reception given in Bane's honor after he was chosen to be Chairman of the newly formed Senate Arts Committee. The new committee was formed to provide some Congressional oversight of the projects being funded by the National Endowment for the Arts.

The reason Senator Bane was chosen to head the Arts Committee was not because he had any expertise in this area. Quite the contrary. The extent of his art background ran from listening to recordings of Buck Owens to watching reruns of *Gomer Pyle* on cable TV. For nearly eighteen years Bane served on the Senate Ethics Committee. When the Chairmanship for that Committee came up for grabs, Senator Bane thought it should rightfully be his due to seniority. But the chair went instead to a younger Republican whose election campaign was financed by the Mafia. To appease Senator Bane, he was given the newly formed Arts Committee to chair. Although not a committee with much power, the Senator's battered ego was assuaged by being told it was a position of great prestige.

(If the laws that govern the Universe are similar to the way the United States Government is run, we can quickly dispel all notions of a rational basis for existence.)

Professor Bormstern warned Senator Bane to shy away from the modern Minimalist composers who were creating quite a stir on the international scene.

"Stick with the Traditionalists," the seventy-five year old Bormstern advised with a cough that sounded like the bark of a terrier. He furnished Bane with a list of sixteen American composers he felt worthy of the task. Some were well known film composers. Others were on faculty at major Conservatories and Universities throughout the United States. All of them responded immediately when they were notified that they were on the short list of composers being considered. All were eager to get the job. It was extremely rare that anyone would commission a new work for chorus and orchestra. An opportunity like this might only come once in a lifetime.

Senator Bane stood before the mirror in the men's room down the hall from his Capitol Hill office. A comb in one hand. Hair-spray in the other. He delicately maneuvered each precious strand of hair into place. Then lacquered it down with the fluorocarbon-propelled spray.

The Public Broadcasting crew was setting up lights in his office. Bane knew the importance of TV. Since the Nixon-Kennedy campaign of 1960, television had become the end-all of political survival.

Bane held his face up close to the mirror to better see the left side of his head. His hair was gray, on the way to being white. But it was there. A whole head of it.

Ever since television became the medium for making Presidents, one of the unwritten qualifications for the job was having hair on top of the head. The last bald President was Eisenhower who came right on the cusp of The Age of TV. Several bald candidates have sought the office since. But none ever made it to the White House. The reason:

they just didn't look "presidential" enough on television. Gerald Ford was partially bald, but then again he wasn't elected. When he finally got into an election, of course, he lost to a peanut farmer who had a full head of hair.

Senator Bane knew the rules. That's why he hired Charles Russell as his publicist. And that's why he was taking excruciating care to make sure every hair was perfectly in place.

The PBS interview went off without a hitch. The Senator had memorized what his speechwriters had written:

"...The Arts are the only thing that sep'rates us hyoo-mans from the rest a' the beasts here on God's green Earth. The role of Government is to support the Arts. To raise the hyoo-man spirit to a lofty place. To keep us from slidin' back into the jungle. Or down into the gutter."

"I think we can wrap on that," said the attractive woman producer. "Thank you for your time, Senator."

"Why, thank *you*," Bane replied, as he stood up from his desk to shake hands with the camera and sound crew — a reflexive response from campaign trails of the past.

Loni squeezed past the TV crew standing in the doorway like a salmon on its way to spawn. She handed her boss a long list of calls that came in during the videotaping. Quickly scanning the list with a brushstroke of his eyes, one name stuck out like a diamond in a goat's ass:

Guy M. Landsworth

Senator Bane cordially hurried the PBS crew out of his office and picked up the phone.

"When did Guy Landsworth call?" he grilled his secretary while frantically dialing the number.

"I dunno. About ten minutes ago, I guess."

"Wha-diddy want?"

Loni shrugged. Bane thought she looked sexy pouting her lips to one side the way she did. For a brief moment, he considered sending his staff home early so he could slam it to her on the reception room couch. But his mind was brought back to more professional matters when a female voice answered on the other end of the phone:

"Lapp City Industries."

"Yes, is Mr. Landsworth in? Senator Lucius Arnold Bane returnin' his call."

"I'll put you through, Senator."

Bane had met Mr. Landsworth at a Republican fund raising dinner several years back. Landsworth was one of the wealthiest men in Alabama. He had contributed heavily to the Senator's campaigns of the past. Mr. Landsworth's self-assured baritone voice finally came on the line:

"Senator, I'm gonna be in Washington next Wednesday on business and I'd like to get together for lunch."

Bane had previously made plans to spend that Wednesday with Loni at his Chesapeake Bay cottage. But even the best-laid plans are subject to change. He would have Loni give him a blowjob in the morning. Then on to meet Landsworth for lunch.

HOLLY PICKED UP two-eggs-over-easy, hash browns and toast and delivered it to table number twelve. It was her first day of work at the *Denny's* next to the exit ramp of Interstate 95. Even though the coffee shop waitress attire was not meant to arouse men's carnal desires, she noticed the male patrons ogling her legs, butt, and especially her bountiful breasts. It was just like it was at the Bulldog Saloon — only the tips weren't nearly as good.

But she'd promised Boo Boo.

A trucker left a fifty-cent tip and a coffee-stained edition of the *Baltimore Sun.* On the front page of the arts section was an article on the 'Christmas 2000 Oratorio' which was what the Media started calling it in spite of its wordy official name. Holly started reading the article when one of her tables started yelling for more cream for their coffee.

I would give anything to write that oratorio, Holly thought to herself while refilling the non-dairy creamer container at table number six.

After the morning breakfast rush, Holly had a few minutes to read the rest of the article. She read how the Senator from Alabama had gotten the idea for the oratorio after attending church just before Christmas. This very same Senator was spearheading the drive to get the work written and ready to be performed by the following Christmas Eve.

Holly thought to herself, while reading the article, *why can't we have more politicians like this?* During the few idle moments she had before the noon lunch hour began, she poured herself some coffee and stared out the window, watching the cars whiz by on the Interstate.

She thought about her Italian grandfather on her Father's side: Giancarlo Bibbleoni. He was born a peasant in Italy. He worked in the coalmines to earn enough money to bring his wife and himself to America. After becoming a United States citizen, World War II broke out and he was drafted into the Army. Since Italy was allied with Germany during that war, Italian surnames were unpopular among GIs. So before his induction into the U.S. Armed Forces, Giancarlo Bibbleoni changed his last name to Bibble. Holly remembers as a child hearing her Grandfather jokingly refer to the change as his "surname circumcision."

Giancarlo was quite an accomplished clarinet player. After basic training he received orders to report to an Officer's Club in the Catskills. He was assigned to play clarinet in the dance band stationed there.

"This horn saved my life," he told Holly after giving her the clarinet when she was eight.

Chances are the clarinet probably did save Corporal Bibble's life. While his boot camp buddies were storming the beachhead at Normandy, he was playing Benny Goodman riffs at a Hudson Riverside resort.

After the war, his wife, Anna, gave birth to their only child, Edward — Holly's Father. Ed Bibble was a fabric salesman when he met Holly's Mom on a plane in 1965.

Deborah was a twenty-one year old stewardess for American Airlines. An attractive Jewish girl with lavender eyes and an ample bustline that Ed just couldn't take his eyes off as she passed by his seat on the aisle. The plane encountered turbulence somewhere between Chicago and Pittsburgh. Deborah accidentally spilled 7-Up on Ed's lap. She cleaned up the mess and they've been inseparable ever since.

Holly grew up in Evanston, a middle-class suburb of Chicago. She was a hyperactive child who talked all the time. In the second grade her schoolmates would teasingly call her "The Holly Bibble Show." Because, like a television always left on, Holly would never shut up.

Once her teacher commented in front of the class: "Holly, I've never known anyone to babble on the way you do!"

The other children found this amusing and started calling her "The Holly Bibble of Babble On." Holly was never offended by their teasing. She rather liked the attention.

"Get ready everybody, here comes The Holly Bibble of Babble On!" a classmate would yell as Holly approached on the playground. She would merely treat this razzing as her special introduction. And then she would commence to live up to her name: talking and talking and talking a mile a minute.

When Holly began school in the fourth grade she was no longer the Bibble of Babble On. She was taciturn. Shy and introverted. Unless someone spoke to her first, she never said anything to anyone. And if anyone did ask her anything, she gave as little response as possible.

That was after the summer her Italian Grandfather gave her his prized clarinet. She began taking lessons soon after that from a woman named Mrs. Martinez. Soon she was practicing all the time. She could play the Mozart *Clarinet Concerto in A Major* by the time she was eleven. When she was twelve, she took up the piano. She became very good and eventually the keyboard became her principal instrument.

While a piano major at Oberlin College, she became interested in music composition. It became her major by the time she got her Bachelor of Arts. She went on to get her Masters at George Washington University in Washington D.C.

Ever since she began playing clarinet, Holly always believed she would do great things with her life. It was this belief that helped her endure the long, grueling hours of practice — sometimes six to eight hours a day. She never went out and played with the neighborhood kids anymore like she used to. And during her teen years she went out on very few dates. But she always felt her self-imposed solitude was for a purpose bigger than herself. That God was preparing her for a great and noble task.

Now here she was: thirty years old with a Masters Degree, waiting tables at Denny's. She wondered if her childhood visions of greatness were nothing more than delusions of grandeur. She wondered if everyone there in the coffee shop had similar yearnings in their youth. All the truck drivers and accountants and telemarketers of the world. Perhaps they had all dreamed of doing great things just as she did. Maybe they were still dreaming them now.

"Holly," the assistant manager called, "table number seven."

She looked up from her reverie. Lunch had begun.

SENATOR BANE AND Guy M. Landsworth were enjoying steak and bourbon at a posh Washington eatery. They began the meal exchanging small talk and home state gossip. Halfway through his mashed potatoes, Landsworth brought the conversation to the point where he wanted it:

"This is a real humdinger of a thing you're doin', Senator, this oratorio thing. It's just what this country needs: more oratorios."

"Why thank you, Mr. Landsworth. I feel the same way myself."

"Have ya decided on a composer yet?" Landsworth asked, washing down the potatoes with a hefty gulp of Kentucky bourbon.

"Not yet," answered Bane, "but whoever the lucky feller is he's gonna go down in hist'ry just like Beethoven an' all the rest. Ain't every day a feller gets to compose sump'm for the two-thousandth birthday of Jesus Christ Almighty!"

"Amen," said the sixty-five year old Alabama businessman as he polished off his glass of hard liquor. He handed the empty to a passing waiter to refill. "You got any kids, Senator?"

Bane and his wife had two sons in their mid-twenties. Both were a continual source of embarrassment. His eldest, Ted, became a Hare Krishna and was living in an ashram in Atlanta. The Senator caught a glimpse of him now and then whenever he had to change planes at Hartsfield Airport and Ted would be there handing out colorfully illustrated pamphlets about Hindu gods.

Bane's youngest son, Biff, lived in Los Angeles. Last he heard, Biff was acting in porn films.

"Yeah, I got two boys," the Senator replied, finally taking a swig on the bourbon he'd been nursing throughout the meal, "One's in the movie business out in California. The other, uh, took up a religious callin'."

"You're a lucky man, Lucius," said Landsworth, putting down half of a freshly filled glass in a single gulp, "I got a son, he's almost forty years old, an' he's the most worthless piece a' scum ever to walk the face a' this Earth. He's a dope addict. Sex fiend. Car thief. Shoplifter. You name it — if it's illegal or immoral — he's done it!"

Landsworth slugged down the rest of his glass and hailed the waiter to bring him another.

"They never turn out how ya want 'em to, Mr. Landsworth. No matter how good an upbringin' ya give 'em."

"Call me Guy."

"It would be an honor to call you that, Sir."

"No 'Sir.' Just Guy."

"All right, Guy. My close friends call me Arnie. Short for Arnold, my middle name."

"Arnie," said Landsworth as the waiter set another drink down in front of him, "you 'n me are a lot alike." Landsworth was beginning to slur his words considerably. His breath smelled like a distillery. He continued, filling

Bane's ears with hundred-proof words: "We're both successful men. We've *made* somethin' of ourselves."

"Yes Guy, we have."

A single tear slid down the businessman's cheek and dropped into his glass like an Acapulco cliff diver. He quickly returned the tear to his system as he took another guzzle. Then his voice began rising in a steady crescendo: "And bein' a Father yourself, you know that no matter how much of a piece a' shit your kid turns out to be, ya still want the best for the little cocksuckin' ingrate. An' you're goddam willin' to do almost anything to help the little piss-ant sonofabitch make somethin' of his-goddamn-good-for-nothin' self!" The Senator tried to hide behind the wine list as heads in the restaurant began to turn.

"I know what you mean, Guy. Whadda you say we continue this conversation over at my office on The Hill?"

Landsworth suddenly lowered his voice and held his shnockered face mere inches from Bane. "You know, Arnie, I own three major TV stations in our home state. One in Birmingham. One in Montgomery. And one in Mobile."

"I've advertised on all three of 'em durin' my campaigns," said Bane, "An' I got a primary just around the b—"

"One thing I didn't tell you about my son," Landsworth stuttered as he picked up the Senator's glass and took a large sip, "I said a lotta nasty things about Roger. But as much of a fuck-up as he is, my boy is one *hell* of a musician."

"I figured he had to have some redeemin' qualities," said the Senator, "after all, he did come from good stock."

Guy looked the Senator straight in the eye and said:

"Now I'm only gonna say this once, Arnie. Then it's up to you whether ya wanna follow through on it or not. If there's any way in Hell my boy Roger could write that Jesus

Christ oratorio a' yours, I'd give your campaign open ended credit on all three a' my TV stations."

Bane knew what Landsworth meant by 'open ended credit.' It meant he could run up a large bill and never have to pay it back. Television eats up the lion's share of a campaign budget. With unlimited TV time, the Senator could crush his competitors into the ground like cigarette butts.

"I'll tell you what, Guy," the Senator said as he picked up his glass and finished off what little bourbon Landsworth had left him, "I certainly will give this matter my utmost consideration."

*

"May I take your ord—? Matt!"

"Miss Bibble! Mom, this is Miss Bibble, my music teacher!"

Holly was surprised to see her ex-pupil and his mother in booth number seven for lunch.

"Miss Bibble, check this out," Matt chirped enthusiastically as he scooped up two forks and began playing a drum solo on the table. He had mastered all the techniques Holly had assigned him at his last lesson.

"Matthew!" scolded his Mother, "stop that this instant!"

"Mrs. McConnahee, I take it?" Holly asked while extending her hand, "I'm Holly Bibble."

"My husband and I have heard a lot about you, Miss Bibble," she said as the two women shook hands.

"Matt has a definite talent," Holly went on, "it's a shame they had to drop music from the schools."

"I know, isn't it?" Mrs. McConnahee agreed.

Then Holly went on: "I'd like to see Matt continue with his music privately—"

"Oh, we don't have the money for that, not the way the economy is—"

"Please, Mom?" Matt pleaded.

"I'll teach him free of charge," Holly offered.

"Can I, Mom? Can I? Can I?"

"Well, in that case, how can I say no?"

"Yayyyy!" Matt cheered as he forked a quick celebratory drumbeat on the tabletop.

"Matthew, *behave!*" chided his mother.

Holly wrote on a napkin and handed it to her. "Here's my number. Call me and we'll set up a lesson."

"This is very kind of you, Miss Bibble," smiled Matt's mother as she folded the napkin and put it in her purse. "Thank you."

"You're welcome," smiled Holly as she flipped another page in her light-green receipt pad and readied her pen, "Now, may I please take your order?"

*

"Ladies and Gentlemen of the Press," greeted Senator Bane in the press room at the Capitol building, "as Chairman of the Senate Arts Committee in charge of the *National Endowment For The Arts Commissioned Musical Work In Celebration of the New Millennium*," he winked and smiled, then added: "also known as the Christmas 2000 Celebration, it is with great honor that I announce to you today, the Amer'can composer we've see-lected to write this new mon-yew-mental work. After much consideration, we decided that if we were to choose an already established composer it would go against the grain of what made this country great.

"Amer'ca's always been, an' always will be, a land of opportunity for the little man. The maverick. The pioneer. The Alexander Graham Bells. The Thomas Edisons. The Wright Brothers. It's the little people with the big visions— the trailblazers — who turned this raw chunk a' real estate into the greatest country on Earth. The Senate Arts Committee wants to honor that tradition by choosin' an Amer'can composer from the ranks of the unknown. Someone who's been toilin' in the fields of art year after year without reward. And by awardin' this commission to this one unknown artist, we hereby pay tribute to all Unknown Artists throughout this great land.

"It is with much pride and honor that I announce to you the Unknown Composer we have chosen to write the Christmas 2000 Oratorio. His name, is:

Roger Milford Landsworth."

Scherzo

Someone was knocking on the door of his apartment. Roger Landsworth woke up in a stupor and looked at the clock. It was twelve-thirty already, but he was used to sleeping till four in the afternoon. His hair was sticking out in every direction. This, in conjunction with the bald spot on the top of his head, gave him the appearance of Bozo the Clown. He buried his bozo head under the pillow like an ostrich, hoping the knocking would go away. It didn't.

"Roger," said Torchena, his fourteen-year-old Puerto Rican girlfriend who was naked in bed beside him, "somebody's at the door."

"Whoever it is can go fuck themselves," Roger snorted from under the semen-stained pillowcase. Roger and Torchy had been up until seven in the morning smoking 'go,' a new designer street drug. 'Go' was a combination of crack cocaine, opium, and mescaline. During their drug induced high, they had sex repeatedly. Vaginal, oral, anal — sometimes the interactions involved inanimate objects. The sheets were still wet on Torchena's side of the bed.

The knocking persisted.

"Roger," she said, shaking him, "they aren't going away."

"Motherfuckers!" snarled Roger as he jumped out of bed. His cock was covered with a clear thin crust reminiscent of the glaze on a doughnut. He stormed across the room, kicking mounds of beer cans and pizza boxes out of the way. When he finally opened the door he blurted: "What the fuck do you assholes want?"

On the other side of the doorway stood reporters from *Time, Newsweek, The New York Times,* and *USA Today.* They stood petrified for a moment, obviously aghast at the sight of a nude thirty-nine year old man who wore his hair like Bozo. His apartment smelled like a cross between an opium den and Cupid's Gymnasium.

"Does Roger Milford Landsworth live here?" the petite blond reporter from *Newsweek* asked timidly, trying not to look at his sex-encrusted genitals.

"Who are you? The fucking cops?" Roger growled, still too stoned to realize he had no clothes on.

"No, we're from the Press," the *USA Today* reporter informed, "we'd like to ask Mr. Landsworth how he feels about being chosen to compose the Christmas 2000 Oratorio."

"What the fuck's a Whor-atorio?" Roger squealed.

The gentleman from the *New York Times* cordially elucidated: "A work for orchestra and voices usually with a sacred text."

Roger turned and yelled to his girlfriend, exposing the Press to the pink maze of fresh fingernail scratches on his back and buttocks, "Hey, d'ya hear that, Torch? I'm gonna jam out some tunes for a fucking orchestra!"

*

LESBIAN COUPLE seeks healthy sperm donor.
— Reader Reply #39-C

Holly read the ad she placed in the *Baltimore Sun*. Even though she and Kim didn't want a child for at least two years, she had no idea how long it would take to find 'Mr. Right in a Bottle,' as Kim referred to it. Kim had suggested using a website called *Craigslist* to find an appropriate sperm donor. But Holly had still not yet embraced the new Internet technology and preferred to do things the old-fashioned way. Besides, putting an ad in the newspaper was more aligned with her motto of 'Think Global — Shop Local.'

More and more Holly's maternal instincts were tugging at her heartstrings, especially after her first private lesson with Matt. She taught him a few complex drumming patterns known as paradiddles. He picked them up right away and was eager to learn more.

Once when she wasn't looking, the freckle-face boy put down the drumsticks and began playing the same rhythms on the keys of the piano. Using the index finger on each hand, he played the piano as if it were a marimba. The exuberance on the young boy's face was highly contagious.

Holly remembered the first time she played a melody on the clarinet. She recalled her teacher Mrs. Martinez and her loving encouragement. Now here she was, years later, the roles reversed. She was now the teacher to the student. It felt as though she were completing an important circle in her life. She imagined childrearing would bring an abundance of the very same sort of circles. Taking the first steps. Saying the first words. Singing the very first song.

Thoughts like these made her biological clock tick loud as a blacksmith striking an anvil. She wanted a baby now more than ever. Holly knew that being queer made motherhood a little more hard to come by. She hoped a healthy sperm donor would send a reader reply soon.

Waiting for the lunch crowd to arrive, Holly sat in the kitchen at *Denny's* thumbing through the rest of the coffee-stained newspaper. She read about all the billions of dollars being spent every day on the Armed Forces. Long, sleek, smart bombs. Big, fat, stupid bombs. Planes to drop the bombs regardless of their IQ. Mobile-launched missiles. Missiles to intercept those missiles. High-tech, big ticket items from the Military-Industrial candy store.

Men and equipment deployed on either side. Waiting for the other guy to make the first move. Unflinchingly held in place by the scourge of their gonads: testosterone. Aiming their armaments with eyes transfixed like two tomcats fighting over a feline in heat. Just like Toes used to do before his castration. Holly wondered if there was a possible way of ridding the world of war, short of taking a sword and lopping off every man's balls.

Holly thought: *What if we took a few thousand dollars from the military budget and built a few billboards that faced the enemy across the desert sand. One of the billboards could read:*

"WRITE MORE POETRY"

Another could say:

"SING MORE SONGS"

And, better yet, still another, with big, bold letters reading:

"LOVE ONE ANOTHER"

Holly wasn't sure if these billboards placed in the desert would have any effect. She knew it was naive to think that trained soldiers would lay down their guns and start to write poetry. Still, she considered writing her Congressman, figuring: *what would be the harm in trying?* She turned to the astrology section. Sometimes she read Kim's horoscope even though Kim didn't think it amounted to a hill of beans. Under *Leo,* it said:

Dramatic changes at hand in the foreseeable future.

Then she read her own:

The planet Uranus is in a favorable position for Libras this month. Expect an important communication soon.

Holly wondered if this "important communication" would be a response to her personal ad. A favorable father on the horizon would sure make her day.

She turned to the Arts section of the newspaper. An article there caught her eye:

UNKNOWN COMPOSER TAPPED FOR X-MAS 2000

Composer Roger Milford Landsworth was asleep Tuesday morning when a group of reporters turned up at his door. The Unknown Composer was evidently caught by surprise. He wasn't even aware he'd been awarded the commission for the coveted Christmas 2000 Oratorio.

He refused all interviews, according to one reporter, possibly because he was caught inappropriately attired. A spokesperson for Senator Bane's office, Mr. Charles Russell, said Landsworth would arrive in Washington "...within the week to discuss the particulars of the commission."

The spokesperson, Mr. Russell, went on to say that the unknown composer was 'tickled pink' to have the opportunity to create the world's first twenty-first century masterpiece.

ROGER LANDSWORTH LOADED HIS Les Paul guitar, his iMac computer and his underage girlfriend onto his Harley-Davidson and roared through the Holland Tunnel on his way to D.C.

As a young boy he became an avid Beatles fan. He started playing guitar at thirteen. At sixteen he dropped out of school and went on the road with a hard rock band. His wealthy Father disowned him during that time. But he could always count on Mom to Western Union him money whenever he got in a pinch.

Which was often.

During the 80's he played lead guitar in a heavy metal band called *Smegma.* They broke up in the early 90's when their album didn't sell. By then he was two years past thirty — over the hill for MTV. He tried wearing wigs and even had plastic surgery done to his face. But he would never again be the pretty boy all the girls buying records wanted to see. He pissed away the remainder of the decade playing blues with burnt-out musicians. And going in and out of drug rehabilitation centers.

During his most recent stay in Rehab, Roger met Torchy, who was thirteen years old at the time. She was placed there by the Youth Corrections Board after they found out she was addicted to heroin.

The Rehab Center had a policy of not allowing mirrors. There were none on the walls. Not even in the bathrooms.

Patients who couldn't shave without mirrors were advised to grow beards during their stay. There was psychological reasoning behind the "no mirrors" policy. An Austrian psychiatrist had recently theorized that all forms of self-abuse from masturbation to drug addiction were symptoms of a 'chronic narcissistic personality disorder.'

Narcissus was a mythical Greek who fell in love with his own reflection. He ended up drowning in a pool of water trying to look at himself too close.

Paradoxically, the mirror-less Rehab center kept its hallway floors highly waxed. The black and white checkerboard tiles had a high-gloss veneer that reflected like glass. That's where Torchy first saw Roger, hunched over his own reflection on the floor. A modern day Narcissus, picking his nose and sticking the boogers in his mouth.

"Hi," chirped Torchy, her cherubic face appearing in the shiny waxed floor tile.

"Hi," Roger parroted, wiping a green glob of snot on his blue cotton sleeve.

He turned and stood up. She was shorter than he was. Her tight little body packed in torn denim jeans reminded him of the girls who used to wait backstage for Smegma. Though he rarely remembered any of their names, Roger always remembered their panties. Cotton and lace and silk and satin, he had hundreds of them packed in an old worn out suitcase. It was all he had to show for ten years on the road. Once the record deal was gone, so was the money. And so were the loose little girls.

"You know," Roger said, finally breaking the silence,

"ordinarily I'd offer ya to come up to my room and smoke a joint but, seein' as we're in Rehab an' all—"

"Yeah, I wish I had a joint right now too," Torchy flirted, flashing a smile from a face with no lines. She batted her lashes like an underage nymph: "Last time I got buzzed was in Joovy," using the street slang for Juvenile Hall.

Roger couldn't resist. Her unabashed availability made him feel like he was in a rock band again. He looked around. The coast was clear. He motioned for Torchy to slip into the closet behind him. She did. He closed the door firmly. They stood in complete darkness.

"Well, here we are," he said, finding her waist with his hands.

"Yeah, here we are," she answered, reaching her own hands around him — squeezing his butt.

Following the sound of her voice, Roger moved his mouth toward the source of it like a panther stalking prey in the night. He found her soft lips adrift in the darkness then pounced on her breath — sucking it into his own. With tongues and teeth gnashing they peeled off each other's clothes as quickly as snaps-buttons-zippers would allow.

The frenzy of flesh that ensued culminated in a cacophonous clatter of brooms, mops, and buckets on the floor. For Roger, it was merely another notch in his failed rock star belt — another Kleenex to blow his nose. But in that moment of post-coital silence while he held her in his arms, Torchy clung to the hope that she'd finally found someone who would love her forever. Someone who wouldn't just fuck her and leave.

When Roger left Rehab he snuck Torchy out with him, taking her to live at his Greenwich Village apartment. Torchy liked living with Roger. What he lacked in the ability to express love he made up for by always having a plentiful supply of dope. Being stoned all the time helped her endure some of her new boyfriend's strange personal habits.

The most bizarre of Roger's personal habits, in Torchy's opinion, was his fetish for photographing his own excrement. In the bathroom, next to the john, he always kept a loaded Polaroid camera. Following every bowel movement, large or small, he would take a picture of his poop before wiping his ass and flushing. Roger kept his favorites in a leather bound photo album. The gold lettering on the cover read:

"My Favorite Dumps
by Roger Milford Landsworth"

Sometimes he would show his collection of Poo Polaroids to his friends when they were high on drugs. Always, they'd become a source of instant amusement. Roger would narrate as his friends flipped through the book. Page after page of his droppings on display. Turds large and small. Floaters and sinkers. Amber and umber and different shades of green. Long ones piled high like Lincoln-log cabins. Some curled like snakes in a pre-striking pose. Corn studded brown-yellow clusters of buck-shot. Bowlfuls of Arabic alphabet soup.

Roger's narrations of the photos were chock full of personal anecdotes. Often he would comment on which restaurant he'd patronized to produce a particular speci-men. Sometimes he'd remember exactly what was ordered, such as: "That one's lasagna!" or "This one was Pad Thai." Other times he would offer more detailed descriptions:

"That Mexican dive over on MacDougal Street. Four enchiladas and the salsa was hot as Hell! My asshole shit fire for a whole fucking week. Can ya believe it? A whole fucking week!"

Roger and Torchy were on his big Harley, roaring down Interstate 95. The cold February wind sharply whipped through their clothes. But they couldn't feel a thing — having both smoked a bong of 'go' before leaving.

As they cruised close to Baltimore, Torchena tapped Roger's leather jacket and yelled in his ear that she was hungry. He took the next exit and pulled into the parking lot of Denny's.

"May I take your order," Holly asked the windblown couple in booth number nine. At first she thought they must be father and daughter. But a closer glance revealed no blood relations. The man looked at least forty, or older. His scraggly blond shoulder-length hair was parted on one side and arched like a rug over the bald spot. Pop musicians had the same problem potential presidents had: a bowling ball head knocked them out of the race.

The girl looked Latin. Obviously in her early teens. Wavy, dark hair that curled in unkempt wisps down over her dark Caribbean eyes. A small, cute, turned up nose and full lips. She quickly scarfed down two hamburgers, onion rings and fries like an aardvark hovering over an ant farm. Her body was slim, in spite of what she ate, and showed contours of a budding young woman.

The bald-headed biker was abusive to Holly throughout the serving of their meal: "Look, Bitch, I want some coffee and I want it fucking *now!*"

It seemed every other word that came out of his mouth was a profanity of one kind or another. Then the last time Holly brought the coffee pot to their table, they were gone like the wind that he broke before leaving. They left no tip and the bill was unpaid. Ketchup was squirted all over the table, spelling:

"DIE YUPPIE SCUM
EAT SHIT"

And to top it off, Roger had discreetly urinated under the table. Holly heard the loud motorcycle leaving the parking lot and caught a glimpse of them riding up the southbound ramp. She called the police and gave them a description.

It wasn't too difficult for the Maryland Highway Patrol to pick Roger out of the southbound traffic that afternoon on I-95. A high-handlebar Harley Hog with an electric guitar case and a cherry-colored computer strapped on the front. A school-aged girl wearing a football helmet with her arms around his waist on the back. And to top it off, Roger always wore a World War II Nazi combat helmet when he rode his Harley.

When the Maryland State Police called Holly at Denny's and asked her to come down and file a formal complaint, she did so at the end of her shift. But when she got to the police station, she was told the ketchup-squirting desperados had already been released.

"Why did you let them go?" Holly asked.

"Connections in high places," said the Desk Sergeant.

Holly wanted to complain to someone. She felt like going off on a long-winded speech about all the injustices in the world. But instead she climbed into her Jetta and meekly drove home before evening rush hour.

Taking a detour down Calvert Street, she stopped by the classified offices of the *Baltimore Sun* to see if any potential donors had responded to her ad. She paid an extra fee to have the mail delivered to a private box at the newspaper offices to avoid having a horde of eager sperm donors showing up at her door.

"Anything for Reader Reply number 39-C?" she asked the pimply-faced, teenage kid behind the counter.

"Lemme check," he said in a high whinny voice as he disappeared into the back room. After a few minutes he came out dragging a large sack of mail behind him.

"You've got to be kidding!" Holly gasped.

He wasn't.

Fugue

Defrauding an establishment of food and beverage.
Vandalism.
Public urination.

When Senator Bane heard the charges against Roger Landsworth he started sweating profusely. *If the Press gets a hold of this, I'm doomed,* he thought. He pulled what political strings he had in Baltimore law enforcement. Roger and Torchy were out of jail in a jiffy.

The moment Senator Bane met Roger and saw his underage girlfriend he knew he had a public relations nightmare on his hands. Every time Roger spoke, obscenities flew out of his mouth like bats out of Carlsbad Caverns. And carting around his fourteen-year-old penis holster was a *National Enquirer* headline ready to explode.

Roger and Torchena sat on the reception sofa in the Senator's Capitol Hill office — the same sofa where Bane had banged Loni many a time. The recent coffee shop fugitives thumbed through magazines and chain-smoked cigarettes while Senator Bane put in an urgent call to his publicist, Charlie Russell.

"Why don't you let them stay at your place on the Bay," Mr. Russell suggested, "you know, the place where you pork your secretary all the time. Post a guardhouse by the road. Make it off limits to the Press. I'll issue a statement that the composer's a recluse and doesn't want to be disturbed while he's creating. It'll add an aura of mystique to the whole thing anyway."

"Charlie, you're a goddamn genius!" Bane lauded, hanging up the phone and re-arranging his genitals in his pants. He walked out to the reception area. Roger had used a cigarette to burn their names into the cherry wood tabletop:

"ROGER -N- TORCH"

The Senator was furious when he saw it but kept his anger contained. "Come on, kids," he said to the girl of fourteen and the thirty-nine year old man dressed in leather, "let's go for a ride in the limo."

*

Dear Lesbian Couple,
Enclosed is a full-length nude photo of myself. I am very healthy, virile, and as you can see, very well hung. I am willing to provide you with as much of the desired ingredient as you require, so long as it can be

administered in a method of my own choosing. I won't go for any of this modern Daddy-in-a-turkey-baster bullshit. You see, I'm what you'd call an old-fashioned kind of guy.

Sincerely Yours, Tom

~

Dear Reader Reply #39-C
I read with great interest your classified ad for sperm donor. I am a 17 year old high school senior with lots of masturbating experience. I really look forward to donating to your cause.

Love, Bradley

P.S. Can we do it as a threesome?

~

Dear Lesbians:
Wow, I'd really get off watching you two go at it sometime. In exchange I'll give you the jizz you want.

Yours truly, Danny

~

Attention Gash-Gobblers:
Ain't nothin wrong with you bitches that a good hard fuck won't cure. Call me if you ever wanna get normal again.

Rick

Holly sat on the corner of the bed, leafing through the responses to her personal ad. There were stacks of them. All with phone numbers and addresses. Some seemed like sincere inquiries. But most were downright seamy.

Kim was still asleep under the covers. Toes jumped up on the bed beside Holly and nuzzled his nose against her arm. He purred like a motorboat as she started to pet him.

Toes adopted Kim and Holly when they were in grad school. Kim heard scratching at the door one day. She opened it. In walked a great big gray tabby who meowed and meowed until she finally fed him some tuna fish from a can.

When Kim first discovered the cat had six digits on one paw and seven on another, she started calling him 'Toes.' The name stuck. Though Toes always showed up religiously at mealtime, he rarely spent the night in their apartment. Instead, he would prowl nearby frat house front lawns and back alleyways in search of stray pussycats in heat. Then he'd come back in the morning all scratched up and bloody from fighting the other male cats over who gets the booty. Holly thought Toes was no different than the men she used to serve drinks to at the Bulldog Saloon. "Fightin' 'n fuckin'!" was their unspoken creed. Holly felt sorry for the males of all species — whipped as they were by the whims of their weenies.

Kim grew very attached to ol' Toes, making sure he always got fed. She sliced a big enough hole in the back window screen so he could come and go as he pleased. When they relocated to Baltimore, Holly and Kim took Toes along too.

Toes was unhappy in his new digs: a small urban apartment on the seventh floor. He couldn't get the hang of a litter box at first. But worse, he couldn't prowl for felines at night. To show his dismay, he squirted on everything — chair legs and sofas and handbags and shoes. The final straw came the night he jumped up on the stove and urinated on one of the electric burners.

The next morning when Holly turned on the stove to boil water for tea the dried urine smoked and smelled up the whole apartment. All of their clothes and the drapes had to be dry cleaned. The smell on the furniture lasted for weeks.

Kim took Toes to the vet and had him castrated. After he got over the initial trauma, he became a very happy kitty indeed. He ate more than ever and became fat. No longer did he spray on the furnishings or yell to be let out late at night. And he started hitting the litter box every time.

"His problem was testosterone," Kim surmised, holding a meat cleaver in one hand after preparing rib roast for dinner, "I think I know the solution to all the problems in the world."

Then she slammed the meat cleaver down hard on the cutting board.

Holly read a few more prospective sperm donor letters. She realized it was a long shot finding "Mr. Right" this way. *A more direct method might be a better approach,* she thought to herself.

Kim began to stir under the patch-quilt comforter: "Good morning, Beautiful," she yawned, stretching her auburn arms toward the ceiling.

"It's afternoon," said Holly on the bed beside her.

Kim sat up and tossed her head, sending her long black hair cascading down her back. Her breasts were small, almost non-existent for a woman. She was taller than Holly, with slender hips, built like a track and field athlete.

Leaning over, she gave Holly a kiss on the middle of her forehead and said: "There's one for the pineal gland."

"I call it the Third Eye," said Holly before pondering aloud: "Why do men have to be such assholes?"

"Because they have a Third Leg," Kim smirked.

Holly cracked a smile and clobbered Kim with a pillow. Kim retaliated with a cushion of her own. Toes jumped off the bed to avoid the commotion. The two women laughed and tumbled together. Tussling and tickling till their laughter peaked. Holly slipped out of her clothes and slid her cold body beneath the pink flannel sheets. Kim quickly warmed her — rubbing her vulva like Aladdin rubbing the lamp.

"You know, Boo Boo," Holly said as Kim's finger slowly slid up inside her, "maybe the sperm bank isn't such a bad idea after all."

THE SENATOR'S LIMOUSINE DROVE southeast from Washington on Pennsylvania Avenue and then south on West Chesapeake Beach Road. The sun was about to set as they arrived at Bane's property on the shore of Chesapeake Bay. They followed the thin gravel driveway that wound its way through a thick forest of tall trees and scrub. It led to a quaint little blue-trimmed white cottage with a cherry-brick chimney and wooden swing on the porch.

Donald, the chauffeur, helped unload their luggage. He was the same age as Roger, but impeccably dressed. His hair was neatly trimmed underneath his black chauffeur's cap.

Roger wore tight leather pants that squeezed his sizable midriff bulge like a large ice cream cone. With his scuffed hobnail boots and bozo blond hair, Roger was the Peter Pan Principle pushed to the extreme.

"What about my fuckin' Harley, Man?" Roger whined as the Senator unlocked the front door to the cottage.

"I'll have somebody bring it out tomorrow," Bane promised. "Now feel free to use anything ya want. The 'frigerator's jam-packed with all kinds a' goodies. If ya get cold there's a big pile a' wood outside the back door to use in the fireplace. An' if there's anything ya need, you just pick up the phone and call this number."

The Senator handed Roger a card with a phone number. A special number Bane usually only gave to women he thought he might be able to have sex with on the sly. Neither his wife nor his secretary knew about the number. It rang a sky pager he kept with him 24 hours a day. The Senator wanted as few people as possible to have access to the Unknown Composer at his Chesapeake Bay cottage. Embarrassing details of Roger's lifestyle had to be kept from the Press at all costs.

"I think you'll both be comf'table here," said the Senator with a forced hospitable smile.

"Where's the fucking bathroom?" Roger blurted.

"Right over there," said the Senator, pointing it out.

"Fucking A," Roger bellowed, heading pronto for the door, "I'm gonna take me a fucking righteous dump! Grab the Polaroid, Torch, I can tell this one's gonna be a fucking Rembrandt!"

AS THE LAST FAINT light of daylight ebbed, Holly and Kim dipped their heads under the covers. Kim propped her knees up, making the bedspread dome up over them like a circus tent.

Holly carefully walked two fingers along Kim's caramel-colored tightrope thigh. Palming at the edge of the lion's mouth, her thumb began circling the soft skin outside. Suddenly the lion engulfed it. The crowd of one roared her hearty approval. Holly dipped her head in between the two Big Top poles (Kim's knees) and came face to face with the curly-maned lioness. She took a deep breath — it smelled cotton candy sweet. Then she opened her mouth and ate fire.

"Dee Dee?" Kim asked as Holly's tongue performed death-defying feats on the rim of her rapturous ravine.

"What?" Holly murmured, immersed in her work.

"Did you ever wonder what it'd be like to have a penis?"

"Yeah," Holly answered as she crisscrossed Kim's chasm. Lifting her head just enough to see Kim's face above the pubic horizon, Holly went on: "Back when I was growing up. My parents took us on camping trips up in Wisconsin. My two older brothers and Dad would just pee wherever they wanted to. It seemed so convenient to be able to take it out like that — instead of having to pull your pants down and squat."

"It would be convenient, wouldn't it?" said Kim as she clasp Holly's head with both hands and pulled her up toward her face.

"Maybe for peeing," Holly said as she kissed her way up Kim's flat chest, "But it's hard enough having to deal with big tits flopping around. I'd hate to think what it's like having something dangling between your legs all the time."

"I shutter at the thought," Kim teased, rolling over on her side.

They kissed, facing each other. Kim took Holly's breasts in her hands and squeezed them playfully like two Harpo Marx horns for the deaf. One hand went lower on a navel expedition. She found Holly's harbor at the height of high tide. Holly lifted one knee to facilitate Kim's finger. In the dark Bermuda Triangle it quickly disappeared. How many vessels have been lost in this abyss? This velvet-soft Venus flytrap of the sea. This curious canal that's lured many a sailor in search of the treasure of consummate bliss. Broken on the rocks, they flounder in the flotsam of history — shipwrecked and shaken. How many wars have been fought o'er this port? This stage entrance door to the passion play of Existence. Was it Helen of Troy's face that really launched all those ships? Or was it, in fact, her vagina?

Kim kissed Holly's mouth as she moaned with delight, forming a brief two-lipped-tongue Bridge of Sighs. Then her nose. Then her cheek. Then her ear as she so softly whispered:

"I have a surprise for you tonight."

AS SOON AS ROGER and Torchy were left alone in the cottage, he pulled out his stash bag of 'go.' They smoked a hefty pipe full. The effect of the cocaine and opium mixture makes a euphoric rush followed by a sensation of floating. Then the mescaline kicks in, providing a few hours of psychedelic hallucinations. During the beginning 'rush' part of the high, Roger fucked Torchy on the Oriental rug in front of the fireplace, their naked bodies glowing gold from the burning fire.

During the 'floating' opium phase, they both lay flat on their backs watching moonbugs on the ceiling till the mescaline started taking affect. Then the roof of the cottage peeled off like the lid on a rusty can of sardines. The rug beneath them laughed as it came alive — becoming a magic carpet that flew them up into the sky and whizzed them like a comet on a rollercoaster course through a luminous nebula cloud on the other side of the Milky Way.

"Whoa!" said Roger like a stagecoach driver trying to rein in the wild horses tugging at his brain.

"Holy shit," exclaimed Torchy, feeling the same.

Their words ec-ec-echoed around the room assuming physical form as tinker toy letters in long vocabulary trains derailed mid-air bounce-bouncing off walls split into molecules back again as munchkins scurrying upwards scaling lampshades twist-twist-twisting their whiskers pulling them tightly into bows with arrows launched in curly-Q flights sail through the air crash hitting the light smash-shattering into porcelain shards rain downward sparks from a cowboy's fire bill-billowing through mosaic window swarm of bees buzz-buzzing through limbs of moonlight making shadows on trees crack-crackling popping sparkling fireflies forming constellations in the steamy star-studded sky.

Roger pulled his finger from Torchy's bum, rolled over and reached for the pipe. Slurring his words like a mouth full of bubble-gum, he merrily marfulled: "Let's smoke some more a' that shit."

Which they did.

LUCIUS BANE SAT UP in bed and punched the TV remote control. He flipped through the vast wasteland of channels. Some intellectual spouting a string of big words about how "the triumph of Liberal Democracy is a clear sign we've reached what Francis Fukuyama called *The End of History.*" Click. A Special Report on the depletion of the ozone layer. Click. A documentary showing the extinction of many of the world's species. Click. Bane stopped changing channels when he came to *The David Letterman Show.*

"Tonight," Letterman announced from the same stage where 36 years before Ed Sullivan introduced the Beatles to America, "our guest is performance artist Jon LaRue."

"Lord have mercy," sighed Lucius.

"I can't believe they're giving that madman all this publicity," Dolores complained from the twin bed next to her husband. Usually she stayed at their home in Birmingham even while Congress was in session. But she was in Washington for the week to attend a benefit for abused toy poodles. Otherwise, the Senator usually had the apartment in the Watergate complex all to himself.

Lucius couldn't wait for Dolores to go back to Alabama so he could start having Loni come over. Now that his Chesapeake Bay cottage was occupied, the only place he could have sex with his non-typing secretary was after hours at the Capitol office. But now in the post-Zippergate era even that was risky. The climate inside the Beltway seemed like every media watchdog from the Washington Post on down to the dreaded Drudge Report was crouched behind every proverbial bush, bus, and park bench ready to pounce, pick, and pummel any government figure with so much as a pubic hair out of place.

Dolores was propped up on her twin bed with pillows. The springs squeaked beneath the enormous strain of her ever-expanding buttocks below. Her pajamas were orange. Florida orange. She bought them on vacation in Orlando. Her Clairol-dyed chestnut hair was pinned in tiny ringlets resembling badly made tortellini. The mucus-green mudpack she had smeared on her face made her look like a Martian on acid. Dried mud cracked around the corners of her mouth as she opened it to stuff in more potato chips and ice cream.

The Senator peeled back a 'scratch-n-sniff' card that was part of his GloptaFast diet kit. He stuck the adhesive backed movie-ticket-sized card under his nostrils and left it there. Then he took a spoon and began eating a large bowl of GloptaMeal, a pudding-like substance with no taste of its own.

The GloptaMeal pudding would taste like whatever Scratch-N-Sniff card was fastened beneath the dieter's nostrils. The card Bane had stuck under his nose was labeled:

"PORTERHOUSE STEAK — MEDIUM WELL DONE"

The Scratch-N-Sniff sniffer made the GloptaMeal taste exactly like a thick, juicy, charbroiled steak.

The GloptaFast Scratch-N-Sniff Diet was the latest fad on the American diet scene. Several afternoon talk show hosts had slimmed down their anatomies using it. They touted its effectiveness in supermarket checkout stand magazines. Charles Russell advised Senator Bane to lose some weight or else he would look like King Henry the VIII in his upcoming re-election ads.

Bane took his publicist's advice and purchased a six-month supply of the pudding and nasal sniff card combinations.

As green-faced Dolores crunched mesquite-flavored chips and Letterman rattled off his nightly Top Ten List on the tube, Senator Bane gobbled glop and sniffed Scratch-N-Sniffers that made the glop taste like Porterhouse. With a tremendous rumble that rattled the room, Lucius let out a machine-gun rectal ripper. It smelled bad enough to curl the hairs in one's nose.

Dolores grabbed an aerosol can of room freshener by her bed. She sprayed the air befouled by her husband's emissions. Thirty years of marriage had well prepared her for the malodorous blasts. Because he was constipated, the Senator's anal orifice emitted much more gases than solids. For this very reason Dolores insisted on twin beds instead of a king-size. She got fed up with the intestinal smog that lingered nightlong under the covers — courtesy of her frequently flatulating husband.

They hadn't had sex together in over three years. To her it was a cumbersome, unsanitary task she could well do without. Which was fine with Lucius. He much preferred slipping it to his secretary.

Since the Senator aspired to be President someday he had a certain decorum to maintain. Otherwise he would gladly divorce Dolores. But she was his decorum. The family. The home. The American Dream come true.

"Ladies and Gentlemen," announced Letterman on the tube, "with us tonight is New York Performance Artist Jon LaRue, performing his latest piece, entitled: *Mapplethorpe's Last Supper.* So without further ado, let's have a warm welcome for Jon LaRue!"

LaRue appeared on the TV screen wearing a stars and stripes G-string. A nine-foot long bullwhip flowed behind him like a tail. The smooth wooden handle was stuffed up his anus. Both hands were handcuffed behind his back. A nun was in front of him on her hands and knees. An assortment of hamburgers and hot dogs and Hostess Twinkies were arrayed on the back of the nun. An air-raid siren went off. LaRue fell to his knees and began eating the junk food with the fervency of a Cub Scout trying to win a pie-eating contest. The siren kept blaring. While eating like a pig, LaRue recited the Gettysburg Address backwards:

"Equal created are men. All that proposition the to dedicated and liberty in conceived Nation. New a continent. This upon forth brought Forefathers. Our ago years seven and score four."

At the conclusion of the recitation, the nun stuck a ruler down LaRue's throat. He threw up all over the front of her habit. The studio audience exploded with riotous applause.

"I can't believe this man is actually making a living with this kind of filth," commented Dolores as she finished off one bag of potato chips and immediately opened another.

"Where do you get your ideas for your work?" Letterman asked as LaRue dislodged the whip from his anus before sitting down on the talk show couch.

"From Life," LaRue answered matter-of-factly, slinging the chocolate tipped bullwhip on the floor.

"This piece you just performed," Letterman went on, "could you possibly, uh, enlighten us as to what it's meaning might be?"

"It's a metaphor for the breakdown of American society," LaRue postulated, scratching his balls through his star spangled G-string.

"Of course," said Letterman, tossing his pencil in the air, "Why couldn't I have figured that out? It must have been the bullwhip that threw me off."

LaRue went on: "We could spend hours dissecting the symbolism of the piece. But that would be a waste of valuable airtime. Because the symbolism in *Mappelthorpe's Last Supper* should be obvious to any human being of even mid-level intelligence."

"Thank you, Jon LaRue," Letterman quickly interjected, "Now here's something we humans of mid-level intelligence can certainly relate to: a commercial break."

A commercial for antacid tablets blared from the TV. Dolores crunched more chips and picked up a *Reader's Digest*. Lucius ate more GloptaMeal that tasted like steak. He lifted one rump and expelled some more gas.

Adding insult to injury of the ozone.

KIM BLEW OUT THE candle and reached under the bed. She took out a box and pulled something from it.

"What is it?" Holly asked.

"Shhh," came Kim's reply in the darkened room.

As Holly's eyes adjusted she could see Kim's silhouette. She appeared to be putting on a garter belt or something.

"Did you buy new lingerie?" Holly questioned.

"Shhhh," hissed Kim as she fidgeted with something around her waist.

"Tell me," begged Holly.

"Damn, this thing isn't going on right!"

"What?"

"Oh, there we go," said Kim climbing back into bed. She laid down on her back under the comforter.

"What have you got?" Holly asked.

"Check it out for yourself," Kim goaded. "Go on, don't be a scaredy cat."

Holly cautiously tiptoed her fingers down below Kim's waistline. She crossed over a leather belt of some sort. Was it a new bathing suit? A —

"Oh, my God!" shrieked Holly, quickly pulling her hand away, "I don't believe it! You didn't!"

"I did."

Holly reached again for the groin of her lover. There, standing straight as a California redwood was a nine-inch strap-on dildo — replete with dangling buckskin balls.

"I can't believe you actually bought this thing, Boo Boo."

"I bought it for you, Dee Dee," came Kim's reply as she rolled over on top and gingerly inserted her key in the lock of Holly's vaginal kingdom.

Kim made love to Holly that night as a man would make love to a woman. It was a novelty for Holly. A playful deviation from their normal sexual flight plan.

For Kim, it was much more than that.

Rondo

After evacuating his bowels into the toilet, Roger was faced with a difficult dilemma. A pimento-sized speck of defecation was stuck on the hairs around his sphincter. He knew if he tried plucking it out with toilet paper, as he had tried on occasion before, it would only smear it and make matters worse. Then, only a hot soapy shower with thorough butt-scrubbing would render him underwear-ready.

If he was in a rush to go somewhere he would have to resort to the smear method. But the better course of action, he knew, was to patiently wait for the force of gravity to coax the stubborn stool sample down from its loft in his soft rectal hairs. Down, down, into the foul smelling toilet bowl waters below. Amongst the acrid armada of excrement ships, the tugboat of a turdlet would be launched with a high-pitched "plop." Actually it's more of a "plip" than a "plop" depending on the tinyness of the turd. (Bear in mind this is not an exact science.)

Since Roger was in no rush to go anywhere he decided to sit this one out. A magazine rack was conveniently located in the space between the toilet and the sink. Roger thumbed past several back issues of *Playboy* he'd already seen back in New York and jerked off to. Finally, he settled on the February issue of *The Johnside Review*.

The Johnside Review was launched late in the 1990's by a New York magazine publisher. A survey found that seventy percent of the American population does most of its reading while on the toilet. This entrepreneurial publisher decided to exploit this untapped market.

The Johnside Review was an instant hit. Its circulation rivaled *USA Today* and sometimes even surpassed *The National Enquirer*. The magazine had no trouble selling ad space to companies hawking enemas, douches, suppositories, crab lice insecticides and feminine deodorant sprays.

Roger opened the magazine and found its contents page divided into three distinct sections: "Long Sit. Medium Sit. Short Sit." He turned to an article in the Medium Sit Section, hoping he didn't have to wait more than ten minutes for the turd to break loose and go plip.

He read part of an article titled: "Solid Waste Management in Fargo, North Dakota." It was about a new fleet of garbage trucks that the city of Fargo just bought. The article had several full-color photos. Roger liked looking at all the pictures of shiny new sanitation trucks — especially the ones that showed attractive young coeds in swimsuits stretched out on the hoods or standing in provocative poses with one high-heeled foot propped up on the bumper. Since the reluctant turdlet had still not dropped from his anal hair entanglement, Roger turned to the 'Long Sit' section of the *Johnside Review* and read a longer article titled:

Life On Earth Briefly Explained
by Jon LaRue

The Universe is an on-going process of matter being converted into energy. Matter exists in three different forms: solid, liquid, or gaseous. Energy exists in waves such as sound, or light, or invisible radiation.

The sun sends waves of radiation to the Earth. Plants convert this energy into matter through photo-synthesis. A hundred million years ago dinosaurs ate these plants — turning them into dinosaur defecation.

Picture, if you will, the magnitude of a Brontosaurus turd. Imagine getting hit with the droppings of a flying Pterodactyl. The dinosaurs roamed the Earth for 125 million years. The amount of shit they produced over this period of time would create a pile as high as the Himalayas.

As the Ice Age approached, this voluminous quantity of dinosaur crap took longer to decompose. Vast accumulations became buried under sediment, which was then covered over with oceans. Over millions of years, the pressure and heat transformed this humungous heap of dinosaur poop into petroleum. The same stuff that powers most of the industrialized world.

From the sun, to the plant, to the dinosaur's sphincter, to the gas tank of the family car. A wave becomes a solid that becomes a liquid and gas that — with a spark — becomes, once again, a wave.

Psychologists tell us that a newborn human goes through three major stages of infant development: oral, anal, and genital — each corresponding to a main orifice of the body. These three main bodily orifices are actually valves for incoming or outgoing matter. Solids, liquids, or gases pass through these ports.

An infant first goes through the oral stage, as this is the valve that takes in either solid or liquid nourishment. Next comes the anal stage, as the tot becomes aware of the valve that releases the solids his body no longer needs.

The genitals, as well, play a role in the emission of unusable liquid forms of matter. But as babies explore the parts where they pee they discover a whole new world of sensations. Most of the body's pleasure receptors have been disproportionately centered in this central region of the anatomy. For good reason. When the genitals are properly stimulated the brain releases endorphins, a natural form of heroin. Without this euphoric "fix" that accompanies an orgasm it is questionable whether human beings would even bother to go through all the messy business that is necessary to propagate the species.

Let's consider the mating process for a moment in the context of matter and energy exchange. At first an exchange of gifts is required: dinner (a solid), wine (a liquid), and flowers (whose fragrance is gaseous.) Then depending on either the prevailing mood or the amount of wine consumed during the interim, the penis (a solid form of matter, especially when erect) is inserted into the valve called vagina. Much writhing and thrashing about is carried on to ensure proper friction to the penis. This causes the solid form of matter to discharge a liquid called semen into the valve called vagina. At this point, the brain secretes an endorphin-opiate as a Pavlonian reward to the male during orgasm. If the male happens to be sensitive to the female's sexual needs he will see to it that she receives this euphoric reward as well. Otherwise, she may later resort to her personal vibrator (a solid, often kept on standby.)

But once a human being has been fed, fucked, and flatulated the more metaphysical concerns of existence start to rise to the fore. This is the mark of Cain, the price we pay for Self-Consciousness. Sometimes these existential concerns pose themselves as questions such as:

Is God a solid, a liquid, a gas — or a wave?

Questions like this are very much on the minds of human beings at the turn of the 21st century. The quest for Truth beyond the physical plane has long been The Holy Grail of human endeavor. But what always seems to get in the way of our spiritual evolution are those same three bodily orifices relentlessly crying out to be fed-fucked-and-emptied on demand.

This is the crux of the human dilemma. Our Bodies crawl through the compost like worms in the shit while our Spirits long to be fluttering with the butterflies.

But unfortunately our spiritual wings are pinioned by our mouths, genitalia, and assholes.

~

Out of the blue Roger heard a tiny plip in the waters below his bare keester. This signaled the end of his reading. He tossed the magazine back in the rack and reached for the roll on the wall. But he stopped in mid-reach as he glanced down through his crotch into the waters of the john.

"Torch, come here, quick!" he trumpeted, "Torchy!"

Torchena came running into the bathroom from where she was avidly watching *The Real World* on MTV. "What is it?" she asked with a look of trepidation on her face.

"Look," Roger exalted, pointing his finger triumphantly toward the waters of the toilet bowl sea.

There in the midst of two medium-sized cruisers was a

battleship. A perfect eleven-inch turd. Roger beamed like a man just informed of his fatherhood by a nurse in the maternity ward.

"Wow," Torchy gushed with feigned enthusiasm after looking in the toilet, realizing how much it meant to him.

"I think this is one for the book, don't you?" Roger asked.

Torchena knew what that meant. "Yeah," she smiled as she reached for the Polaroid camera next to the sink.

Roger took a picture of his recent rectal accomplishment. With the solemnity of a priest, he reached for the handle and flushed. The unbreakable brown fecal flagship spun slowly around like the needle of a compass. As the waters swirled into a whirlpool the bowel movement twirled like a majorette's baton. Then faster — like an airplane propeller — finally breaking in half as it slipped down the watery chute.

"It's a fucking masterpiece!" Roger boasted, as the Polaroid developed before his eyes. He would add it to his collection of *My Favorite Dumps* that he left back at his apartment in New York.

Torchena thought Roger's fascination with his poop was peculiar, for sure. But she considered it a relatively harmless pastime and cheerfully played along. After all, she'd been privy to a lot worse traits in men during her years as a child prostitute.

Roger wiped his ass and walked out to the living room. Picking up his guitar, he adjusted the strap and slung it over his shoulder. He wore it real low — just above his knees — a remnant of his days as a rocker. In musician's slang, an "axe" is someone's personal musical instrument. Roger's "axe" was a gold Les Paul guitar of custom vintage.

Reaching for the cord that hung from his axe like an over-sized spiraling penis, he plugged it into a MIDI interface connected to his computer.

Seeing that he was about to play, Torchy turned off the sound on the television. *The Real World* was over and the cable channel was now playing music videos. As Roger prepared for his live living room performance, she silently watched a video of her favorite band, *The Mutant Gay Love Nodes from Texas.*

As Torchy stayed glued to the MTV images, Roger stood naked in front of the window. There was snow on the ground around the cottage. He smoked some more "go" and began to play his Les Paul. Convincing himself that the wind through the trees outside was caused by his guitar playing, Roger looked out across the bay and imagined he was God.

As the InstaNote software was booting up on his computer, Roger played sloppy guitar licks left over from his youth. Once it booted up, the computer transcribed every note Roger played into musical notation. Roger didn't know how to read or write music. He taught himself guitar by listening to records and mimicking what he heard— the same way a parrot learns to speak.

Roger turned away from the window and looked at the small computer screen. He watched with fascination as the notes showed up on the staff lines a split-second after he played them. Dark little dots with stems appeared like clothes strewn across a clothesline.

He plucked a single string and held it. A hollow whole-note plopped itself in the middle of every bar. Each one connected by a series of tie marks like cables on the George Washington Bridge. Strumming a chord made six separate whole notes pop up like a totem pole. Roger was amazed at the miracle unfolding before his eyes.

When he would pluck the same string repeatedly the notes became birds on a telephone wire. A series of scales played up and down made mountain peaks and valleys (much like the digital displays on the Life-Cycle bikes he rode in Rehab).

After a few minutes he got bored, put down his guitar and turned on the printer. He hated the sound of the printer. So he went into the bedroom and smoked some more "go" and Torchy turned the sound back up on the TV. *The Mutant Gay Love Nodes from Texas* were lip-syncing the end of their latest hit song:

> *"Tell me what to say-hey,*
> Tell me what to say-hey,
> Tell me what to say
> 'Cause I don't know."

When the printer went silent, Roger tore off the ten-page printout and swung it around the room as if it were a long Chinese kite. Then he picked up the phone to call Washington. Since he'd lost the slip of paper Bane gave him, he had to dial 411 to get the number.

"Yeah, lemme talk to the Senator! Roger. Roger Landsworth, you stupid cunt!"

Suddenly a video of Torchena's second most favorite band, *The Donkey Condoms*, played on MTV. They had a song on the charts titled: "Bungee Cord Mating Ritual." Their lead singer sounded like Donald Duck with his nuts in a vise grip. They just released a new CD called "Tied Up & Tank Topped In Tijuana."

"Turn that fucking thing down!" Roger barked, "Can't ya see I'm fucking talkin' on the phone?"

Torchy turned the sound off again. She wondered why Roger was so angry. Maybe she hadn't heaped enough praise on his recent toilet bowl extravaganza. Perhaps she hadn't screamed loud enough while faking her orgasm with him earlier that morning. Whatever it was, she wanted to make amends right away. If he told her to leave she would have to go back to sucking off strangers on street corners. Unsolicited, she got down on her knees in front of him and began giving him a blowjob. Roger came quickly and let out a high-pitched scream just as his benefactor finally got on the phone.

"Roger, you all right, Buddy?" came the Senator's voice on the other end of the phone, obviously concerned.

"Fucking A, Man!" Roger answered as Torchena coaxed the last drops from his penis.

Bane dispensed with the chit-chat and cut to the chase: "How's the oratorio comin' along?"

"In-fucking-credible," Roger bragged as Torchy pulled her head away from his crotch, "I just got done with the first fucking movement!"

"How is it?" asked Bane who coincidentally happened to have Loni going down on him under the large oak desk in his Capitol office.

"It's a fucking masterpiece!" Roger boasted, "the greatest fucking thing ever written in the history of mankind!"

*

"It can't be as bad as all that," Bane protested.

"It's worse than bad," Professor Bormstern informed, looking over the computer printout of Roger's First Movement, "it's abysmal. Worse than abysmal, if there is such a thing."

The Senator wheeled around in his desk chair and looked out his office window. The long grassy stretch of the Capitol Mall was like a bowling alley for the Jolly Green Giant. Midway between him and the Lincoln Memorial stood the Washington Monument like a solitary bowling pin on the verge of being knocked down.

The Senator's tit was in the proverbial wringer. He had just won the Republican primary back home. But he'd barely squeezed past his opponents. He would have lost were it not for all the TV ads he ran on the Guy Landsworth stations. And he would need even more airtime in the fall if he hoped to beat Rupert Conyers, who was ahead in the polls.

Conyers, who won the Democratic primary, would be a formidable opponent indeed. If Bane fired Roger and hired a competent composer to write the oratorio, he would have to pay off the twelve million dollars owed to Landsworth's stations. Even worse, he would have to "pay as he played" in the upcoming fall campaign. And it was doubtful he'd be able to raise enough money to finance the kind of TV blitz that would be necessary to keep his seat in the Senate.

"What about a ghostwriter?" the Senator proposed.

"You mean someone to compose the score and put this joker's name on it?" Bormstern asked incredulously.

"You betcha," Bane retorted, "Hell, in politics we use speechwriters all the time. Even the President. Who's got time to sit around writin' speeches all day long? We got more important things to do."

The Senator looked at his watch. He was meeting Loni at a hotel later on so they could have sex in bed for a change.

"If this were composing a score for television or the movies," Bormstern went on, "it would be an entirely different matter. Ghostwriting goes on in those fields all the time. But not with a serious work of art, Senator. There has to be some integrity left somewhere, don't you think?"

"Sydney, I'm locked in with this no-talent low-life," Bane sighed, wadding Roger's printout score and tossing it in the trash. "Don't ask for the dee-tails. You don't wanna know. Now I hired you as a consultant an' now I need some consultin'. Quick. Hey, you're a composer. Why don't you write the damn thing. I'm sure I kin squeeze ya an extra fifty grand or so outta the federal budget — even though things are gettin' kinda tight."

"If I were ten years younger, I'd jump at the chance," said Bormstern, "and I wouldn't even care about the money. But my health hasn't been good; I doubt I'd have the stamina to see it through. It's hard work and it takes a lot out of you. But, you know, Senator, I've had a couple grad students over the years whom I'm sure would be able to do an excellent job. But as to whether they'd be willing to prostitute themselves like this and put someone else's name on it, that's another—"

"Everybody's got a price," the Senator interrupted, "you just gimme some names, and leave the rest up to me."

HOLLY COULDN'T QUITE FIGURE out the message on her answering machine when she got home from Denny's that day. She played it over several times:

"Hi, Ms. Bibble, my name is Charles Russell. When you have a spare moment please give me a call at 301-555-6269. I have what I believe could be a very fruitful proposition to make to you. Thank you and have a wonderful day."

"What do you think?" Holly asked Kim who was just waking up.

"Obviously calling about your sperm donor ad," Kim answered, "I think the key word is 'fruitful' as in 'be fruitful and multiply.'"

"But I didn't put my phone number in the ad."

"They have your phone number down there at the newspaper office, don't they? Probably some punk who works there got your number and passed it along to his friends."

Holly began dialing the number.

"You're not going to actually call this jerk, are you?"

"Why not? Maybe he's got a big dick," Holly laughed, then kissed her lover on the lips and added: "but nowhere as big as yours, Boo Boo."

Kim began tickling Holly under her ribs just as the phone was picked up on the other end.

"Charles Russell Agency," came a female voice through the phone.

Holly, laughing hysterically said: "Charles Russell, please. Holly b-b-b-b-Bibble calling — Boo Boo, stop!"

"Are you all right?" came a man's voice on the other end.

"Yes. Ow, Stop it, Boo! I said *stop!*"

"I hope I'm not interrupting anything," said the man on the phone.

Holly pulled away from Kim and walked to the other side of the room with the phone.

"Hello, Mr. Russell?"

"This is he. Am I speaking with the infamous Holly Bibble?"

"Do I know you?" Holly asked.

"No." the man answered. "Ms. Bibble, I'm calling on behalf of a client of mine in the Washington area."

"And?"

"I apologize for leaving such a vague message on your machine. But the nature of what I have to propose to you dictates, well, shall we say, the utmost confidentiality. I was wondering if we could meet at a place of your choosing to discuss the particulars in person."

"Are you a lawyer?" asked Holly.

"No. I'm a PR man, M'am. Public relations."

"I'd like to know how this client of yours got my number?"

"He's very well-connected, M'am."

"Stop calling me M'am."

"Sorry, I'd be happy to address you in whatever manner you prefer."

"Listen, Mr. Russell, I can save us both a lot of time and gasoline if you'll just answer me this: this 'client' of yours wants to be a donor, am I right?"

"A donor?" asked Mr. Russell, perplexed, "Oh, now I see what you're saying — yes, my client is willing to make a donation. A very sizable donation. You could consider it as a form of endowment, if you wish."

"Uh huh," said Holly," well, you can tell your well-endowed client to go take his big donation and shove it!" She slammed down the phone in a huff.

"Bravo," said Kim, clapping her hands. *"Bra-vo."*

The phone rang immediately. Kim picked it up.

"Yes?"

"Is Holly there?" asked the male voice.

Holly, who had her ear up next to the receiver silently mouthed to Kim: "It's *him*."

"Yes, Holly *is* here," Kim informed, "but I'm afraid she's in the bathroom right now, masturbating with a rather large dildo."

Holly had to bury her face in the pillow to keep from laughing out loud.

"Is there anything I can help you with?" Kim continued.

"I need to talk to Holly," Mr. Russell pleaded, "it's very urgent!"

"How urgent is it, Big Boy?" Kim baited.

"Listen, I think we're getting our signals crossed here somewhat—

"Oh, are we now? Well, listen, I think Holly's almost done with the dildo now," Kim held the phone away from her mouth and yelled: "Holly! Are you done with the dildo yet? Somebody wants to talk to you on the phone! And when you're done with it bring it in here to me, I wanna use it too! No, don't bother to wash it off!" Then back into the phone she said: "Yes, she says she's almost through with it, Sir. By the way, what's this I hear about somebody being well-endowed?"

"Look," said Charlie, who was getting a hard-on from all the dirty talk, "just ask Holly Bibble if she'd be interested in composing the Christmas 2000 Oratorio?"

Holly heard the words. In the moment of pin-drop silence that followed, Kim peered into her lover's eyes and saw a light that only shines when an impossible dream comes true.

Polonaise

Holly followed the directions Charlie gave her. Second gas station after the bridge. There it was: a long black limousine parked in the back of the Phillips 66. Holly pulled her Jetta into the lot, splashing through several puddles — remnants of a recent rain. She parked next to the limo with government plates and tapped on the dark tinted windows. The back door opened up and two middle-aged men bearing a resemblance to Laurel & Hardy motioned her inside. One was tall and thin, the other one fat.

"Hi, Miss Bibble, I'm Senator Bane," said the fat one, "and this here's my attorney Marvin Hamelstein. Care for a drink?"

"No thanks," Holly replied, "I'm a teetotaler, really."

Hamelstein went on to explain in detail the contents of the contract. He pulled the multi-page document from his important looking briefcase. She would compose the oratorio. But she would relinquish all claim of authorship. Also, she would have to initial a 'confidentiality clause.' This meant she could never publicly reveal that she was the oratorio's composer. If she did she would be subject to a civil lawsuit. For all this Holly would be paid the sum of fifty-thousand dollars in cash. No taxes taken out.

Holly signed the contract. But she felt uneasy about the ghostwriting aspect of it.

"How does this Roger Landsworth person feel about having his name on someone else's work?" Holly asked as the ink of her signature was still not quite dry.

"He doesn't know," said the lawyer.

"An' we don't want him to find out neither," Senator Bane quickly added while pouring himself a *Jack Daniels* from the backseat mini bar, "that's why I want ya to meet him this afternoon. We told him every big time composer uses a copyist to copy the music into all the little-bitty parts for all the instruments. We gave him a list of names, and fer some dang reason he picked your name outta the bunch. Now all you gotta do is go talk to him an' the job's yours."

"Paragraph forty-three letter 'F'," Hamelstein cut in, turning to a specific page in the contract, "This agreement is contingent upon COMPOSER'S approval of COPYIST."

"All ya gotta do is meet with him," said Bane, "and let him know you're just a copyist, and *he's* the one who's actually writin' the dang music."

"But as soon as he hears it performed he's going to know it's not what he wrote!" Holly argued.

"By then it won't matter," Bane replied. "Besides, I think the poor bastard is so dim-witted, he won't know the diff'rence anyhow."

"If this guy's as bad as you say he is," Holly pried, "why don't you just fire him and get a real composer instead of going through all this rigmarole?"

The Senator slugged down the rest of his whiskey and said in a patronizing tone: "Now, Miss Bibble, you just write us a nice piece a' music and don't you worry your purty little head about those kinda dee-tails. Take it from me: there's some things in life you're better off not knowin'."

*

"Torchy, get the camera!" Roger demanded as he stood up from the toilet and beheld his glorious work. The compliant teenager grabbed the Polaroid InstaMatic and rushed to the bathroom like a messenger on an urgent mission. Roger took the camera from her, aimed it straight down at the bowl and clicked a picture. But the flash failed to go off. Roger quickly looked at the row of flash bulbs on the top of the camera. They were all spent. He pulled the flashcube bar from the Polaroid and slung it across the room like a GI in combat ejecting a spent rifle clip.

"Get me another one a' those fucking things!" he snapped.

"There's none left," said Torchy, "you used 'em all up last night takin' pictures of me stickin' beer bottles up my twat, remember?"

"You fucking bitch!" he reprimanded, "you should a' gone up to the store today and got some more! You stupid cunt!"

"Fuck you," Torchy said, not meaning to. The words just flew out of her mouth like a cuckoo clock striking one.

Roger hit her. Hard. "Nobody says 'fuck you' to me, you fucking little whore!"

Torchy ran out of the cottage. It was starting to drizzle. The rain and tears ran across her swollen cheek where Roger hit her. She kept running even as he came to the back porch and yelled out into the forest: "If you don't come back here right now, you little slut, I'm gonna call the fucking social worker and have your ass sent back to Joovy!"

Torchy kept running into the woods. The tall trees overhead dripped bigger drops than the ones the sky was offering. They hit Torchy's head like Chinese water torture. She kept running. Through the soaked shrubs and brambles, some bristling with tiny green buds with high hopes of becoming flowers. She slipped in the mud and slid face first along the soaking wet forest floor. When she came to a halt she was a tar baby of detritus and leaves.

She stayed there on the ground with Roger's gutter-mouthed yelps echoing through the woods. Calling her "cunt" and "whore" and saying he would smash her face in if she didn't come back that very instant. And she cried and cried and cried as she realized she had nowhere else to go.

HOLLY FOLLOWED THE SENATOR'S limousine three miles down winding Maryland State roads. Along the way she had a spiritual revelation of sorts. She metaphorically saw her body as being a car. Her soul, or consciousness, was the driver. Everyone is issued a car at birth to get them around this existence. Some cars run better than others. Some are much nicer to look at. Plastic surgery can change a bumper here, a hood ornament there. But you're basically stuck with the car you were issued at the outset of the trip. Proper maintenance will help the vehicle run smoother. But sooner or later it'll sputter and wheeze. One day you'll ditch it alongside the road. Then the soul gets out and starts hitchhiking again. The wanderer who's been wondering for a lifetime through weeping-windshield-eyes. The wanderer who was the driver inside the car.

The long black limousine turned down a gravel driveway. A recently built guardhouse stood in front. The guard controlled a gate that barred unauthorized vehicles from entering. Financed by the Senate Arts Committee, Bane had it installed to keep away the Press.

The Senator rolled down his window and signaled to the gatekeeper — a middle-aged African-American named Clarence Green. Clarence pushed a button. The gate automatically lifted.

The Jetta pulled alongside the limo. The Senator waved Holly on in. "What should I say to him?" Holly asked as her engine idled like a child with a very bad cold.

"Just tell him you're the dang copyist and you're lookin' forward to workin' for a great genius like him," Bane answered.

"He's a very deluded individual," Hamelstein added.

"Look," said Bane, "I'd go in there with ya, but I gotta get back to The Hill and vote on that dang Funeral Home Bill. Just go in there for a half hour or so and babble on about nothin' in particular. Ain't nothin' to it. We politicians do it all the time."

Holly drove down the gravel road toward the cottage. The spring rain started up again. Senator Bane got out of the limousine and walked over to the gatekeeper.

"Clarence, ol' Buddy," the Senator said, "you see that sweet young thang who just drove in?"

"Yessir."

"I want you to forget you ever saw her here. And if she comes back any time in the future, let her in. But for gosh sakes don't never tell nobody she was here. If anybody ever asks, you never seen her before in your life. Got it?" The Senator handed the gray-haired black man a couple folded-up hundred-dollar bills.

"Ain't never seen her," Clarence said, stuffing the bills in his pocket, "No sirree, never seen the purty lady at all. Never."

Torchena, still covered with mud and leaves, was walking back toward the cottage. The Volkswagen Jetta pulled up in the driveway. Holly got out and ran through the rain to the porch.

Thinking Holly was a social worker, Torchy turned and ran back into the woods. Fast as she could. Without the slightest idea of where she was going.

Holly shook the rain out of her hair on the porch. Water poured off the rafters all around her. Quickly checking in her pocket mirror for any hair out of place, food between teeth, eye-gook, or visible boogers, she straightened her blouse, put the mirror away and knocked on the door. She heard footsteps within. Each one getting closer. Till they stopped. The hinges of the door creaked eerily as it opened.

"Hi, I'm Holly Bibble," she said to the figure in the dimly lit doorway. Her eyes had not yet adjusted to the dark.

"Yeah, I'm high too," the silhouette replied. Holly's irises expanded to where she could faintly notice a few details. He was tall and thin. Very thin. Except for a big potbelly. And naked from head to toe.

"You the copy bitch?" the nudist man grumbled.

"I am the copyist," Holly answered, biting her bottom lip to contain the urge to put this relic from the Chauvinistic Era in his rightful place.

"I told 'em to send me a good-looking one," Roger muttered arrogantly, "I'm glad to see our fucking Government finally do something fucking right for a change. Come on in. You wanna bong hit?"

As Holly followed the crude Neanderthal inside, her eyes finally adjusted to the low light and she recognized him as the vandal from Denny's. The same one who stiffed her on the bill, left no tip, squirted ketchup and emptied his bladder on the floor.

"You look familiar," he said, scratching his head while his other hand was dawdling his dangling balls.

"A lot of people say that," she blushed, doing a juggling act with her eyes, trying not to look too long at his face — or his genitals.

"Come check out my new masterpiece," he said, ushering her in. She followed. The floor was quite littered with beer cans and trash. Something told her she was entering a dangerous zone. Her horoscope that day had warned:

Be wary of strangers bearing gifts.
And steer clear of dark, foreboding places.

The way Roger kept the cottage, it qualified for a "dark, foreboding place" if there ever was one. Holly felt like turning back. But one thing kept her going: composing the oratorio. She wanted it more than anything in the world.

This is my trial of fire, she thought. She would be subjected to the most vile and degenerate displays of human behavior imaginable. Roger was Orpheus, taking her on a tour through the perilous Underworld. She was determined to prevail. For truth and beauty. For Art. For Music. For Love.

And Underworld it was. Inside the cottage was the most unfathomable depth of human squalor she had ever seen. Garbage strewn all over the furniture and floor. Walls with food splattered and spray paint graffiti so vulgar it would make even Howard Stern blush. And the stench! There were slaughterhouses in Iowa that smelled better!

"It's in here," Roger noted, guiding her into the bathroom where it smelled even worse than the rest of the house. Then, with the smile of a Proud Papa, he pointed down into the bowl.

There, floating in the toilet were two humungous turds. Cucumber-shits held together like Polish sausage.

"Fucking incredible, isn't it?" he boasted, proud as a peacock, "Hey, you wouldn't fucking happen to have a camera on ya by any chance would ya?"

Holly assessed her predicament and measured her response accordingly. She had to make a good impression on this poor excuse for a human being so he would approve her as his so-called "copyist." Then she would be paid fifty-thousand dollars to compose a symphonic work that would bear his name, for all time, instead of hers.

Holly wondered why reality always had to be so twisted. Her fantasies, by comparison, always seemed so orderly and just. But standing in the cottage bathroom with a naked nincompoop praising his recent defecation, Holly's just and orderly world seemed light-years away.

The options before her were perfectly clear: if she did not win this derelict's approval she would have to continue waitressing at Denny's. Or she could play along and pocket fifty-thousand tax-free dollars for doing something she loves — something she would gladly do for free given the opportunity. Holly witnessed in herself how quickly one's personal integrity goes right out the window once a large sum of money is involved.

Roger stood there, awaiting her critique of his foul-smelling fecal spectacle. Holly thought of a recent magazine article she read on Jon LaRue.

"I think you missed your calling, Roger," she said glancing into the bowl, "have you ever considered a career in Performance Art?"

"Whadda ya mean?" Roger asked, not being one for nuance.

"I mean, I think something like this would really go over in New York."

"I'm from New York. An' I got lots a' friends in New York. You got somethin' against people from fucking New York?"

"No, not at all," Holly hastened to say, "I've got a lot of friends in fucking New York myself."

Holly never used the word 'fucking.' But she figured *when in Rome, do as the Romans do.* Apparently, her resorting to the use of gutter vocabulary succeeded in breaking the ice — as Roger abruptly warmed up to her.

"Yeah? Fucking A. You wanna get high?" Roger asked, taking out his pipe and filling it with 'go'.

"Uh, no thanks, really," Holly muttered uncomfortably, "I don't use anything artificial."

"Hey," he said, lighting the pipe, "I don't know if I can have you bein' my fucking copy bitch if you don't get high. I gotta have someone who knows where the fuck I'm coming from with my music."

Holly suddenly saw her prospects for composing the oratorio going up in smoke. Quickly she headed that possibility off at the pass: "I guess there's a first time for everything," she said — taking the pipe from Roger and putting in her mouth.

Roger lit it. Holly had smoked cigarettes for a short time while in college so she knew how to inhale smoke. But this was no Virginia Slims Extra Light.

This was holymindfuckfuel. One tiny puff and she felt

like the top of her skull lifted off. Her brain was shot out like a cannonball into the upper regions of the stratosphere where Bugs Bunny & Friends enticed her to sing in their opening toon.

Her knees turned into rubber. Unable to support her weight, she fell to the bathroom floor. She tried lifting herself up by the rim of the toilet. And did so. There nestled in the porcelain commode was Roger's bowel movement. While on drugs she could 'see' where he was 'coming from.' The turds were like eggs in a nest. Jewelry in a jewelry box. Why couldn't she see that before? Why did she have to smoke dope to realize that Roger Milford Landsworth was a genius on the level of Vincent Van Gogh and Goethe?

Then Holly threw up into the bowl, adding her own inner truth to Roger's creation. Like filmmaking in Hollywood, Roger's toilet art had become a collaborative medium.

"Now look what you've done, you stupid bitch!" he reprimanded, "Ya went an' fucking ruined it!"

"I'm really sorry," said Holly as the opium started to kick in, putting her into a stupor, "I didn't mean to. Really I didn't."

Holly felt like her entire body had become like Casper the friendly ghost. The air became a thick blue fog, like a blanket wrapping itself around her making everything in the world seem perfect as possible. She tried lifting herself off the floor again. The blue fog was warm and kept her from moving. Finally she managed to grab onto the side of the toilet.

She pulled herself up bit by bit. As if scaling Mount Everest one foothold at a time. Toward the top of her ascent, she unwittingly grabbed on to the chrome handle and ker-*FLUSH* — the shit was sent swirling to the depths with the accompaniment of gurgling water sounds.

"No!" Roger cried as if losing a loved one, "I didn't even get a fucking picture! My fucking masterpiece! And not one lousy fucking shitty motherfucking picture! You stupid cunt!"

Holly thought it was the end. Surely now he would ask for another 'copy bitch' since she had just lost his 'fucking masterpiece' down the john. But then, out of the blue, Roger spoke to her in a friendly tone of voice:

"Hey, you got a really nice ass."

Holly didn't know quite what to say. She was so high on the 'go' that her mind felt like pickled herring. Her body felt absolutely incredible. Waves of delight surged through her capillaries. Her mind felt free. Perfect Buddhahood. All her troubles and worries evaporated like mist in the early morning sun. For a fleeting moment, she had a very clear understanding of why humans abuse illegal drugs.

Laying flat on her back on the cold tile floor she saw the ornate glass light fixture on the ceiling. Its bulb became a prism refracting liquid rainbow ribbons that swirled around the room like a Maypole in motion.

Roger appeared over her. His head eclipsed the ceiling light. A halo appeared around him. His long blond hair became sun flares shooting into space. His naked body was beautiful. Holly thought it was ugly before. Roger wasn't Orpheus of the Underworld. He was Zeus — riding a lightning bolt down to Earth from the heights of Olympus.

Holly watched her body turn into a swan. Her arms grew long and covered with feathers. She opened her wings and wanted to fly! Lightning struck and thunder pounded like armies of ten-ton tympani. Water-soaked windows trembled in frames. Torrential tap dancing. Rooftops of rain. From the woodwork the wind pulled out long banshee cries as Zeus crossed the Equinox atwixt Holly's thighs.

Reaching his zenith. He made the Swan sing! It was March twenty-first. The first day of spring.

HOLLY DROVE HER UNHEATED Jetta out the long gravel driveway. She passed the guard who purposely looked the other way. The well-worn tires on her car screeched as she swerved out onto the shiny wet blacktop. Her metronome-like windshield wipers click-clacked a persistent *prestissimo* rhythmic refrain.

Coming down from the high feeling like she'd been hit by a train, all she could think of was getting home. And crawling in bed with Boo Boo.

Turning the bend in the road that wound like a ribbon through the barren trees, she saw a figure up ahead. She thought it was a mailbox at first. Until the mailbox moved. Soon she could see it was a young girl hitchhiking in the rain. Holly pulled over. The girl quickly climbed in.

"Oh, shit," Torchy muttered, "you're the social worker, aren't you?"

She was sopping wet. Leaves and mud stuck to her body like too many magnets on a refrigerator door.

"No, I'm not," Holly replied, "I'm a teacher, no, actually a waitress. Wait — no, I'm quitting that today. I'm a composer, really. That's what I really do."

"Phew!" Torchena sighed as she sat soaking the seat, "well, whatever y'are I'm glad you're not who I thought ya were. For a minute there I thought I was soooo busted."

Normally it would have been an hour's drive from the Chesapeake Bay cottage up to Baltimore. But the storm turned the roads into rivers and lakes. And the sky became a giant shower stall. Holly was still coming down from the 'go' as she drove, following the road signs that led the way back to reality. During the two and a half hour drive home, the fourteen-year-old girl covered with mud and leaves poured out her entire life history:

Torchena grew up in a one-room apartment in a bad part of Spanish Harlem. A rat-infested slum shared by her mother, six brothers and sisters, and a dog. Her Father deserted the family when she was four, never to be heard from again.

When Torchy was nine, her mother had a new live-in boyfriend named Reuben. One night while her mother was working her janitor job in a tall office building, Reuben took Torchy into a vacant room on their floor and molested her. This went on every night for almost a week until Torchy lost her virginity to Reuben. When Torchy told her mother about it the next day, her mother called her a liar and told her to get out of the apartment and never come back.

After spending the night in a trash-strewn alley, scared out of her wits, Torchy started panhandling to get money. It didn't take long before a man named Harold, who looked to be in his forties, said she could stay with him in his hotel room. There was only one bed and it turned out he wanted to do the same things that Reuben had been doing to her the previous week. The next morning Harold checked out and Torchy found herself homeless again. She learned quickly that sex was the coin of the realm in the cold, cruel world of the streets of New York. By simply allowing men to do whatever they wanted to do with her body she was provided with cigarettes, shelter, food, liquor and drugs in plentiful supply.

But everything changed when Torchy met Lamar. She was living with Chuckie, a 20-year-old cocaine dealer she met in Central Park. One day Lamar, a well-dressed African-American man in his mid-twenties, came over to score some coke. Chuckie wasn't there. Torchena was. Lamar was real nice to Torchy. He took her out shopping for clothes. He paid for it all with a big wad of cash that conspicuously bulged in the pocket of his pants.

"How old are you, Girl?" Lamar asked in his deep, friendly voice as Torchy tried on a dress worth two-hundred dollars.

"Eleven," she answered.

"Girl, you sure be lookin' good for eleven," he said with a smile as his eyes appraised the merchandise from hair to toe — dollar signs dancing in his head.

Actually Torchy looked younger than her years. She could have easily passed for nine. Her body was thin as a rail except for a slight budding curve to her hips. Her face had a cute little turned up nose. Full pouting lips. And a flawless complexion that always looked tan from being Puerto Rican. But her eyes were her most predominant feature. Dark eyes that seemed a tad too big for her face. Lashes so long, when she blinked, it appeared as if gypsy moths had landed on her eyelids. Eyes that — in spite of the sadness they'd seen — still exuded a certain innocent wonder.

Lamar paid for the dress. They got in his big red El Dorado. He drove her to his condo on the Hudson River in Hoboken. His place had the best furniture, carpeting, and stereo that money could buy. They got drunk on champagne, snorted cocaine, and had sex in front of the window till the sun came up over the Statue of Liberty.

Torchena never went back to Chuckie. Lamar gave her something she'd never had before: a sense of belonging. Sure, he had sex with her several times a day — but from her experience that was normal behavior. On their third night together, Lamar licked her between the legs for the longest time. Torchy had her very first orgasm. Afterward, wrapped in his strong African arms, Torchy fell in love. As she drifted off to sleep, all seemed perfect and beautiful in the world.

The following night Lamar came home with "a friend." The friend was a white, fifty year old businessman from the Bronx. The three of them drank vodka. Then Lamar took Torchena aside.

"You love me, Baby?"

"Yeah, of course I love you."

"I wanchoo to prove how much you love me, Baby."

"How?"

"I wanchoo to make it with my friend Bob. Will ya do that for me, Baby? Will ya?"

"But he's too old. And fat," Torchy protested.

"Do ya love me, Baby?"

"I wanna make it with *you,* Lamar," she said, throwing her arms around him. "Nobody else."

"You gots to do it for me, Darlin'. You gots to do it with my friend Bob."

"Why?" she pleaded, her eyes getting watery.

"Cuz dare ain't no free lunch, Baby. How d'you think I pays for all dis shit? It shore ain't be growin' on no trees."

That evening Bob from the Bronx sampled two out of three of Torchy's main bodily orifices. He spanked her when he was through.

She cried after that. But not from the spanking. It was the last time Torchena cried for a very long time.

She stayed with Lamar for almost a year. During that time, her three body valves were made available to an onslaught of Lamar's so called "friends." Stockbrokers, lawyers, politicians, and such. All paid big bucks to fuck or be sucked by the nubile pubescent Puerto Rican. It got easier and easier each time she did it.

A few months before her twelfth birthday, Torchy had her first menstrual period. Lamar had his doctor friend put a Norplant in her arm. The slow release of hormones would keep her from getting pregnant for five years — until her sweet sixteenth birthday.

One day Lamar caught her stealing his cocaine and threw her out on the street. She worked a couple months hustling 42nd street. Customers weren't "friends" any more. They were "tricks." Not even thirteen yet, Torchy learned the words and the ways of the street from the veterans already working. Veterans — sixteen and seventeen years old — servicing their two-thousandth customer.

Torchy soon found she could charge a higher price than her far more experienced elders. She was actually learning the hard facts of supply-side economics. On the street hustling market, there was a high demand for twelve-year-old girls and a scarcity of suppliers. This drove up the rental value of her three main bodily valves.

After a few months on her own, she took up with another pimp. A big, fat white man named Chester. She liked the protection that came with having a pimp. A father figure of sorts.

By the time Torchy was thirteen she was addicted to heroin. It made her feel better than she had ever felt before. Better than even the orgasms she'd had with Lamar. Not only did the high from the heroin last longer — but never once did it break her fragile young heart.

One Saturday night Torchy was doing better than usual. She had earned enough money to buy a week's worth of dope. A man propositioned her for a blowjob. They negotiated a price. She got in his car. He would have been her seventeenth customer that evening. But instead of his penis, he pulled out a badge.

After two days in Juvenile Hall, she began to go through withdrawals. All the state-run drug rehabilitation centers were full. But a privately-funded center took her in as charity. It took several days of vomiting, screaming, and feeling the worst pain she'd ever felt in her life, but she kicked her heroin habit. Then, going from one bad habit to another, she met Roger on the hallway floor.

"I'll give you a ride where ever you need to go," Holly offered, deeply saddened by the young girl's story. It made her own problems seem minuscule by comparison.

"I don't have anywhere to go," Torchy admitted, "except back to New York. Back to the streets."

"You can come live with me and Kim," Holly said as she turned off the exit ramp that ran by their building.

"Cool," Torchy replied.

At first, Kim was reluctant about letting the homeless girl stay with them. The apartment was cramped as it was with just the two of them and their castrated cat. But while Torchena was taking a shower, Holly gave Kim an encapsulated version of the young girl's story.

"And I thought I had a rough childhood," said Kim after listening to Holly's recount of Torchy's life. As the nubile ex-prostitute stepped out of the shower, Kim said to her: "You can stay here as long as you'd like."

"Awesome," Torchy beamed, dripping water all over the floor.

AS FAR AS SENATOR Bane was concerned, all the elements were in place for making the Christmas 2000 Celebration a big success. The composer, the conductor, the orchestra, the choir. He was being hailed in the media as 'the conservative Southern Senator who supports the Arts.' His standing in the polls kept rising from all the favorable publicity, eating away at Rupert Conyers' lead. And all the free airtime on Guy M. Landsworth's stations was helping his campaign considerably. It would especially come in handy in the fall. He knew the plan would work as long as Roger was under wraps. Sequestered in the cottage. Out of sight and out of the Media's mind. And as long as this female composer that Sydney Bormstern so highly recommended is able to deliver the goods.

THE VERY NEXT DAY the doorbell rang to her seventh floor apartment. Holly answered the door. Standing in the hall was a medium-height thirtysomething man wearing a dark suit and tie. His tie was an inflamed-hemorrhoid-red that clenched his throat like a hangman's noose. His neatly groomed hair was thin, sandy-blond, receding from his forehead like the ocean from a beach at low tide (no chance for the Presidency here). In one arm he held a large brown paper bag as if he'd just come from the grocery.

"Holly Bibble, I presume?" the man asked in a voice that sounded somewhat familiar.

"Yes?" Holly replied with caution, wondering if he was a mass murderer or a Jehovah's Witness.

"I'm Charlie Russell," the man introduced, extending the hand that wasn't holding the groceries.

"Oh," sighed Holly, relieved that she would neither be stabbed nor proselytized to death.

"Here's the first payment," said Charlie, handing her the bag.

Inside was ten-thousand dollars in cash. All in small bills, mostly fives, tens, and twenties. Holly had never seen so much money at one time. Her mouth dropped a mile. Her eyes opened wide.

"There's no need to report this on your income tax," he informed. "There's no record of this money ever changing hands."

Holly was so flabbergasted she didn't even invite him in. She just thanked him and closed the apartment door in his face. She poured the money into a pile on the floor, fell to her knees and ran her fingers through it. Scooping up wads of the green paper bills, as much as her hands could hold, she tossed them in the air. The money rained down on the rug around her like maple seeds scattered by the late March wind. Holly smiled like a child on early Christmas morning.

Filthy lucre.... Holly thought...*That's what Jesus called it. The root of all evil was a standard cliché. Consumption of goods and services is the inescapable nature of earthly existence. Just as cars need gasoline to run, humans need food and clothing and cappuccino machines. But the funny thing about money is: the more of it you have, the less it means. The less you have, the more it means. If you have no money at all, it means everything in the world. If someone had all the money in the world, it would probably mean absolutely nothing at all.*

But what the money on the floor meant to Holly was much more than what she could buy with it. It was tangible proof that the past twenty-four hours had not been a dream she was about to wake up from. All the Lincolns and Jacksons and mostly James Madisons she held in the palms of her hands brought her face to face with the rapturous reality:

She would compose the Christmas 2000 Oratorio!

Within days Holly found a two-bedroom house in the suburbs. She agreed to rent it on a twelve-month lease. It was further out than she had wanted, since Kim would have to drive the extra miles to the hospital each day. But the house had a den Holly could use as a studio. And Torchy could have her own room. But what really sold Holly on the house was the large picture window in the den that looked out on an untended garden.

Holly hired professional movers. At the end of the week they were all moved in. Holly painted the spare room a light pale green. The color of freshly budding leaves. She rolled out a rug with a Persian design. Faded and frayed, its value was sentimental — bought at a yard sale during her Oberlin days.

Two burly movers with forearms like Popeye rolled in her piano along with its bench. On top of it she placed her cracked china light. An oval-shaped vase of delicate porcelain. An old family heirloom from her Jewish mother's side. It survived Hitler's Holocaust only to be vibrated off her piano while playing an Etude by Liszt. It took several nights, three tubes of Super Glue and all the jigsaw puzzle skills acquired in her youth to restore the china light to its original configuration. The lamp provided much more than mere illumination for her studio. It served as a constant reminder that some things, no matter how badly damaged, are repairable. Holly set up her desk. Sharpened some pencils. A fresh pad of musical manuscript was laid out.

It was a new moon night in early spring. Kim was at work. Torchy was soundly sleeping. Holly sat at her desk and pondered the task that was now set before her. She picked up a pencil, but still lost in thought — placed the eraser in her mouth. It was a small harmless habit leftover from childhood. Most people have them. From picking one's nose or popping zits on one's back, old habits die hard, like cigarettes or heroin addiction. As with boomerangs, the harder we try to throw them away, the faster they're back in our face.

With the number 2 pencil dangling from her lips like a cigarette in an old Humphrey Bogart movie, Holly turned out the small china light on her piano and swiveled in her chair to face the picture window. Outside, the multitude of stars winked their promise of a Universe perfect in conception of design.

"Thank you, God," she said aloud, "Whoever You are. Whatever You are. I know all things of beauty must emanate from You."

Keeping her eyes on the stars, Holly fixated on her own constellation of Libra — the dim little pinpoints of suns burning light years away. She was about to embark on a journey. A journey within her own soul. She would make the oratorio the best it could possibly be. Like a mountain about to be scaled, she stood in awe of the task set before her. Fulfilling a yearning from childhood, this was her chance to do great things. It was what she had lived and breathed for.

All these years.

Trio

Less than a week after moving into the house, Toes was run over by a car and died. Kim dug a hole in the backyard garden with Holly and Torchy looking on. In a silent ceremony they all understood, she laid the cat carcass there. And placed his favorite kitty toy beside him.

None of them spoke as Kim filled in the grave. A solitary bird in a tree nearby sang a song of spring — but it sounded sad.

Holly wondered what happened to Toes' soul, the driver of his gray tabby car. Would he come back as a cougar? A panther? A giraffe? Or maybe a human being she would encounter later on. Holly wondered what it would be like to be a cat. There were times she had wished she could be one. But most of all she wanted to be a bird. To fly and sing would be the biggest thrill of all.

Kim transplanted a rosebush in the freshly turned soil. Torchy found a large flat rock that she set in the ground as a headstone. She wrote on its surface with bright red lipstick:

> HERE LIES TOES
> WHERE HE WENT
> NOBODY KNOWS

Kim walked into the house and went back to sleep. Torchy stayed in the backyard a while, rearranging the dirt around Toes' tombstone. Holly went back in her studio to write.

The bird in the nearby tree kept on singing.

Holly didn't like the popular title: "Christmas 2000 Oratorio." She thought it was tacky. And she thought the official title: *National Endowment For The Arts Commissioned Musical Work In Celebration of the New Millennium* was even worse. She called Senator Bane and told him so.

"So what would you rather call the darn thing?" the Senator asked over the phone.

"I think *Hosanna Millennia* is a better title," Holly answered, "it's more befitting of the sanctity of the subject."

"What the Hell's a Ho-zanna Mill-ennia?" Bane asked in his thick hillbilly drawl.

"Hosanna means praise," Holly informed in her teacherly tone, "and "Millennia," of course, is the plural form of 'millennium.' Using the plural form implies we're not only praising this particular millennium, but the prior millennium and all future millennia to come."

"Sounds high falootin' to me," said the Senator. "I don't want this to be somethin' only the dern intellect-shals understand. I want this to be for ever'body. So leave the name as it stands. The Government calls it one thang, but the people call it The *Christmas Two-Thousand Oratorio.* And it's what the people call it that matters. It's simple and to the point. That's the first thing ya learn runnin' for public office, Miss Bibble. Never aim too high or you'll end up confusin' the common man on the street. And if that ever happens, you better start lookin' for another job.

I remember as a young boy listenin' to Adlai Stevenson on the radio. Barely understood a dang word the man said."

After her brief talk on the phone with Senator Bane, Holly went into her studio and closed the door. It was sparsely decorated. She liked it that way. With few distractions. Her piano was there. An upright Baldwin that Lulah, her Jewish grandmother, bought her as a graduation gift. A waist-high walnut bookshelf held her music textbooks, piano literature, and several orchestral scores. Her Mac laptop computer sat on the desk. She had several programs for musical notation. But Holly preferred the old-fashioned way of writing the notes by hand.

On the wall was a picture of Mozart she'd torn out of a book when she was in high school. It hung crooked to one side, held by a thumbtack inserted just above Wolfgang's eye. Since she'd first played his *Clarinet Concerto in A Major* as a child, the composer had always been an inspiration to do great things.

Holly decided to make the oratorio a work in eight movements. She wanted each movement to depict a certain milestone in the life of Jesus. Choosing the first was easy. She took out a large blank sheet of orchestral manuscript and inscribed across the top:

"Immaculate Conception"

When Holly first began composing music at Oberlin, she used to always write at the piano. She liked to hear the notes with her ears. But she remembered Professor Bormstern's words when she first began studying at George Washington U: "Learn to write away from the instrument," he advised, "otherwise, your composition will be limited by the technical abilities of your fingers."

Holly had a hard time writing music in her head. She wanted to hear it vibrate her ears. Composing away from the piano was like a kitten being weaned from its mother's milk. But slowly she trained herself to hear the intervals between each note. To hear whole chords. The different blends of high and low registers. Eventually her mind became the instrument on which she composed.

Beethoven wrote his *Ninth Symphony* while he was completely deaf. He composed it entirely in his head. His brain had been trained to be an orchestra since childhood.

Once Holly had mastered composing this way she felt like a horse let loose from a corral. She could write the melodies and harmonies that came to her without using the piano as an interpreter. From that point on her music would never be hamstrung by the skills of ten fingers. The music within could be put on the page.

After pouring a cup of coffee from the thermos, Holly made a toast to Amadeus on the wall. Then she had a vision of a dark enclosed place. The space within Mary's womb. A single seed. Dividing on its own. Conceived by God's Love. A Love without penetration.

She began with high sustaining strings. Then a single flute melody emerged. Four-four time. Slow and plaintive. Whole notes held. Progressing into half notes, quarter notes, then into eighths.

An oboe soon joins in counterpoint. Together they weave. Then one by one the other woodwinds join. Then the brass. Then percussion. Melodies emerge and musically intertwine. Modulating through different key changes. The orchestra builds with a steady crescendo to the cadence of a minor to a major chord!

Holly decided the first movement would be wholly instrumental. During the Second Movement she would bring in the Tabernacle Choir. The second movement would be titled: "Virgin Birth."

She remembered her high school biology class studying the reproductive habits of aphids. These teensy-tiny sap-sucking insects have no need of males, since they give birth while they're virgins. In a process called parthenogenesis, aphids become pregnant without fertilization. Holly wondered why God couldn't make all His creatures reproduce this way, with no penises involved. It seemed like it would make things a whole lot less complicated.

Holly heard the phone ring in the other end of the house. It was close to midnight. Kim had already left for work. She decided to let the answering machine pick it up.

But instead, Torchy got it.

"Hello?"

"Hi," said the voice. It was male; "I hear you've got a dildo over there."

"Oh, yeah," said Torchy, "*lots* of dildos." Torchy knew how this game was played. It was called 'phone sex.' She did it all the time when she lived with Lamar. He would have his clients call her while they were at work. Presidents of multinational corporations would take time out from their busy workloads to have an eleven-year-old girl talk dirty to them over the phone.

It was an easy game to play. And Torchy liked pretending a lot better than doing it for real, especially with overweight, middle-aged men.

"How many dildos?" asked the man on the other end of the phone.

"Hundreds," said Torchy, "all different kinds."

Holly got hungry and went in the kitchen to snack. While spooning pickled artichoke hearts from a jar she decided to call Kim at the hospital just to tell her she loved her. But when she picked up the phone she heard Torchy's voice on the line:

"Yeah, I got this dog. A big ol' German Shepherd. He's licking my pussy right now. Oh, yeah, it feels so good. Oh, yeah, he's just licking my pussy with that big ol' tongue a' his. Lick, lick, lick. Oh, no, what's he doing now? Oh no, he's climbing on top of me. Oh, God! He's shoving his dick up my twat! His big ol' doggie dick is going in 'n outta my pussy right now. Oh, I'm so wet! I've never been this wet!"

Then Holly heard a man's voice, breathing hard, say: "How big is the doggie's dick?"

"Big!" Torchy answered, "big as a corn dog with chili!"

Holly had a good ear for recognizing voices. She immediately recognized the man's voice as Charles Russell, the Senator's publicist. The one who delivered the money to her doorstep.

"How far is he ramming his big corn dog dick up your twat right now?" he pleaded to know.

"Mr. Russell, you should be ashamed of yourself!" Holly interrupted, "Do you know the girl you're talking to is only fourteen years old?"

Torchy hung up the phone. But Holly stayed on as Charlie Russell poured forth an avalanche of apologies. Working in public relations had made him a maestro of saying "I'm sorry." He explained how he thought she and Kim were "into phone sex" since the first time he called they had gone on about the dildo.

"I thought you were a prank caller then," Holly explained, "calling about an ad I'd placed looking for a sperm donor."

"Hey," Charlie said, "if it's sperm samples you want, I got plenty! Believe me, I get myself off maybe three or four times a day. At least!"

"I believe you," said Holly. Her maternal instincts were murmuring again. He did seem like a semi-attractive man when he showed up at their city apartment the month before. Good teeth and good bone structure. Then Holly asked: "Have you ever been tested for HIV?"

"Don't need to," he replied, "I've never had sex with anybody in my entire life. I'm still a virgin at thirty-three years old."

"Why haven't you ever had sex?"

"I'm impotent. The only way I can get off is by looking at pictures of naked women or talking dirty over the phone. The minute I get with a real woman — psssst! — just like letting the air out of a tire."

"Have you ever tried to get professional help?"

"I've been through the whole shebang. Psychologists, sex therapists, palm readers, dick doctors. They all scored a big goose egg with me. I've tried *Viagra, Cialis,* and every off-brand E.D. medicine known to mankind. I can't get it up no matter what. The Good Lord gave me a whizzer that's afraid of women."

A little bell rang inside of Holly's brain. *A man who was impotent,* she thought, *would be the perfect surrogate father. At least she wouldn't have to worry about his penis getting out of hand.*

"I might be interested in a sperm donor next December," said Holly, "after the oratorio is done."

"The Christmas 2000 Oratorio," said Charlie, citing its popular name.

"Oh, I hate that title," Holly groaned.

"So you like the official title better?"

"No. That one's even worse. I called Senator Bane about changing it. But he wants to keep it the way it is."

"Senator Bane's got his head up his ass."

"I'm surprised hearing that from *you*. You're supposed to be his publicist."

"This is off the record, you understand."

"Obviously."

"Hey, you wanna change the name of the oratorio?" asked Charlie, 'Lemme talk to the fat-ass."

Later that afternoon, Holly got a call from the Senator.

"Miss Bibble, how are you today?"

"Just fine, Senator. Working away."

"Good. Good. Listen, I was doin' some thinkin' 'bout changin' the name a' the oratorio. By the way, what was that name you wanted to call it?"

"Hosanna Millennia."

"Yeah, yeah, that's it. The Hose, Ann — how d'you spell that?"

"H-O-S-A-N-N-A M-I-L-L-E-N-N-I-A," Holly answered as if she were performing on Sesame Street.

"I think that's a good name for it," Bane acquiesced, "I think we should run with it."

"I do too," she said.

"It's done then," came the Senator's reply, "Carry on with the Hose Ann Millen-yum."

"Thank you, Sir," Holly said as she hung up the phone. She immediately called Charlie Russell.

"How did you get him to do it?" she asked.

"I appealed to his vanity," the public relations man replied, "It works like a charm every time. Especially with politicians. I told him the oratorio would live on long after he's dead. I convinced him that the official name or even 'The Christmas 2000 Oratorio' wasn't the sort of name that lends itself to longevity. I said to him: 'Senator, since your name's gonna be attached to this thing, you want it to be a *classy* title.' That was the word that got him, I think. Classy.

I said: 'Senator, if you want this oratorio to last longer than a rap song on the charts you better come up with a classy title.' I guess that's what clinched it."

"Mr. Russell, I owe you one for this."

"Call me Charlie."

"What sign are you, Charlie?"

"A stop sign with a penis rising."

"Oh, come on."

"I'm Virgo. September eleventh."

"I usually get along with Virgos just fine," Holly mentioned, "Even though the book says we're incompatible."

"Fuck the book," said Charlie. "Look, whenever you and your girlfriend start talking about having a baby, just remember: when you think of sperm, think of Charlie Russell."

"Thank you, Charlie. We just might be thinking of you next Christmas."

The two said goodbye. She hung up the phone and went back to composing the work that would now forever be known as *Hosanna Millennia.*

KIM TOOK A FEW hours every afternoon to teach Torchy how to use her PC computer. She took to it quickly. Lamar once bought her a Nintendo gaming console so she would have something to do in between tricks. Roger had taught her some games on his Macintosh.

A computer aptitude test showed Torchy was already reading at a sixth grade level. But she had a lot of catching up to do to be able to enter the eighth grade in the fall. With Holly sequestered in her studio, Kim tutored her whenever she could. But once Torchy learned how to use the self-teaching programs on the CD-ROMs, the teenager was off and running on her own.

One day Torchy walked to a nearby drugstore to buy some aspirin for Holly. While in the store a picture on a spiral notebook caught her eye. It was a picture of Pegasus. A great white horse with wings flying through the clouds. Torchy had never ridden a horse. But all her life she'd always wanted to. Ever since she was a very young girl she had seen them in movies and magazines. And the ones that pulled the carriages through Central Park. But she'd never seen one with wings before. Not even in her wildest dreams.

She counted the money that Holly had given her. There wasn't quite enough for the notebook. Torchy looked around the store. No one was watching. She stuffed the notebook under her blouse. Then went and paid for the aspirin.

Torchy's bedroom was next to Kim and Holly's. Late at night, sometimes, she would press her ear to the wall and listen to the sounds of their lovemaking. That particular night, before making love, Holly and Kim were discussing something called *karma*. Holly said the law of karma was expressed succinctly in the Bible: 'As a man soweth, so shall he reap.' Kim didn't believe in karma, calling it: '...a human desire for poetic justice.' But to Holly, the law of karma was just as inescapable as the law of gravity. She went on to explain:

"If somebody steals something, it creates a hole in the Universe that has to be filled. So someone has to take from somewhere else to fill that hole, which creates another hole that has to be filled from somewhere else. Eventually the hole goes all the way around the Universe till it comes back to the person who originally created it in the first place, only by that time the hole is a lot bigger."

Torchy pulled her ear away from the wall. She thought about the hole in the Universe she'd created by stealing the Pegasus notebook. It was the first time she'd ever felt guilty about something she did. She laid awake most of the night, worrying about how big the hole would be by the time it got back to her. Taking her allowance, she walked to the drugstore as soon as it opened the next morning. She paid the cashier. Apologized for taking it. The manager thanked her for being so honest. Walking out of the store, Torchy felt good inside. Her life had enough holes in it as it was.

Torchy kept the notebook under her pillow. She took it out at night to write down her thoughts. Some of her thoughts she would weave into poetry. They were awkward at first, like a young bird's first fledgling attempts at flapping its wings. Eventually she wrote a poem she liked. At dinner one night she showed it to Holly:

> "if I could be anything I would be a bird
> just fly all day and never say a word
> no one could tell me what to do
> where to stay or who to screw
> just sing all night in a tall maple tree
> cuz birds don't need pimps
> they fly for free."

"Torchy, this is very good," Holly praised while they were eating spaghetti together at the dinner table. "You keep going and someday you'll be another Emily Dickenson."

"Who's that?" Torchy asked.

"Here," Holly said, going over to the bookshelf in the living room. She pulled out a thin book of Dickenson's poetry. It hadn't been cracked since her freshman year at Oberlin. "You can have this book if you want it," Holly offered.

"Cool!" Torchy blurted while slurping a strand of spaghetti into her mouth. She was truly grateful. But the basic nature of her upbringing had never taught her simple things like saying "thank you."

During the rest of the meal Torchy read Emily Dickenson. The only other thing Holly had ever seen her read were the backs of cereal boxes in the morning. Holly wondered why cereal boxes couldn't be printed with poetry. What a perfect way to expose children to art. She thought about writing her Congressman about it. Along with her idea for Middle East billboards.

After dinner Holly went back to her studio to write while Kim helped Torchena work on a computer math lesson. Torchy didn't like math as much as she liked poetry. But Kim kept on insisting: "math is important in this day and age."

While working at the computer together, Torchy let her hand rest on Kim's leg, the way she'd seen Holly do it when the two of them were ready to go to bed. Kim didn't think anything of it at first. But when Torchy started rubbing her hand back and forth in a highly affectionate manner, Kim felt she had to address the situation before it got carried away.

"You keep doing that, Young Lady, and you'll end up getting us *both* in trouble."

"I made it with a girl in Joovy once," Torchy boasted.

"Did you like it?" Kim asked.

"Yeah. I liked it a *lot,*" Torchy answered, placing considerable emphasis on the word: 'lot'.

"Better than with boys?" Kim pressed further, genuinely curious.

"Well, maybe. Yeah. Definitely better than with most dudes." Then the precocious teenager went on: "I wanna make it with you and Holly, both. Donna, the girl I did it with in Joovy, told me about when she did a threesome once with all girls and she said it was *awesome.*"

Torchy put her hand back on Kim's leg.

"We can't, Honey," Kim said, gently moving the girl's hand from her leg and holding it. "Holly and I have a commitment to each other. We'd be taking a risk of weakening our relationship."

Torchy knew the word "commitment" from watching daytime soap operas on TV. But since the people with "commitments" on those shows were always having sex with someone else besides the one to whom they were "committed," the ex-child prostitute was a little confused as to what the word really meant.

"So you don't really want me here. Is that what you're saying?"

"Oh, no, Torchy," Kim said, giving the young girl a motherly hug, "that's not the situation at all. Holly and I love you dearly. But our love for you has nothing to do with sex. Do you understand that?"

"Sorta. Yeah."

"We both care about you and we want to see you make it in life."

"But you *have* seen me naked."

"Not naked — I said: 'make it'."

"That's what I wanna do: *make it.* With you and Holly. At the same time."

"Let's get back to math, Young Lady," Kim said as her patience ran thin as a string from Tinker Bell's tampon, "now, how do we find the square root of thirty-six?"

Because of her life experiences, Torchena didn't know how to have a relationship with someone that wasn't centered on one of her three main bodily orifices.

Like math, it was something new she had to learn.

Dolce

The doorbell rang to his Watergate apartment. Bane looked through the peephole, then quickly unbolted the door and opened it. Loni slipped into his apartment with the stealth of a spy. The Senator closed the door and locked it.

Ordinarily they would have rendezvoused after office hours at the Chesapeake Bay cottage. But since Roger was there "composing," the cottage was out of the question. Sleazy roadside motels on the outskirts of D.C. were okay on occasion. But places like that were risky around Washington. The Press was always hard up to expose someone dicking around. The Senator figured that if Loni was seen going in and out of his apartment — as long as it wasn't overnight — he could say she came over to deliver some papers. Or dictate a letter. No one had to know she couldn't even type.

Loni let her knee-length overcoat slide off her shoulders and fall to the floor. It curled around her high-heeled shoes like a cat. She was wearing a French maid outfit underneath as her boss had requested earlier. Also a pair of see-through crotchless panties.

"Boy, am I glad you're here," Lucius snorted as he pushed Loni down on the couch. He ripped her bodice open down to the navel, then attached a CHICKEN 'N' DUMPLINGS Scratch-N-Sniff sniffer under his nose. "I'm hungry as Hell!" he roared.

His tongue found the breech in her blue crotchless panties like a hound chasing a fox down a wet gopher hole. She grabbed his white hair in her hands — tussled and mussed it — as he munched on her muff like a madman.

Bane had grown tired of the GloptaMeal pudding that came with the Scratch-N-Sniff sniffers. But he found that the nose-attached sniffers worked well in conjunction with cunnilingus. He began performing oral sex on his obliging secretary several times a day. As a result, he lost over thirty pounds in six weeks. The nose sniffers could give her blond-haired vagina over forty-seven different flavors. From beef stew to egg-foo-young to chicken fricassee. Crème Brule to carrot cake.

On Bane's Scratch-N-Sniff Cunnilingus Diet, Loni was the perfect in-between meal snatch.

Loni grew up in nearby Arlington, Virginia. She spent her teen years getting drunk and having sex with most of the high school football team. After high school, she got a job as a cashier at K-mart during the day. And at night she would go to bars, get drunk, and get laid by traveling rock musicians. This went on until she was twenty-three years old.

At that point, she began to notice small lines around her eyes. Also on her forehead and the corners of her mouth. Too much alcohol and too little sleep had taken its toll over the years. And the rock bands began passing her up for the girls eighteen and under.

She saw the older cash register girls at K-mart: fortyish, fat, and forcing an increasingly wrinkled smile on their overly-made-up faces while saying: "Thank you for shopping K-mart" a zillion times a day.

Loni realized her sex appeal was the only marketable commodity she had. And like produce at the supermarket, its shelf life was limited. If her three main bodily orifices were ever going to upgrade her standard of living, she had to act fast before the wrinkles got any deeper.

She began frequenting some of the more upscale drinking establishments across the Potomac. It was at one of these, *The Draconian Inn*, where she met Senator Bane. He took her to his Chesapeake Bay cottage the first night he met her. She had never had sex with someone as old or overweight as him. Not even the linebackers in high school came close to his girth. And rock musicians are notoriously anorexic.

But the Senator from Alabama turned her on even though he was a hippopotamus. Loni found that Power was indeed the ultimate aphrodisiac. The Senator had the power to make laws that others had to obey. He had the power to wage wars. But most of all, he had the power to raise her up from her meager station in life. Which he did.

That very first night they met, after depositing seminal fluids inside her, he made her his secretary at eight hundred dollars a week. The next day she kissed her K-mart career goodbye.

While Loni was reminiscing her recent past, Bane was stroking his tongue up and down her pudenda as if painting a white picket fence. A LASAGNA sniffer was stuck under his nose. Loni tasted Italian.

He climbed up on top of her. Slid his pecker deep into his leftover meal. Loni was glad he was losing weight.

When the Senator was three-hundred pounds, missionary position was like being attacked by a refrigerator. Bane banged away like a samurai Sumo wrestler till he came and collapsed in her embrace.

"I wish I could marry you," the hard-breathing Senator muttered.

Loni felt crushed under his weight. But she endured it. She had worked for the Senator for nearly five years. Her feminine intuition told her this was a moment to be seized. If she played her cards right, she would never have to work at K-mart ever again.

"Why can't you?" she purred.

"You know," he answered, "I got a wife back home."

"Why don't you divorce her?"

"I cain't. Not durin' a 'lection year."

"What about after the election?"

"It could ruin my chances a' becomin' President."

"Not if you do it right after the election," Loni goaded. "There'd be four years in between. People forget a lot in four years. Besides," she said, pulling her body a little out from underneath him and shoving her naturally well-shaped breasts in his face, "don't you think I'd be a much nicer looking First Lady than Dolores?"

The Senator started kissing her breasts — slurping her nipples into his mouth and sucking them like candy. He opened another Scratch-N-Sniff sniffer and fixed it to his nostrils without missing a beat. (This one had the scent of spumoni ice cream.) "You're right," he said in between the newly-flavored slurps, "but we gotta wait till *after* the election. You can't tell a soul. If the Press gets a hold a' this I'm deader'n a doornail. They'll rake me over the coals like they did Gary Hart."

"My lips are sealed," Loni whispered before tracing an imaginary zipper across her lips with her index finger and thumb. But the seal was soon breached after Bane tired of the taste of spumoni and Loni obliged him with an after dinner blowjob.

HOLLY BEGAN WORKING incessantly. Composing music was a tedious task even when the Muse was with her. And when the Muse was — the music came gushing like a flash flood roaring through a dry river gully. But still it took time to put it on paper. Sorting melodic murmurs from the chaff of stillborn motifs.

Each separate note she would pluck from her consciousness and place on the page with a jeweler's precision. Setting tones in time. That's what she was doing. Making a mosaic of a million and one tiles. Setting them in place. One by one.

Twelve different tones, each a half-step apart. From these she would build an hour-long oratorio. Like the twelve days of Christmas. And the hours on the clock. From these twelve tones: a sacred symphony of psalms.

Each separate note was an entity unto itself. Until it was joined with another. Then the intricate laws of harmony took hold. Laws described thousands of years ago by Pythagoras in Greece. Holly knew that each note placed down on the page could change the tonality of all the notes around it. Like a musical matchmaker she labored alone trying to fit twelve lonely tones into perfect harmonic relationships.

And the Muse was with Holly. Filling her sail. Sending her soaring on high open C's! Her soul was consumed by a passion not felt since the old days in college. Living on coffee and unsullied dreams. Her pencil strode feverishly across the lined page dotting eighth-note staccatos of a violin phrase. Occasionally she would catnap on an old Army cot that stretched perpendicular to the piano. These would rarely last more than an hour or so. Then, like toast, she would pop back up to her desk and resume where she last left off.

The only time she'd come out of her studio was when her thermos of java was in need of refilling. And of course when she had to go potty. Even then she would wait till the very last minute — holding it in till her bowels or her bladder or both were about to burst like balloons.

Kim noticed Holly wasn't eating. So she made it a point to bring her a sandwich and milk as she left for the hospital each night. Holly would eventually pick up the sandwich and munch it in rhythm with the music in her mind. Holding the turkey on rye in her right hand while penciling notes with her left she worked in an unbroken stream of consciousness without so much as a quarter-note rest.

She wrote by sunlight till night fell. Then she wrote by the light of her lamp. Days turned to nights turned to days turned to nighttime.

Once Torchy burnt some toast in the kitchen and set off the loud smoke alarm. Holly wrote right through it. Never missing a beat. She ate and slept and breathed the oratorio. Anything else just bounced off her brain like Ethiopian spears against the tanks of Mussolini.

"Myopic work mode," Holly called it.

Kim called it: "Going without sex."

But the idea of sex meant nothing to Holly while the creative juices were flowing. Like a horse wearing blinders she stuck to her task. No tempestuous tonguing nor fingering technique, not even a virtuoso vaginal caress could compare with the ecstasy of music being born.

But after a month's worth of *myopic work mode,* Kim became frustrated and laid down the law. They would set aside Thursday nights to be with each other. The one night of the week Kim wasn't on call at Johns Hopkins.

Holly agreed. Her relationship with Kim was important to her. Like fine, precious silver, she wanted to keep it. And silver needs a good polish now and then.

TORCHY SAT IN THE backyard beside Toes' grave, smoking a Marlboro cigarette. Holly and Kim wouldn't let her smoke in the house. She took the last puff and crushed the filtered butt into the soft soil of the garden. She was tired of studying on the computer. And she didn't feel like writing poetry.

Torchy walked up to a local mall and met some boys outside a video arcade. She had never really been with guys her own age. After talking with them a while she came to the conclusion they were doofusses. On her way home she purchased a three-dollar dildo from a Love-Sandwich vending machine.

That night, after Kim went to work and Holly was busy in her studio, Torchy tried out the cheap dildo. But she stopped after the initial foray. It reminded her too much of Roger. He often used dildos instead of his dick. There was something about being fucked by a real cock that just couldn't be duped with a mass-produced decoy. Frustrated, but horny as hell, Torchy reached for her hairbrush on the shelf by the side of the bed. Running the brush through her hair, she began to undo the windblown tangles. Then she noticed the shape of the handle she held in her hand. It was made of smooth plastic. With slightly curved edges. Torchy laid on her back and slowly began inserting it into her vagina.

It didn't go in easily at first, so she lubed the smooth handle with Vaseline. That enabled her to take it in all the way up to the lower edge of the bristles. She imagined herself with the lead singer of a new band called *Krot Shot* who was on MTV. She didn't know his name but she pretended the brush handle was his erect penis going in and out of her while he was fucking her hard. Suddenly an orgasm swept over her like a thousand just-under-the-skin pin prickles. It was the first time she came since the last time she'd slept with Lamar.

Torchy soon became addicted to the handle of the hairbrush the same way she'd become addicted to heroin. She started doing it three or four times a day. Sometimes ten. Whenever she got bored or lonely, she would reach for the brush that she named 'Brett' after she finally found out the lead singer's name.

SINCE HOLLY AND KIM moved to the suburbs, Matt could no longer ride the city bus over to have his music lesson. His mother would have to drive him the eight miles each way. But on the Thursday of the first week of May, Matt's father brought him over.

Holly was busy working on the *Hosanna* when they arrived. She had never met Matt's father before. He was a factory worker in a canning plant. The plant recently closed, so he was presently unemployed. Holly could tell by the tone of his voice that he didn't think highly of his son studying music.

While Holly gave Matt his lesson, his father waited in the living room. He thumbed through some of the magazines on the coffee table: The *New England Journal of Medicine, Feminism Today, Downbeat, Mother Jones*. None of it interested him.

He grew restless and went to find the bathroom, hoping to find a copy of *The Johnside Review*. He didn't. But when he opened the cabinet under the sink, he found something else that made the red hairs on his testicles curl:

The strap-on dildo.

Mr. McConnahee flushed the toilet in the bathroom even though he didn't use it. He didn't want anyone to think he was in there masturbating.

When he stepped out, he came face to face with Kim. She had just woken up. Her hair was sticking out in every direction like an African witch doctor. And she was wearing nothing but an old, moth-eaten T-shirt from her childhood that read:

SHIT HAPPENS

The unemployed Irish cannery worker barged into Holly's studio, grabbed his son by the arm and said they had to leave "...before traffic starts to get bad." Holly could tell by the look on his face that he was disturbed about something. She thought it might be due to his being unemployed. She knew all too well what that felt like.

Kim was taking a shower, getting ready for their big night out on the town. The doorbell rang. Holly answered it. It was Charlie Russell with another big bag of money.

"I left a little something in the bottom of the bag," he informed. Then he turned around, got back in his car, and drove off into the night.

What Holly found in the bottom of the bag, under the stacks of tens and twenties, was a small glass vial. Holly showed it to Kim and asked her what it could possibly be.

"Semen," Kim replied, stepping out of the shower.

"Really?" said Holly, holding the small glass receptacle up to her eye. She thought of how the milky-white substance was home to billions of squiggly little long-tailed sperm. Each held the blueprint for half a human being. Once a month her ovaries were host to the other half. If ever the two halves got together — a whole human being would form. Her womb would be transformed into an elaborate factory where a wandering soul would become the proud owner of a brand new flesh and blood car.

Holly decided to keep the vial of Charlie Russell fluid just in case she never found the right sperm donor through her ad. As she walked into the kitchen, she held the small container in the same palm she once held a snowflake. She marveled at the miracle of birth that brings each one of us into existence. And how the Lord sometimes works in very strange ways.

A chipmunk stores walnuts for the winter. A dog buries bones in the dirt. Holly placed the precious semen behind the ice-trays in the freezer. Like money in the bank, she would save it for a rainy day.

Life starts out a single snowflake falling from the sky
melts up on a mountaintop turns into a trickle becomes
a babbling brook leaps and gurgles grows into a stream
twists and turns and tumbles becomes a river raging
waterfalling rapid surging growing ever wider
current swiftly moving empties out to sea
sun boils off the surface rising steam
becomes the clouds briskly billow
churn a fresh new batch
of snow

Torchy found the handwritten poem on a sheet of paper tucked between the pages of the book by Emily Dickenson. But the poem was not by Dickenson. It was signed by Holly Bibble. Torchy liked the poem. But more than that, it inspired her to write more poetry. It made her feel camaraderie with Holly, knowing they both shared a need for personal expression.

Taking out the Pegasus book she kept beneath her pillow, Torchy began to write another poem of her own.

KIM PRESSED HER FOOT on the accelerator pedal, pumping refined dinosaur shit into the cylinder. A spark ignited the liquid, turning it into a wave. The wave of energy propelled the little green Fiat up the Interstate entrance ramp. During the conversion of a liquid into a wave, a gas was produced called carbon monoxide. This gas, which is lethal to human beings, went into the air and stayed there.

Slowly but surely, the dinosaur poop that is powering the world is rendering the planet uninhabitable, Holly thought as they whizzed by a gas station. *But, unlike those large prehistoric defecators who survived for hundreds of millions of years, we humans are neither big enough, nor have we lived long enough, to have future wars fought over our shit.*

After shifting into fourth gear and merging with the Interstate traffic, Kim let out a sneeze.

"God bless you," said Holly.

"You know I don't believe in God," Kim corrected.

"Well, bless you all the same."

The Fiat hummed along with many hundreds of cars burning dinosaur shit and spewing out poison.

"Boo Boo?" squeaked Holly.

"What?" Kim replied.

"Do you think Immaculate Conception is possible?"

"No."

"Why not?" Holly pressed.

Kim looked over at her lover's face, framed by the lights of downtown Baltimore through the passenger window, "Takes an egg and a sperm. No way around it."

"How do you think Mary got pregnant with Jesus, then?"

"The possibilities are limitless," said Kim as she drove her car down the exit ramp into a bad part of town: "a horny Roman soldier taking advantage of a young woman in an occupied country. A wayward masturbationist passing through Nazareth jacks off on a spot where she later sits down. Who knows?"

Holly thought that if Hollywood ever makes a movie about The Wayward Masturbationist, Charlie Russell would be the perfect person to play the part.

Kim downshifted to stop for a stop sign. Then she rolled down the window, coughed up a wad of phlegm and spit it across the street. "Spermatozoa doesn't just fly around like parakeets," Kim insisted as she accelerated through a deserted intersection, "so it had to come from someone. And that someone had to have functioning testicles. Those are just the facts of life."

Holly was quiet for a while. She had never given much analytical thought to this basic tenant of Christian faith:

Mary was a virgin who was impregnated by God.

The Catholic part of her upbringing taught her that this was Absolute Undeniable Truth. To question it was blasphemy.

Her simultaneous Jewish upbringing taught her the Messiah had not arrived yet. That Mary was a loose *shlooche* with a sucker for a husband. She thought that if

Jesus really was the child of Mary and a horny Roman soldier, He would be the same ethnic mix as she: half Jewish and half Italian.

But how can I really know the Truth? she thought. *If I believe something on faith alone, I could be suckered into believing anything. I could be talked into worshipping a stuffed alligator from a roadside stand outside Miami, Florida. Or, Heaven forbid, become a Hare Krishna. Or a Moonie.*

"Do you believe there're such things as miracles?" Holly asked.

They drove past a group of homeless people bedding down in cardboard boxes for the night.

"There's a scientific explanation for *everything,*" Kim answered.

"What would the scientific explanation be for Jesus feeding the multitudes with just five loaves and seven fishes?"

Kim thought for a minute, then said: "Maybe all those people who went to hear him speak already had food with them, hidden in their clothing. They weren't about to pull it out in the middle of a hungry crowd. But when they saw a few people give away the only food they had, and Jesus passing it around, maybe they pulled out the food they were hoarding and started passing it around, too. So everybody ate, and still they had baskets and baskets of food left over. And everyone got to take home a doggie bag, too. Jesus got them to overcome their fear of going hungry. He got a crowd of strangers to share with each other. That's a miracle if I ever heard one."

Kim swerved to avoid a dead dog sprawled in the middle of the street. She pulled to the curb. Got out and dragged the dog's body off to the side. The dog had been dead for a while. Rigor mortis had already set in. Kim wondered if anyone had loved the poor dog. She knew how much people could become attached to animals. She'd never really known that until she knew Toes. *The worse thing about losing someone to death*, she thought, *is that the loss is definite. And irretrievable.*

Kim got back in the Fiat. They took off again through the desolate streets.

"I think we got off on the wrong exit," Kim said. There was a weighted silence between them. The same sort of silence that sank in their hearts during dearly departed Toes' backyard burial.

Holly broke the sullen silence by asking Kim something she had never asked her before: "Boo Boo, do you think there's a purpose to life?"

Kim coughed another hawker-wad and spit it out the window. The small mucus jellyfish spiraled spinelessly through the air and splattered on a yellow sign that read:

WATCH FOR CHILDREN

Kim rolled the window back up and answered:

"I think it's up to us to define the purpose of our lives. Then it's up to us to fulfill it. I think the only hope we have for the future is through technology. We can't go back to living primitively. At least not voluntarily. Once you *know* something you can't go back to pretending you don't know it. Unless you get a lobotomy.

"Someday we'll be able to digitalize human consciousness. We'll store the information on a silicon chip. These 'consciousness chips' will be connected to some sort of hardware. Say a six-inch-square titanium cube, or something. The cube will be equipped with sensors far beyond what our eyes, ears, and skin and noses are now. We'll be able to see into the infrared and ultraviolet spectrums, with both telescopic and microscopic capabilities. We'll be able to hear ultra and subsonic sounds. We'll each have an onboard supercomputer making trillions of calculations per millisecond. We'll have instantaneous access to the sum total of human knowledge at any time. All packed within our self-contained titanium cube.

"Since our new cube-bodies will be made of indestructible or self-repairing components, we'll have life-spans of billions and billions of years. There won't be any limit to whatever we wanna do — since we won't have death to cut our time short anymore. We'll all be able to compose symphonies. Write epic novels. Be quantum physicists. We'll be able to do things we can't even conceive of now. It'll all be possible.

"We'll communicate with other cubes through microwave or cellular radio frequencies. We'll have interface ports so we can hook up to air-mobiles and fly wherever we want to. Using an inexhaustible fuel supply like solar or fusion, or some technology we haven't even discovered yet.

"Instead of cruise ships that just sail to the Bahamas and back, we'll hook into spacecraft that'll explore distant galaxies. And think about it: if we have infinite space to explore, and infinite time to explore it — Time itself will cease to exist."

Their conversation came back down to Earth as Kim parked in a spot next to O'Keeffe's Flower, a lesbian bar in the Inner Harbor District. The place was packed to the gills with gay women of every discernible stripe. Everything from mini-skirted centerfold types to butch-burred, khaki-trousered army boot dykes.

Behind the bar was a bull dyke pouring drinks. Above the bar was a painting by Georgia O'Keeffe. A painting of a flower so unabashedly vulvic it made one want to lick right through to the canvas. Next to the painting was the State Motto of Maryland engraved on a long piece of wood:

Fatti maschii, parole femine

It meant "Manly deeds, womanly words."

Although still socially unacceptable in the mainstream of society, lesbianism became relatively popular during the latter part of the 1990's. They were the one sexually active group who were at low risk of contracting the HIV virus.

"In the future," Kim projected, as she and Holly drank beers at the bar, waiting for a pool table to open, "the only people who'll be left in the world will be lesbians. There'll be a few males left who'll be kept for semen production. Some girls will be sperm farmers. So when we wanna have kids we won't have to resort to personal ads anymore. We'll just walk down to the corner store and buy a shot of baby juice."

When Holly thought of sperm farming, she thought of Charlie Russell. She imagined a whole stable of Charlie Russells raised on a "Dude Ranch." Each would be kept in their individual stalls. Their penises hooked up to a milking machine. Five or six times a day the machine would suck them off automatically. Then an industrious female spermatozoa farmer would gather the produce. Separate the sperm into X and Y chromosomes. And market the stuff to lesbian couples who want to bear daughters of their own. Almost like aphids. Holly wondered how this sort of reproductive arrangement would affect the story lines of daytime TV.

Finally, a pool table opened up. Shooting pool was a sentimental thing for Holly and Kim. They first met in a billiard hall near George Washington University. Holly was in Music and Kim was in Medicine. They met and fell madly in love during a hot late night game of eight-ball. The two grad students hung up their cue sticks, went back to Kim's apartment and made passionate love till the slow rising sun turned the eastern sky a perfect shade of labia-pink.

After a few games and a buzz from the beer, they stepped out of O'Keeffe's and walked down to the water. By day, the Patapsco River was a festering soup of slick city sewage and industrial waste. But at night, with the moon shining bright and the silhouette tugboats toot-tooting across the way — the river could be magical for the romantically inclined. Waves lapping rhythms beneath their four feet as they walked hand in hand on the seawall.

Kim and Holly liked being in this part of town where they could display their affection for each other without raising eyebrows from the people they passed. It was nice to not have to pretend they were sisters. Or roommates. Or college coeds. Or any such socially acceptable form of female to female togetherness. They were lovers. Soul mates. Bonded for life. And in this moment, walking on the seawall, all they wanted to do was hold hands.

In the distance they heard music. Voices in the air. Echoing through alleyways. Vibrant and alive. They followed like bears follow the scent of honey — knowing what sweetness awaits at its source. It grew more intense. More beautiful. Jubilant. Beckoning more the closer they got. Like two fluttering moths on a quest toward the light.

They could walk no more. They had to run as fast as their feet would carry them over passed-out bums and bottles and foul-smelling trash till they came to a small white-brick church several blocks from the waterfront nestled in between a lingerie boutique and a liquor store. From inside the church came the sound that they sought.

The front of the church had four round stained-glass windows. Each depicted a scene from the life of Christ. The Nativity, Walking on Water, The Crucifixion, and The Resurrection. A plaque by the front door said the church was built in 1907 — after the Great Fire of 1904.

Holly pulled at the paint-peeling doors. The music hit them like wind. A black Baptist church congregation singing *a cappella*: no instruments accompanied their voices. Some forty strong, with a preacher who led them. He sang out the phrase and they answered in kind. Singing and swaying with the wildest abandon; a glorious exaltation!

Holly and Kim stood transfixed in the foyer. Still holding hands. In awe. Stricken. These voices from Africa shook every wall. Even Christ on His cross appeared ready to tumble.

Kim's eyes welled up like a cup overflowing. Spilling down on to the floor. She had gone to a black Baptist church once before with her father, a carpenter, after the Vietnam War. While driving through Louisiana they stopped at a place where an orphanage had burned to the ground. He said he was raised there. A bastard from the bayou. An old ramshackle church was still standing nearby. He'd converted to Buddhism when he married her mother. But he couldn't resist a quick peek at his past.

Kim was just five when she first heard this singing. There in that church. Holding Daddy's hand. But she hadn't remembered it since. Till now. It filled her with longing to see them again. Like the old faded photo she kept in her purse. She longed to hug Mommy and Daddy. Just once. Just one more time.

Kim never did cry when her parents died. She never cried about anything. But the black Baptist singing had stripped her defenses. And left her soul naked in the House of the Lord.

"I've got to incorporate this into the Hosanna," Holly said to Kim as they left the small church.

For a while, as they walked, neither spoke. Only listened. The sound of their footsteps kept perfect time with the singing that slowly grew fainter and fainter. Kim wiped the last tears from her almond-shaped eyes.

The two of them stopped by the edge of the waterfront. The city lights danced on the dark, gentle waves. They still heard the singing way off in the distance. And then it was still. The two women embraced.

"Don't you think we would miss this," Holly asked, holding tight, "if we traded in our bodies for titanium cubes?"

"Do we miss clubbing Mastodons for dinner?" Kim countered. For an instant she smiled. Then looked out on the Bay. A few stars broke through the thick Baltimore haze.

"Whenever humankind has moved forward," she said, "there's always something that gets left behind."

"But I like your behind," Holly giggled while squeezing Kim's buns through her tight leather jeans. Then they kissed. Eyes closed. Heads turned. Arms tangling. A lip locking, tongue twisting, mouth-wrangling kiss.

Back in the car Holly rested her head on Kim's shoulder for the half-hour drive. The radio played Rachmaninoff. No words were exchanged. Just caresses.

While she was driving, Kim kept trying to analyze what she was feeling. What had happened to her in the church seemed like so much more than a chemical reaction. And what of her feelings for Holly? They, too, seemed to be much more than a release of endorphins in the brain. Her feelings in the church and her love for Holly seemed to be cut from a similar cloth. Maybe the Universe was more than a mere exchange of matter and energy. More than an endless swirl of solids, liquids, gases, and waves.

Holly was wearing her Pendleton sweater. The same one she wore on the night they first met. Never in her life had she loved anyone as much as she loved Kim. They had differences, of course. Philosophically, most certainly. But sensually, emotionally, they were perfectly combined. But, more than her body, she loved Kimberly's mind.

Conversations with Kim always compelled her to push beyond the limits of everyday thinking. Holly had a need for cerebral stimulation as well as her need for its clitoral counterpart. Although they had differing viewpoints, in essence what both of them sought was the same: love, beauty and truth, and a sense of adventure.

The one thing more precious to Holly than Kim was music. It was her center. Her soul. But without love, she felt like an empty oboe, alone with no wind in its reeds. And even though Holly couldn't fathom a life without music —the music within— neither could she imagine spending her life without Kim.

They pulled in the driveway. Turned off the car. Crept in the house on tiptoes. Torchy was already asleep in her room. A teddybear tucked under her arm.

Quiet as mice the two went to their bedroom. Left the lights off as they slow-shut the door. Kim lit a candle on the shelf of the headboard. By the mirror they embraced and fell down on the bed. Clothes came off quickly — flung in every direction. Lips met with lips met with hips met with lip-song. Sheets became wrapped rumpled bibs 'round their rib-song. Together they made sweet and passionate love till the hours were wee and their bodies exhausted. Like their very first night after sinking the eight-ball, they collapsed intertwined in each other's arms.

The next morning Holly threw up for the third day in a row.

Recitative

Blue. It was blue. Ocean hue. Robin's egg. *Something borrowed something new.* Sinatra-eyed, internet hyperlink blue.

"Boo Boo," Holly whispered to Kim as she shook her from her slumber. The sheets were still scented from sex the night before.

"What, Sugar?" Kim purred, eyes still closed with a smile draped across her dark complexion.

"I'm pregnant," Holly answered.

Kim's smile vanished like fairy dust. Her eyes opened wide as the windows. She sat up suddenly — like a switchblade sprung.

"You're *what?*"

Holly held out the home pregnancy tester. The clear plastic cap held the blue-turned solution. Kim knew what blue meant. She had used the same kit herself some years back — after her one heterosexual encounter.

Holly stared at Kim's full sensuous lips that just hours before had sucked and caressed her clitoris to the peak of elation. Lips still glossed and reddened from the act. Holly leaned forward to kiss those lips with her own. But Kim pulled away with punitive swiftness. The mouth Holly longed to engulf in her own hung half-open in simmering disdain. Out of reach, barely heard, uttering a single, one-syllable word:

"How?"

"I'm not sure," Holly replied uneasily. She averted Kim's inquisitive eyes. She focused instead on the flower box outside on the window ledge. The posies were beginning to bloom.

"What do you mean, you're not sure? It sure as shit wasn't the strap-on."

"It must have been Roger."

"Roger who?"

"The composer. Well, he's not much of a composer."

"You had an affair?"

"No. I was on drugs."

"What kind of drugs?"

"I don't know. It was a grayish-brown color. We smoked it out of a little-bitty pipe."

"So you fucked the Unknown Composer, is that what you're saying?"

"I don't know. I don't remember. He must have taken advantage of me when I was high."

"So he raped you."

"I guess if you wanna call it that."

Kim picked up the phone and started dialing.

"What are you doing?"

"I'm calling the police."

Holly quickly pushed down the receiver. "No, you can't!"

"He raped you! Men like that belong in jail!"

"I'll lose the commission if you call. I'll lose the *Hosanna!*"

"We can't let that prick get away with it!" Kim said as she started dialing again, "it's a matter of principle."

"Kim, no! Don't! I'll tell them I let him do it! I'll tell them *I let him!*"

"Did you?" asked Kim, with her ear to the phone.

"Yes! I let him fuck me! I gave him my permission! It was consensual!"

Kim slammed down the phone. "You little whore!"

"Please don't call me that."

"You fucked him to get the commission, didn't you?"

"No, I didn't!"

"No different than a streetwalker and a trick!"

"No, it wasn't like that! Boo Boo, I love you!"

"Don't 'Boo Boo' me, you little tramp. You don't really love me."

"I do!"

"No you don't. You're probably not even really gay! You just do it to get back at your parents or something."

"That's not true! I love my parents! They disowned me because I'm gay. And I wish they hadn't."

"You're lying to yourself, Holly."

"I am not!"

"You're in love with the idea of being in love with me."

"That's not true. I know what I want. I want to spend the rest of my life with you, Boo Boo!" Holly threw her arms around Kim, sobbing.

Kim brushed her fingers through Holly's hair, pushing it away from her tear-streamed face. The tears poured across Kim's flat chest, forming tributaries around her pert, dark nipples, meandering downward toward her belly and disappearing into the soft bramble of her pubic forest. "I can set up an abortion at the hospital," she said. "We can have it done this afternoon."

"I don't want an abortion," Holly meekly replied.

"Come again?"

"I want to have the baby."

"Not now. It's too soon. The time has to be right."

"When will it be right?"

"As soon as my practice is established."

"Who knows if the time'll be right even then? I have a little life inside me now. And I didn't even have to resort to the personal ads to get it."

"You planned this whole thing, didn't you?" Kim accused.

"No, I didn't."

"You went and got pregnant behind my back without even consulting me—"

"It was an accident!"

"Bullshit!" Kim jumped out of bed and started dressing hurriedly.

"Where are you going?"

"I'm outta here."

"What do you mean?"

"Look, Holly, let's stop bullshitting each other. Why don't you and Roger the Unknown Composer get married and live happily ever after."

"I hate him. I hate his guts. I only love *you!*"

"Well, you either call the police right now and report this fucking rapist, or you can forget about it between you and me," said Kim, holding the phone toward Holly.

"I can't. You know how much the *Hosanna* means to me."

"Obviously much more than I do," Kim said, throwing the phone on the bed. "Goodbye!"

She stormed out of the house. Got into her car. Burnt a twenty-foot stretch of black rubber in the driveway. Holly heard a distant high-pitched "Fuck you!" accompanied by the sound of Kim's car speeding angrily away.

Torchy came into the room dressed in a long cotton nightie and rubbing her sleepy eyes. She took one look at Holly and knew something was terribly wrong.

"Where did Kim go?"

"She'll be back," Holly said, rubbing her own eyes then walking to her studio with a sudden urgency of purpose. She picked up a worn-down pencil and began notating a melody. It came to her in a dream that night after making love to Kim.

Now it was coming back to her. Note for note. Exactly as she had dreamt it. Played by a distant oboe. The singular melody enveloped her with its haunting beauty. It filled her emptiness. Watered the inner flower of her soul. The music danced across the canvas of her consciousness like a paintbrush. Sweeping away her sorrow.

And turning her pain into joy.

ON THE SENATE FLOOR a debate was raging over an amendment to House Resolution 581 — The Funeral Services Regulatory Act. The Bill already passed in the House of Representatives. All it needed was Senate approval before being sent to the President for his signature.

With the aging of the post-World War II baby-boom population, funeral services were rapidly becoming the number one growth industry in America. Resolution 581 sought to regulate all the casket retailers, funeral homes, and crematoriums that were popping up like mushrooms all over the country.

Senator Hotchkins of Utah was sponsoring an amendment to Resolution 581 that would make it illegal to use profanity in the presence of a dead person. Because his amendment was just shy of the votes needed to tack it on to the Bill, Senator Hotchkins was on the Senate floor in the midst of a filibuster.

"The use of foul language in the proximity of a corpse is an affront to the dignity of the deceased," Hotchkins ranted as the C-SPAN cameras rolled. The Senator from Utah continued his speech (it had already gone on for six hours): "The law needs to protect those who otherwise cannot be protected. That is our mandate. And in all of God's Creation there's no one more defenseless than a person who is no longer among the living."

While Senator Hotchkins railed on, his supporters canvassed the Senate, trying to muster the needed votes for the Amendment's passage.

But Senator Bane had a more personal matter that he desperately wanted to get passed: a large backlog of solid waste material impacted in his colon. The grumblings of his lower abdominals rose to a fevered pitch — rivaling Hotchkins' overwrought oratory.

Bane made a beeline for the bathroom down the hall. He already planned on voting for the Amendment. Not out of any moral conviction to protect future dead people from the profanities of morgue attendants and their ilk. But rather because Senator Hotchkins of Utah had been instrumental in booking The Mormon Tabernacle Choir for the oratorio. Voting for the Amendment was Senator Bane's way of paying Senator Hotchkins back.

This is how the parliamentary system works in a nation that is ruled by testosterone and runs on dinosaur shit.

Lucius latched the door in an unoccupied stall in the Senate restroom. He reached for a thin paper toilet seat cover from the dispenser next to the john. The doughnut-shaped bottom-bibs were supposed to protect a person's hiney from the onslaught of bathroom borne diseases, but they looked more like life preservers from a two-dimensional world. Bane dropped his drawers and carefully lowered his enormous posterior onto the toilet seat. The paper-thin fanny-gasket crinkled but held firmly in place. The overweight Senator reached for his favorite reading material from the rack on the stall door. On the cover of *The Johnside Review* was Jon LaRue — holding a corncob.

The Senator opened *The Johnside Review* and perused its contents page. Since he suffered from constipation, his eyes went automatically to the 'Long Sit' section.

There was an article on an Amish bran muffin bakery. Also a do-it-yourself guide to home plumbing. But he couldn't resist the *Johnside* Interview with his nemesis: the notorious New York performance artist.

The first page of the interview showed a full-color photo of LaRue nailed to the outhouse door. Under the photo, the caption read:

"OUCH!"

Like the up-chuck of a badly cooked dinner, the photo brought back unpleasant memories for Bane. The backlash from the trial. The analogies to Hitler. Six months of flaccid penis imposed celibacy.

The first half of the interview dealt mostly with LaRue's up-coming world tour. Advance tickets were selling briskly. Six nights at the newly opened Staples Center in Los Angeles were already sold out.

The interviewer asked LaRue about the Crucifax Trial that brought him so much notoriety. The wily performance artist answered with a long rambling speech about First Amendment rights and the rise of neo-fascism in America. LaRue also mentioned he would never perform *Crucifax* again. He claimed that after the one performance his hands were so bandaged he couldn't masturbate for over three months. He professed an aversion to Love-Sandwiches, saying he was really a "traditionalist" when it came to self-abuse.

Senator Bane stopped reading for a moment. His bowels were gridlocked as bad as the Capital Beltway at rush hour. He closed his eyes and tried visualizing a full tube of toothpaste in his mind. It was a technique he learned from a video called *Curing Constipation Through Mind Control.* He ordered it with his credit card after seeing it advertised on late night TV. The video he bought ran only five minutes. It showed a toothpaste tube slowly being squeezed until it was empty. A deep, Darth Vader-esque voice gave detailed instructions on following the 'Toothpaste Tube Technique:'

"Visualize a full toothpaste tube in your mind. Picture it with the nozzle facing down. Envision it being squeezed from the bottom of the tube. Imagine the toothpaste being expelled from the nozzle like icing all over a cake. Now visualize the same tube of toothpaste down in your lower abdominal tract. Continue squeezing it. Imagine the tube is

your bowel. The toothpaste is the stuff that you want to be voided. Picture it. Squeezing it. Toothpaste oozing out the end. Things should be moving very soon."

The video had New Age music playing as background. Senator Bane had tried the Toothpaste Tube Technique on several occasions — to no avail. He decided this would be the last time he would try it. If it didn't work he would demand a refund and report the video company to The Department of Consumer Affairs.

After several vain attempts at squeezing the metaphysical mind-tube in his colonic consciousness, Senator Bane gave up. He went back to reading the interview with Jon LaRue:

JOHNSIDE: On your current tour, the piece that is getting the most response is the one titled: *Sobriety Checkpoint* –

LaRUE: Oh, yes, I enjoy performing that one very much.

JOHNSIDE: In this piece, you are naked, as you are in most of your works—

LaRUE: Yeah, that way I don't have to pay a wardrobe person to go on the road with me. *(laughs)*

JOHNSIDE: Right. Now in *Sobriety Checkpoint* you walk a white line that's painted across the stage. Your wrists are handcuffed in front of you. A yardstick is imbedded several inches up your ass. A nun leads you across the stage, pointing a flashlight in your face while you recite the alphabet backwards. I'm curious as to the significance of the nun?

LaRUE: Again, it's a costuming thing. I try to reduce my conceptual imagery down to its most simplest form. That way the audience doesn't get confused. Instead of a nun, I could have made it a cop holding the flashlight. Or a judge. In this case, any symbol of authority would do.

JOHNSIDE: And what about the yardstick extending out of your rectum?

LaRUE: Again, *Sobriety Checkpoint* is a statement about Authority. The yardstick signifies how our lives are constantly being measured. Too much. Too little. Too big. Too small. And so on.

JOHNSIDE: Are you an anarchist?

LaRUE: Religions and governments were explicitly set up to enslave people. To keep them from doing what their instincts tell them to do. We're all like birds kept in cages with these beautiful wings and we can only fantasize how to use them. Through my art I hope to convey to people a glimpse of what that freedom will be like when the human spirit can truly fly.

JOHNSIDE: Another conceptual piece in your show, titled: *Hemorrhoid Boomerang*, you stand — naked again — eating a slice of watermelon skewered on a pitchfork. You have a wooden boomerang protruding from your anus. And you sing German polkas while spitting seeds at an archery target fastened to the nun's crotch.

LaRUE: Brilliant, isn't it?

JOHNSIDE: The protruding boomerang. The yardstick. The bullwhip. Do I detect an "anal theme" emerging in your work?

LaRUE: There is a lot of untapped power in the anus, the kundalini yogis have known this for thousands of years. To them, the asshole is the center of the base root chakra. A source of energy. I try to incorporate certain common denominators in my art so that everyone can relate to it. The thing about assholes is they're like opinions — everybody's got one. Eating is another thing we all have in common. Eating is the first major event of a newborn baby's life. After birth, that is. Defecating is the last thing a person does when they die. When you die, the muscles holding everything in your bowels just let loose and everything comes pouring out like a cement mixer. And funny that you should use the term "anal theme" in your question. Because what I plan on doing with the millions of dollars I'll have when this tour is over is open an "Anal Theme Park" in Orlando, Florida. The entrance to the park will be this gigantic pink doughnut that visitors will walk through. Once inside they'll be greeted by Gerry Gerbil, Hieronymus Buttplug, and Poopy the Appendix. They'll guide you down Peristalsis Path to Sphincterland. There you can take a suppository cruise through the Intestinal Flora Gardens. Or, for the thrill-seekers, there's brownwater rafting down the treacherous Colonic Falls. And for the kids there's always Mister Turd's Wild Ride. There'll be a wide assortment of restaurants within the park and, of course, lots and lots of restrooms...

....

Senator Bane threw the magazine down on the floor, disgusted. *What kind a' society is this?* he thought to himself, *where we heap fame and fortune on a degenerate who really belongs in a straight jacket.*

"You've been in there a while, haven't you, Lou?" came a New England voice from elsewhere in the restroom.

Bane peeked through the crack on the side of the stall door and saw the Democratic Senator from Massachusetts, who was emptying the product of his kidneys into a urinal.

"Yeah," Bane replied, "you could say I've been havin' a little filibuster in here a' my own."

"I think they'll be getting to the vote any minute now," the Democrat said as he zipped his fly and checked his hair in the mirror. Because he still had a full head of hair, the Massachusetts Senator posed a possible threat to Bane's future aspirations toward the White House.

"Thanks," Bane replied as he turned and looked down into the toilet. The only reward for his efforts was a single brown bullet that he'd managed to pinch off a few minutes earlier. He wiped and flushed and left in a hurry. As usual, his work was left undone in these hallowed stalls of government. It seemed easier to pass bills through Congress than it was to get anything to pass through his own intestines.

But Lucius Bane looked on the bright side as he walked back out to vote on the fate of funeral workers: at least during his next sit he would be able to read about the Amish Bran Muffin Bakeries.

Instead of that lowlife LaRue.

Andante

Holly encouraged Torchy to grow a garden in the backyard. She was reluctant at first, till one day Holly brought home seeds and got her started. Once she got in the groove of things, Torchy actually enjoyed it. She planted tomatoes and cucumbers. Onions and summer squash. And a bed of petunias all around Toes' grave.

Torchy liked the planting and watering. But she hated pulling weeds. Holly convinced her it was "all part of the process." When the first sprouts came up, Torchy was "totally psyched." It gave her inspiration to pull more weeds. Between the computer, the garden, and the hairbrush in her room, Torchy had her hands full all summer.

*

Dear Holly,

I have tried to call you several times but your answering machine always picks up. I declined to leave a message, since I am bound by a confidentiality clause in my contract, just as you are. It would be reckless of me to leave a message not sure who could possibly overhear it.

When you get to be as old as I am you often look back and say, "What have I done with my life?" Since I retired from teaching this year, I began thinking that my entire life has been a waste. When I was about your age, I still had a dream in my heart to become a composer. But when the harsh reality set in, I settled for a chair at the University. I always considered this to be a retrenchment — an abandonment of my goals.

But reading your scores for the Hosanna has changed my perspective completely. I used to think the energy I put into teaching was wasted — that my life was a failure. But, Holly, your Hosanna Millennia has proven me wrong! The beauty of your second movement brought tears to my eyes. Tears!

'Fishers of Men' and 'Beatitudes' are exquisitely conceived and executed. (Although be careful of writing the French Horns in that upper register. It works — but it's risky.)

I avidly await with eager inner ears the completion of the entire score. I regret that your name won't be on it, Holly, because I sense longevity with this work. It's a magnificent piece of music and I am so proud of you.

You have completely changed my perspective of teaching. Culture would wither and die without the people who pass it on from one generation to the next.

These days are difficult times for true artists. The media hypes mediocrities and the masses follow like lemmings. The Music of our age sounds like the clatter of trashcans banging in a litter-strewn alleyway at night. You must continue the struggle to bring beauty into the world, Holly. Whether anyone pays you to do so or not.

I trust you will destroy this letter after reading it, in accordance with the confidentiality clause. Keep up the good work!

Sincerely Yours,

Sydney Bormstern

Two days after Holly received the letter, Professor Bormstern passed away. Holly drove down to Alexandria for his funeral. She ran into some friends she hadn't seen since grad school. Because of the confidentiality clause in her contract, she couldn't tell any of them that she was ghostwriting the *Hosanna Millennia* that they were all buzzing about and seemed so eager to hear come Christmas.

The funeral was open casket, Holly saw the Professor's body and thought of it as his car. The car wasn't running any more so the driver had gone on elsewhere. Holly wondered if Professor Bormstern's soul was standing in some Great Big Valet Parking Lot in the Sky.

As the final garage for the Professor's used car was lowered down into the ground, Holly reminisced about her Grandpa Bibble. His was the last funeral she had been to (except for her backyard service for Toes.)

She was fifteen at the time her Grandfather died and was living at home with her parents. They flew to New York and stayed several days at her Grandmother's house on Long Island.

Holly remembered the house being filled with flowers. The funeral procession stretched a mile behind the hearse. Poor Grandma Bibble cried for days over her husband whom a heart attack struck down at the age of sixty-three.

Giancarlo was a kind man. And loved by many. Holly remembered him giving her chocolates as a child. Then he gave her his prized clarinet. If it were not for that clarinet, her Grandfather might have been killed in the Second World War. Then *her* father, of course, would never have been born. And neither would Holly. So, in essence, she owed her very existence to her Grandfather's ebony horn.

Holly thought: *Everything in life is interdependent. Connected. Every mountain and molehill and molecule. You can't change one without affecting all the others. Music is passed down from one generation to another — like a harmonic progression. Now she had a child of her own, slowly growing inside her like the backyard garden. She would nurture it to grow strong and sing a song of its own.*

There was birdsong in the trees reminding Holly of the *Hosanna.* She watched as dirt was shoveled on Professor Bormstern's grave. The man who had taught her to write music in her mind was no longer in the Realm of Matter and Energy. He had returned to the Realm of Idea, that Infinite Abyss from whence he came.

Every step Holly had taken in life had led her to where she was standing. If she changed a single step, she would be in a completely different place. Just as each note follows the note before it in the miraculous Symphony of Life, Holly was grateful for all God's blessings. Even in the cold face of death.

ROGER GOT HORNY AFTER Torchy left. He wanted to go looking for women to fuck but couldn't get his Harley-Davidson started. Unbeknownst to him, Senator Bane had a CIA friend sabotage Roger's motorcycle so it would never start ever again. Not even the best mechanic in the world would be able to figure out what was wrong with it. The Senator did this to keep Roger from roaming around outside the Chesapeake Bay property. He took every precaution to keep him away from the Press.

Roger spent his fortieth birthday alone. Age forty for a rocker is synonymous with death. There were no dildo candles to lick like last year. Roger spent the day thumbtacking his most recent poop pictures to the ceiling.

Then despair set in. The emptiness resulting from a

lifetime badly squandered. A life adding up to a photo album full of shit. Roger called the Senator and told him he was going back to New York.

"I can play my fucking guitar just as good there as I can here," he complained.

Senator Bane babbled on about how Roger needed to stay in seclusion until the oratorio is finished. "It'll create *mystique*," he added, using a word he'd picked up from Charlie Russell.

But mystique alone couldn't keep Roger Landsworth in Maryland.

"What is it you got in New Yawk that ya ain't got there on the Bay?" the Senator asked over the phone.

"Pussy," Roger replied.

"Don't you fret none," Bane assured, "you kin order that jes' like ya order pizza."

The Senator set Roger up with an outcall service in Annapolis, a little less than an hour away. It was expensive with all the extra mileage charges. But there was no length the Senator wouldn't go to keep Roger out of the public eye until after November.

After the first week, the outcall service called Senator Bane to inform him they would not be sending any more escorts to his cottage: "The guy's a real wacko," the proprietor explained, "None of the girls are willing to go back. For any price."

At that point, Senator Bane suggested that Roger invite some of his friends in New York to come down and spend the summer with him at Chesapeake Bay. Roger thought it was a 'mega' idea.

Roger called his ex-girlfriend named Marsha, a large-breasted amphetamine freak. She supported her habit by having men view her valves in a peep show on 42nd Street.

A peep show is a form of entertainment where a girl dances naked while men in private booths jack-off while watching her. Charlie Russell often frequented these establishments in Baltimore. To some he had a season pass.

Marsha jumped at the chance to come party with Roger, even though she hated his guts. His name had been mentioned in the papers. Even on TV. Word on the street was that "Roger finally hit the Big Time."

After Marsha was there for a week, she grew tired of constantly having cucumbers shoved up her ass and being forced to take photos of Roger's turds. But she grew fond of the money that Roger had in abundant supply. Drugs were expensive. So were cigarettes and liquor. Marsha decided to spread Roger's wealth. She called all her friends and invited them down. Soon these friends called their friends. Then those friends called others.

Toward the end of the summer, a full-on party was raging twenty-four hours a day. Everyone stayed drunk and smoked 'go' all the time. Burnt-out musicians, bikers and strippers, lushes and losers and lowlifes alike — some stayed for a day, some a week. Some longer. Others stayed until they had to be hospitalized.

Clarence the gatekeeper saw all sorts of degenerates ride down the long gravel driveway that summer. As long as they didn't look like reporters, on Senator Bane's orders, he would smile and wave them on in.

About once every couple months or so, Roger would feel a compulsion to do something besides having sex, taking drugs, and playing rock-n-roll. On these rare occasions he would take his Les Paul, plug it into the computer and 'jam' till his fingers got tired (which usually wasn't very long while the party was going on and he had an assortment of fur-pies to fondle). Then he would print out the meaningless jumble of musical notes and have it Fed-Exed up to Baltimore. Holly would then take one look at his score and immediately throw it into the trashcan where it belonged.

Holly called Charlie Russell. She had forgiven him for the episode with Torchy and the imaginary dog. She thought about how lonely it must be for a man to only be able to have sex with himself. Charlie Russell was not in his office. So Holly called him on his cell phone.

Charlie was on his way back from Washington, cruising the I-95 Corridor in his navy-blue Infiniti with the Acu-Jack attached to his prick.

(An Acu-Jack is a device that fastens to a man's penis and sucks him off while he's driving a car. It runs off the DC power from the car's cigarette lighter. The Acu-Jack has three variable speeds: "Highway," "City," and "Gridlock." The United States Department of Transportation tried to ban Acu-Jacks, claiming they were a menace to public safety. But in a celebrated countersuit brought before the Supreme Court (*Acu-Jack Inc. vs. The U.S. Dept. of Transportation*), lawyers for the plaintiffs claimed the Acu-Jack could actually reduce traffic fatalities. They argued that men with unrelieved sexual tension have trouble keeping their eyes on the road. Statistics showed this was especially true when large breasted women drove by in small foreign sports cars or any type of convertible. In a 5-4 ruling the Justices decided in favor of Acu-Jack Inc. This opened the door for Acu-Jacks to be distributed nationwide. Sales were poor in New York City where dildos and Love-Sandwiches reigned supreme.

But they sold like hot cakes in Los Angeles where everyone has a car — and a broken dream.

With his car stereo blasting The Mutant Gay Love Nodes from Texas, Charlie Russell answered his cell phone while the Acu-Jack hummed along at 'Highway' speed.

"Charlie, I'd like to write a section of the *Hosanna* for a black Baptist congregation," Holly said over the phone, "about forty people, including the preacher. I was wondering if you had any ideas about how I should present the idea to the Senator?"

"I got the perfect angle," said Charlie Russell as the Acu-Jack began to make his cock tingle — a harbinger of the orgasm that was on the way. He clicked off his phone without saying goodbye. Within fifteen minutes Holly got a call from Senator Bane.

"Miss Bibble, I got a great idea," Bane blurted enthusiastically over the phone, "Let's get a black Baptist church to sing in the *Hosanna.* It'll help get the black vote — I mean, it'll help get the colored folks involved."

After telling Senator Bane what a truly wonderful idea he came up with, Holly said yes, she would love to write a part for the Baptist singers. When she got off the phone with the Senator, she called Charlie Russell. He didn't answer his cell phone so she called him at his office. He picked up the phone while his secretary was washing his Acu-Jack in the sink.

"How'd you do it this time?" Holly asked.

"I told him we could get *beaucoup* TV coverage having an all black church group involved," Charlie laughed while flipping the pages of the most recent *Penthouse* magazine. "I told him if nothing else, it would help get some of the African-American vote back home."

"Charlie, you're a genius."

"If I'm a genius and you're a genius," he said, "just think of what our kids are gonna be like."

"That's certainly something to think about," Holly added.

"You know," said Charlie, sitting behind his desk in his office high in a building in downtown Baltimore. He took out his limp prick and started stroking it in his palm. Ogling the wide open centerfold spread across the desk in front of him, he asked Holly: "Did you get my gift?"

"Yes, I did, Charlie. Thank you."

"I just wanna let you know there's plenty more where that came from."

"If I need any more I'll be sure to let you know."

"Just remember: when you think of sperm, think of Charlie Russell."

"Thank you for getting the Senator to let the Baptists into the *Hosanna*, Charlie. You're a real sweetheart. Now, I've got to get back to work. Goodbye."

After Holly hung up, Charlie reached in his desk and took out a *Love Sandwich*. He tore open the wrapper, pulled down his zipper, and started going to town. Once he ejaculated, he carefully squeezed the juice into a small glass vial. Then he had it messengered over to Holly along with a dozen red roses.

Like the other one she'd received two months earlier, she put it in her freezer. Even though she was pregnant, she might want to have another child somewhere down the line.

But the next day another vial arrived at her doorstep, delivered by a singing telegram. Every day for a week, Charlie had sperm samples sent over. Once by a tap-dancing gorilla. Finally Holly had to put a stop to it. She was running out of available space in her freezer.

"Charlie," she said over the phone, "I appreciate the gesture but there isn't any need to send any more of your personalized gifts."

"Why not?" Charlie asked, "Don't you want to get pregnant?"

"I already am," Holly replied.

Charlie asked if he could take Holly out to dinner. Holly said she was too busy with the *Hosanna*. He called every day for a couple more weeks but all he got was her answering machine.

TORCHY ORDERED SOME LADYBUGS through the mail to put in her garden. The ladybugs ate the aphids that sucked the sap out of her seedling plants. The delicate balance of Nature is often violent. Sometimes cruel. The higher we go up the food chain, the more savage a species can be. Humans, being the highest, can be the most ruthlessly barbaric of all.

At the bottom of the food chain are plants. The flowers and trees. Each converting waves of sunlight into solid petals and leaves. Fed by liquid rainfall and carbon dioxide from the air, they create a useful gas called oxygen. But the flowers and trees are more than mere matter. More than makers of gas and converters of energy. They bring a sense of beauty into the world for whoever has the open doors of perception to perceive It.

And Beauty is beyond all solids, liquids, and gases — and even waves.

WRITING THE THIRD MOVEMENT of the *Hosanna Millennia* was not as simple as Holly thought it would be. It would be *a cappella:* no instruments, only voices. She had a title she liked: "Good Young Carpenter." And she wanted it to be about Jesus as a boy. But what she had written was too rigid and refined. She wanted the third movement to have the raw power she and Kim heard that night in the church near the waterfront. She wanted the notes to leap off the page and wag their long stems like two lover's tongues in a tizzy!

The melodies she'd heard the black Baptist congregation sing were simple enough in theory. Blues-based. Almost like folk songs. But her classical training couldn't help her with this. More than anything it had to have the right *feel*. She had to rely on her instinct.

For her, writing the music first and then trying to fit words to the melody didn't work at all. She realized she would first have to find the right text. And then let the music grow out of the words.

Holly was dissatisfied with the Third Movement as she had written it. So she tore up the manuscript and threw it in the air. Weeks of work rained down on her in confetti-snowflakes that stuck in her hair. With a sigh she decided to start it all over. From scratch.

In her search for text for "Good Young Carpenter," Holly remembered her high school boyfriend. Paul was a folk-singer with strawberry blond hair down to the top of his back. He wrote songs and played acoustic guitar in local coffee houses. Some words to one of his songs came to Holly one night while she sat in her studio:

It is said: 'He who lives by the sword dies by the sword',
True, Jesus was a carpenter who was nailed to a board.
I am but a poet and following that trend:
Will I stab my heart out with a ball-point pen?"

Holly thought about Paul's song lyrics and realized they might be too abrasive for the general public. But the line: "Jesus was a carpenter who was nailed to a board" managed to stimulate her thinking.

She thought about Joseph and his Son getting a purchase order from the Romans for, say, fifty crucifixes. What could Joseph do? Would he have the gall to tell the Imperial Rulers: "Sorry, my Son and I don't *do* crosses." In all likelihood they would have filled the order. And since most of the big construction jobs of the time were probably built of marble and brick, the Roman demand for large wooden crosses was probably Joe and his Son's bread and butter back then. As Marx said: "Everything in society is governed by economics."

Paul was the only male lover Holly had ever had in her lifetime. Until Roger, of course, but that was rape and didn't count. Paul was the only person she could talk to in high school. They would take long walks along the Lake Michigan shore and discuss heady topics like the origin of the Universe.

In Paul's view, the Universe is a colossal Work in Progress. An infinite tapestry being spun from an inexhaustible Source. Paul once told her when humans created — say, a painting, a poem, or a play — they were tapping into that Limitless Source from which all Creation springs.

Holly and Paul got along perfectly. Except for one minor detail: Paul liked having sex on a frequent basis. Holly, at that time in her life, didn't like having sex at all.

Obviously, this became a point of contention. A sore spot, if you will, on an otherwise good relationship. Eventually their relationship came to an end — like a pulsar imploding into a black hole in space.

Holly last saw Paul at their ten-year high school reunion. He had a beer belly then and was going bald. (This didn't matter since he had no aspirations to be President.) Paul was separated from his second wife and he had his new girlfriend with him. He showed Holly snapshots of his three lovely children, divvied up between his two marriages. He told her he worked in an auto assembly plant an hour's drive south of Chicago, building Japanese cars in Joliet. And he'd sold his guitar some several years back.

"Don't you miss playing music?" she asked him.

"Only when I'm really drunk."

It had been two years since that high school reunion. Holly hadn't really thought of Paul much since. She realized his song of the ballpoint-pen-poet would probably not play well in Peoria. Mozart looked down from the wall without rancor. Even *he* must have had bouts of writer's block. She put down her pencil. And turned off the small china light.

Holly walked into the living room. It was dark. She peeked into Torchy's room. The streetlight shone through the window, casting an almost moonlight pale on the young girl's face. Come fall she would be entering school. Having scored well on her placement tests, she would enter the ninth grade. A friend of Holly's in the school system helped Torchy enroll without too much rigmarole. After all, she was still technically a runaway, under the auspices of the New York Youth Authority. Holly was proud Torchy was doing so well and wanted to see her continue. And the garden in the backyard was coming up like gangbusters.

Holly closed the door to the young girl's room and tiptoed into her own. The new life that was stirring within her womb was now three and a half months along. Her stomach was bigger. She wore looser clothes. And felt like a kangaroo with a passenger in her pouch.

The telephone rang. Ordinarily, Holly would let the answering machine take a message. But she was hoping it would be Kim saying she was coming home. Last she heard: her ex-lover was housesitting an apartment on East Monument just across the street from Johns Hopkins Medical Center. But it wasn't Kimberly who called. It was Matt's Mom. And her voice sounded strangely befuddled.

"My husband and I talked it over and we decided not to have Matthew take music lessons any more."

"Why?" Holly asked, "I'm giving them to him for free."

"I know. And we appreciate that, Miss Bibble. Me and my husband both do. But we just thought it was best for Matthew to work on his schoolwork."

"Mrs. McConnahee," Holly countered, "school lets out for summer in three weeks. Would you like him to start his lessons again after that?"

"No, I don't think so, Miss Bibble," Holly heard Matt's Father say something in the background, "I've gotta go now, Miss Bibble," Mrs. McConnahee blurted, "I've got something in the oven!"

Holly hung up; puzzled. Why wouldn't parents let their eleven-year-old son take free music lessons? Resting her head back down on the pillow, she turned out the light.

She wanted to sleep. But all she could think about was Kim. How she missed her. As long as she was working, immersed in her music, she was perfectly content to be alone. But as soon as she stopped, as soon as the pencil dropped from her hand, as soon as the melodies evaporated from her head, a deep-seated loneliness set in like a thick fog rolling in from a cold, dark ocean. At times like this, she understood why Paul had given up "dangling on the edge of a precipice" to work in an auto assembly plant. Times like this, she fully grasped the reason why people get married, promising *forever* — in spite of the hardships and dissonances that inevitably will arise. Because love can never be saved. It can only be spent as each passing moment goes by.

Holly couldn't take it anymore. She broke down and called Kim's cell phone number. A pleasant woman's voice answered:

"The number you have dialed has been disconnected or is no longer in service. Please check the number and dial again or—"

Holly tried the number three times and got the same recording. The permanence of their breakup was only now sinking in. It was just before midnight when Holly finally fell asleep hugging the pillow. Wishing it was Kim.

Good young carpenter working in wood
Working in wood, working in wood...

Holly awoke with these words singing in her head. Not by the Tabernacle choir. By the Baptist congregation in the church near the harbor. She jumped out of bed and rushed across the living room. Once in her studio she turned on the china light. Grabbing a blank sheet of manuscript paper she began jotting down the notes and words as fast as her fingers could go.

Then she heard a sound that wasn't inside her head. She heard it again. It was outside her window. Something was rustling the bushes out there. She glanced at the clock. It was quarter past one. The new moon had made the night dark as black tea. Then a face pressed up to the pane of the window. She slowly edged back. Out of her chair. Ready to run for the phone. Then the face became clearer. She saw it was Matt.

"And just where were you planning on running away to?" Holly asked as she brought the suitcase-toting youngster into the house.

"Here," he answered.

"Don't you think your parents will look for you here?"

"Why don't we run away someplace. Together. I know where there's a neat cabin my uncle owns in North Carolina. He won't be there all summer."

"Matt," said Holly, getting her car keys, "let's talk about this in the car."

"Where are we going?" he asked.

"I'm taking you home."

Matt was silent during the ride back toward the city until Holly asked: "Why don't your parents want you studying music any more? Haven't you been using your drum practice pad?"

"Yeah."

"Then what is it?"

Matt was quiet for a while. Then he spoke: "My Dad says you and your roommate are muff-divers."

"Oh, he did, did he?"

"He told Mom that if I kept going over there, you'd turn me into a faggot. Dad says that all fags and muff-divers are gonna go to Hell on Judgment Day. That's why I wanna marry you, Miss Bibble, so you won't have to burn in Everlasting Hellfire."

"That's very thoughtful of you, Matt," said Holly, who was deeply hurt by what he had just said. It brought back memories of her own parents when she told them she was gay. They disowned her and immediately cut her off from her college trust fund. That's when she first became a cocktail waitress, which of course turned her off to men even more.

Matt reluctantly gave her directions to his house. Holly pulled to the curb in front of the modest tract home.

"I appreciate the offer, Matt," Holly said carefully, "but you're way too young to get married. I hope someday when you're older you'll be able to understand things a little better."

Suddenly Matt's pajama-clad Father came running out into the yard, yelling at the top of his lungs, waking every dog in the neighborhood:

"You leave my son alone you God-forsaken dyke!"

"But Dad—" Matt protested.

His Father opened the car door and yanked the redheaded boy and his suitcase out. "Get in the house!"

"But, Dad!"

"Don't you cross me!" he bellowed, striking his son with his fist. Matt started crying and ran into the house.

"Mr. McConnahee," Holly interjected, "I think this is the result of a big misunderst—"

"Listen, *you!*" Mr. McConnahee yelled, pointing his finger in the car window for emphasis. His words were orchestrated by the neighborhood dogs barking up a storm. "I don't give a goddamn whatever you do with your lezbo girlfriends! But you leave my boy alone or I'll kill you! You hear me? I swear to God, I'll *kill* you!"

Lento

As soon as Congress recessed at the end of July, Bane went home to Birmingham to coordinate his re-election effort. Recent polls showed him trailing Harvey Conyers, the Democratic candidate, by eleven points. His campaign staff planned on whittling those numbers down by producing a series of malicious attack ads for TV. One showed a salivating Charles Manson look-a-like prowling the streets of Birmingham wielding a knife. The voice-over read:

"Harvey Conyers believes prisoners should be rehabilitated and returned to society. But would you want THIS man moving in next door?"

At this point in the ad the Charles Manson look-a-like sneers and swings his knife toward the camera. The picture freezes as the voice-over continues:

"Return Lucius Bane to the U.S. Senate. He'll see that hardened criminals are kept where they belong..."

A jail door is slammed over the freeze-frame picture of Charles Manson — the perennial poster boy for the capital punishment crowd.

Utilizing the free airtime of Guy M. Landsworth's three stations, Senator Bane planned to barrage the voters with TV ads like the Manson spot. His media consultants would find one small thing his opponent said at one time such as "...we should try our best to rehabilitate criminals..." and twist it in such a way that the Average Joe Sixpack will think Harvey Conyers is a friend of mass murderers. This is the way elections were won at the turn of the twenty-first century. "And by golly," said Bane to his staffers, "we're gonna win *this* one by a landslide!"

Seated toward the back of the room during Bane's pep talk to his Birmingham staff was Lisa May Hartley. Lisa was seventeen years old and cute as a button. In the fall she would enter the University of Alabama, majoring in political science. For the summer she hoped to gain practical experience working on Bane's re-election campaign.

Lisa May Hartley could barely contain her excitement when she was first introduced to the Senator. It was the first time in her life she had ever shook hands with someone she'd seen on TV. Sure, Senator Bane was a fat old man. But he was a celebrity. And that was all that mattered. So when the rotund legislator asked her if she could work late that evening, of course she could only say yes.

The Senator sent everyone home early that night — around nine o'clock daylight savings time. Nobody noticed that Lisa May Hartley was not among those who were leaving. She was back in the copy room dutifully xeroxing a brochure the Senator had given her. After locking the door and switching off the front lights, the Senator walked back and joined her there.

"How's it comin'?" he asked.

"Just fine," Lisa May answered with a sweet home Alabama twang, "But I was jes' wonderin' how my makin' a copy of *this* is gonna get you re-elected?"

She held up the pamphlet he had given her to xerox. It was titled: *Sexual Norms in Khoi-San Society.* Bane apologized. He had meant to give her a different pamphlet that outlined various procedures for registering voters.

"Can you believe it?" Bane huffed, "Our Government spent seven-hun'ert 'n fifty thousand of our hard-earned tax dollars to study the sex lives a' these darn Pygmies in Africa."

"There's some purty int'restin' stuff here," Lisa May concluded as she thumbed through the pages of the pamphlet, "Like this here: *The very short life-expectancy of the pygmy races put evolutionary pressure on pygmy women to begin reproduction at an earlier age—*"

"You shouldn't be readin' this smut," Bane scolded, grabbing the pamphlet away from her. Safely hidden within his extra-large pants, the head of his penis protruded from the top of his underwear like a one-eyed child peering over a white picket fence, longing to pluck the ripe apples from his neighbor's tree.

"It reminds me of a joke I heard at summer camp," she bragged, "Ya wanna hear it?"

"Sure," the Senator answered, hoping it would change the subject.

"Why do Pygmies eat so much pussy?" Lisa May asked.

The Senator's face turned red as a beet. He couldn't believe such talk was coming from the mouth of such a sweet-looking girl.

"I don't know," said Bane, his penis swiftly stiffening.

"Because they don't call 'em *bush*-men for nothin'!"

Lisa May's laughter was so full of exuberance that the middle-aged Senator lost all control. He fell to his knees like a sorry ol' hound dog and stuck his face right up her dress. He lapped at her calico undies as if they were ice cream. He whiffed her warm peach-pie through the thin covering of cotton that was getting wet as a kitten in a Georgia rainstorm.

Lisa May Hartley spread her legs wider, stroking Bane's white head of hair with her hands. She reached down in front of his slobbering face and pulled her soaked panties aside. He grabbed both her buttocks and pulled her as close as he could. His nose became drenched in the maelstrom. Lisa May wrenched on his chin as his tongue went within her. And she wailed: "Oh yay-yes! Oh *yay*-yes!"

He lifted the curvaceous sweet Southern belle up onto the glass plate of the copier. Peeled her sopped panties down long slender legs and tossed them like a candy wrapper on the floor. His blood-engorged prick was straining at the bit like a thoroughbred horse primed for running. Down went his zipper like an opening gate. Out shot the stiletto-stallion. Hitting the pink bulls-eye crevice with the dead aim of a crack archer's arrow slung from a taut bow.

During their frenzied fornication they accidentally flipped the 'on' switch of the copier. Riding back and forth, the bright light illuminated the wildly gyrating ham hocks and testicles. One by one, the Xerox machine began churning out a series of X-rated photocopies — capturing their pumping posteriors for posterity.

The following morning Senator Bane announced to his staff that he was promoting Lisa May to assistant office manager. During her first day on the job Lisa May learned a lot about getting ahead in politics. She also learned a few things about pygmies.

HOLLY OPENED HER BIBLE for the first time since she was a child. She began reading the first book of the New Testament: The Gospel According to St. Matthew. When she got to Chapter Five, she was emotionally stirred by Jesus' teachings in The Sermon on the Mount. She decided to devote an entire movement of the Oratorio to the Beatitudes, as they are commonly called.

Blessed are the peacemakers: for they shall be called the children of God.

When she was a child, reading the Bible was something she did because her parents expected it of her. A lot of it made no sense to her at all. Now she was reading these words through the eyes of experience. She saw what a revolutionary Jesus was.

The history of civilization is not much more than a chronicle of man's inhumanity toward man. Might was right. Whoever had the most powerful army ruled. But here was a humble carpenter's son from Galilee telling people:

Whosoever shall smite thee on thy right cheek, turn to him the other also.

It was contrary to the most basic instinct of survival. But, for the first time, Holly understood what seemed to be the essence of Jesus' teachings: Our animal nature is but a fleeting episode. Experience here in the physical world is only a passing dream. Our true eternal being is the spiritual self. The consciousness. The Perceiver of the Perception.

Blessed are they that hunger and thirst after righteousness: for they shall be filled.

Holly read. And re-read the chapter. She realized the hunger for righteousness, the hunger for Truth, was something that had been with her as far back as she could remember. She wondered if many other people had this hunger. Why did she always feel there was so much more to Reality than what she was seeing and experiencing with her senses? What was it she really wanted from life? More orgasms with Kim? A new car with a heater? More money? Fame? A cappuccino machine?

For where your treasure is, there will your heart be also.

Holly's treasure was music. Most of her life she had labored long and lone to be able to understand its workings. Theory. Counterpoint. Orchestration. All geared toward creating a perfect moment in song. To her, music reflected life: a series of dissonances seeking harmonic resolution.

Holly read on. Into Luke. On to John. The simplicity of Jesus' prescription for living was so simple and pure. She thought of how wonderful the world would be if everyone abided by His Golden Rule:

Do unto others as you would have others do unto you.

But then again, she wondered how this rule would apply to masochists.

SENATOR BANE FLEW TO Mobile to speak at a political fundraiser that evening on the private jet that was loaned to his campaign by Mr. Landsworth. Lisa May Hartley was also on the flight since she had just received another promotion: she was now officially in charge of the campaign's "Get Out The Student Vote Drive."

Since Lisa May was still seventeen, she wasn't yet a registered voter. But since she was starting classes at the University of Alabama in a little over a week, at least she qualified as a college student. This was the reasoning Bane explained to his statewide campaign manager in adding Lisa May to the payroll. What Bane failed to mention to his campaign manager was how truly thankful he was that the Age of Consent in Alabama was only sixteen. Otherwise, the Senator would have really been in deep shit.

Just before midnight Lucius took the emergency stairs from the top floor of the Hilton one flight up to the roof where lovely Lisa May was waiting — leaning against a large air-conditioning unit that roared like a jet engine blowing her hair. She was dressed very Republican in a loose knee-length skirt. A white collared blouse. Brown Oxford shoes. As the Senator walked toward her, she lifted the skirt and showed him her black see-through panties. Slowly she slithered them down her long, slender thighs and carefully stepped through the leg-holes.

Tossing the tiny wisp of underthing upward into the starry dome of sky, they tumbled off the side of the edifice and floated on an updraft of warm summer air around the periphery. Like one of the 4-and-20 blackbirds that miraculously escaped from the proverbial pie, it flew over the tops of tall oaks surrounding the building. Gliding past branches all draped with Spanish moss so long they looked like an army of Rip Van Winkles, the pretty little panties finally landed like a leaf on the turquoise-lighted water at the deep end of the hotel pool.

The Senator and the seventeen year old fucked like wild animals on the air-conditioner that rumbled beneath their frenetically banging buns. The wily Southern filly faked an orgasm so convincingly she could have won an Academy Award. She timed it to coincide with the Senator's ejaculation at which point she screamed:

"Oh, Arnie, you're the best! The best I've ever had! Oh, yay-ess! Yay-ess! *Yay-yes!*"

The moment his pecker was squirting fluid into the teenager was the first time Senator Bane thought seriously about divorcing his wife. But he would wait till November. After the election. The divorce would be final six months from then. If the resultant publicity harmed his future bid for the Presidency — so be it.

The Senator was in love. Totally in love. And he didn't want the feeling to ever go away. At the center of his Penisentric Universe now was the soft, sweet vagina of lovely Lisa May.

Cantata

Summer eased into fall. Congress was back in session. Roger continued his marathon party at the cottage. Torchy went back to school and was now officially a ninth grader. Holly was six months pregnant and working long hours to finish the *Hosanna* on time.

Charlie had one more delivery of ten thousand dollars that he brought in mid September. Holly invited him in and fixed him some tea. He seemed to be elated when he saw her stomach all swollen. While dipping his tea bag, Charlie asked Holly to marry him.

"But, Charlie," she blushed, "you know I'm gay."

"But a child needs a father," he insisted, "and I'm the perfect man for the job. Since I'm impotent I'll never have to bother you about sex. And you can do it with all the women you want — all I ask is that you let me watch now and then."

"You've got a lot of gall," Holly scolded as she stood up from the couch and walked over toward the door.

"Is that a 'yes' or a 'no'?" he asked.

"Charlie, the answer is an emphatic no!" Holly walked to the front door and opened it, "Now if you'll excuse me, I have an oratorio to compose."

"Think about it," he said as he finished his tea and walked out to his car, "Take your time and think about it."

Charlie got in his Infiniti and drove off into the descending dusk. His Acu-Jack was on the blink. So he stopped at a 7-Eleven and bought a six-pack of Love-Sandwiches. By the time he got home there were only three left.

HOLLY'S BIRTHDAY WAS October 5th. She didn't tell anyone. Not even Torchy. She didn't want anything to break her musical stride. But she was hurt that she didn't even get so much as a card from Kim, her ex-lover.

How she missed running her fingers through her long black hair. And nibbling her flat-chested nipples. Weaving their light and dark fingers together like threads through an angel's loom. Traversing the dark Delta of Venus with the tip of her tongue. And cuddling with love-dripping bodies. Looking deeply into those coal-black eyes and connecting with the driver inside the car.

The day after Holly's birthday, Torchena was too sick to go to school. At first Holly thought she might be malinger-ing to stay home. But after a few days she knew she wasn't faking when her condition went from bad to worse. Holly did what she had wanted to do for several months — only under different circumstances, of course. She called Johns Hopkins Medical Center and asked for Kim. When she finally got on the line it was all Holly could do to suppress her own overflowing emotions and focus instead on the needs of a teenage girl she had taken under her wing.

After describing Torchy's symptoms, Kim told Holly to bring her to the hospital right away. Holly was shocked to see Kim at first. Her long black hair was cut short into a butch.

"Why did you cut your hair?" Holly asked as Torchy was led into an examining room.

"It was time for a change."

"Time to change your cell phone number too?"

Kim didn't answer that one.

Tests revealed Torchy had cervical cancer in advanced stages. Her cervix and most of her uterus would have to be surgically removed. Even then she had less than a fifty-percent chance of survival. Since Kim was specializing in brain surgery, Torchy's malady was outside her field of expertise. So she enlisted a colleague, Dr. Lambowitz, to perform the operation the following day.

"She was doing so well in school," Holly sniffled, wiping her eyes after hearing the diagnosis.

"Dr. Lambowitz is one of the top surgeons here," Kim consoled, running her fingers nervously through her crew-cut black hair.

"But what are her chances?" Holly asked with a motherly concern.

Kim looked out the window. It was getting dark outside. "I'd be lying if I said they were good," she reluctantly replied.

Torchy was given a sedative to help her sleep. But she had a high tolerance to drugs and woke about eight o'clock that night. Some nurses were talking in lowered voices near her bed. She overheard them mention that her cervix would be removed. One of her ovaries too.

"Maybe even more," the elder nurse speculated, "Once the doctors open her up and find out how far the cancer has spread."

Torchy pretended to be asleep until the two nurses left. Then she tiptoed to the door and listened for the *clip-clop* of their shoes to eventually disappear down the hall.

Holly spent the night with Kim at the apartment she was housesitting across the street from the hospital. They didn't have sex. They just held each other close in silent sadness. A faint light through the window barely illuminated the room.

"Boo Boo?" Holly chirped, breaking the stillness.

"What?" Kim responded as she opened her eyes.

"I'm not really sure if there's a God any more."

Kim didn't answer. But she pulled Holly closer. Letting her face lay across her right breast.

"And if there is no God," Holly continued in half-whisper, "then I'm not really sure if I can finish the *Hosanna*."

Kim stroked the wavy brown hair from Holly's eyes and said: "You should finish it come Hell or high water."

"Why?"

"Because God or no God, you're bringing something beautiful into the world. I know from my experience, there's nothing like music to make someone feel the joy of being alive."

"What do you think of Christianity?" Holly asked as she heard Kim's heart beating strong in her ear.

"I think the Church is a scam perpetuated by the remnants of the Roman Empire."

"I don't think I'm following you, Boo Boo."

Kim, whose minor was Comparative Religion during her undergraduate years, went on to explain: "When the

Emperor Constantine converted to Christianity, everybody in the crumbling Empire had to become Christians as well. They formed a church and forced everyone within their control to join it or they would be persecuted and even put to death.

"So when Rome couldn't hold its Empire together with armies and physical terror any more, they switched to another ploy. The Emperor became the Pope. His Ministers became the Bishops and Cardinals. The priests and nuns, his foot soldiers.

"The symbol of the sword was turned upside down — the handle of which resembled a cross. This new method of Empire building worked better than anything Caesar could have possibly imagined. No longer were chariots and archers required to coerce the populace into sending money to Rome. All it took was the promise of a paradisiacal afterlife in return for unyielding obedience.

"After the Empire was chipped away by the invading Germanic tribes, the Church remained latent in the midst of the rubble. Softly and subtly the missionaries and priests subdued the invaders by controlling their minds. Once all of Europe was controlled by the Vatican, the church sought to wipe out all remaining vestiges of Paganism.

"Paganism is a religion that sprang from the forest. It was matriarchal — run by women, worshipping nature and the multiplicity of living things.

"Judaism, Christianity, and Islam, all came from the desert. Patriarchal, monotheistic — focusing on death. And in this male-dominant view of the world, women are nothing more than brood mares. A spare rib whose natural curiosity committed Original Sin. Because in a religion that celebrates death, the inception of life itself is considered a sin.

"So the male-dominant Roman Church had to use everything in its power to eliminate the pagans from the continent. They called them "witches" and had them burned. Threw them in dungeons. Broke them on the rack. A far cry from *the meek shall inherit the Earth.*

"Whereas the forest religion celebrated life by enjoying sex, laughter and merriment, the desert religions venerated death, celebrated celibacy, and wallowed in punishment and penitence. The paternalistic Church of Rome had to extinguish the maternalistic pagans quickly. Not only because these enlightened "witches" didn't fit into their subjugated *Whore-Madonna* categories for women. But primarily because there's nothing a celibate hates more than knowing that somebody somewhere is getting laid.

"So here we are, two thousand years down the pike, and the Roman Empire is still going stronger than ever. The Catholic Church is the wealthiest organization in the world. And they'll keep getting stronger, breeding like rabbits, as the rest of the world struggles with population control."

"What about the Protestants?" Holly interjected after Kim's long-winded dissertation.

"Still the same basic mind control, with fewer icons. The result of a lone German priest who felt guilty about perpetuating the Roman Empire scam. They still foster the same Judeo-Christian Adam's rib line: that women are unclean and the cause of all sin. And that all we're really good for is providing men pleasure and cleaning up after them and breeding their offspring. And Muslims are even worse in the way they regard women. They treat them like chattel."

"So really what you're saying," Holly interjected, "is that you think all religions are basically bullshit."

"Not only do I think they're bullshit, I think religions are a major impediment to a lasting peace in the world. Protestants fighting Catholics in Ireland. Muslims and Jews in the Mideast. Hindus and Muslims and Sikhs in India. All these divisions dividing people. Them and Us. When will we learn that we're all voyagers sharing the same ship?"

Holly remembered more lyrics from one of Paul's songs:

"Many one and only answers under many names,
Many, many differences with so many sames..."

"If you don't believe in any religion," asked Holly, "what *do* you believe in?"

In the faint light that shone on their faces, they both gazed searchingly in each other's eyes — the windows of their souls. Kim's onyx-black eyes sparkled for an instant as she answered:

"I believe in humanity. And I believe in Love. Sometimes I feel I'm an incurable romantic trapped in the mind of a cynic."

Holly lifted her head from its perch on Kim's shoulder. Tenderly touched her lips to her lover's skin just above her nose. Her hand dipped down into Kim's cotton panties. Their lips pressed like pancakes all hot and syrup-steeped. Holly's hand felt the bushfire at the juncture of Kim's femurs. Silk-soft and warm, exactly as she remembered it.

Suddenly, Kim's cell phone rang. Evidently somebody had her new number.

"Dr. Jackson," came the nurse's voice in a tone of urgency, "The patient in 304 is missing!"

Holly and Kim both jumped out of bed, pulled on some clothes and rushed across the street and up the elevator and down the many corridors to where Torchy was last seen.

"I should have stayed in the room with her," Holly lamented, feeling guilty as hell, "what was I thinking? I can't even imagine what she must be going through right now. I should have never left her alone."

The early October air was chilly on the streets of Baltimore. The light green hospital gown Torchy wore was thin and provided little warmth. Soon her skin was a rash of goose bumps. She was shivering. Turning blue. Her teeth were clattering like castanets in the hands of a Spanish dancer. Faster and faster and faster she ran as if trying to outdistance the cold.

An open doorway dead ahead. A sign reading:

"REVIVAL TONIGHT"

Torchy ran inside. Into the light. It was warm. Full of people with love-shining faces. A man in a suit and tie on stage beseeched her to come forward. She walked down the aisle lined with bright eyes and smiles and knelt before the man with outstretched *Armani* arms.

He asked: "Do you accept the Lord Jesus Christ as your personal Savior?"

Torchena said: "Yes" and was filled with a glorious light that kept shining even with her eyes tightly closed.

Lost in the Light from inside she heard the man's voice saying: "Lord, cleanse away the sins of the world from this child. And let her be whole again in Your eyes. Bestow upon her your everlasting Heavenly Grace. And give her the fortitude to go and sin no more. Amen."

Torchy heard the group of people behind her chant "Amen" in a long and resonating unison. Then she opened her eyes. It was like seeing the world for the very first time.

The smiling Evangelist warmly clasped Torchy's hands. Then turned her around to the audience. They began to applaud. A camera on wheels rolled in for a close-up. Her face filled the wall-mounted monitor screens. Tears flowed down her cheeks — washing away years of pain. Still, she was smiling. Beaming. *Radiant.* Like sunshine in the rain.

Another well-dressed man led her off to the side of the stage. There, a girl her own age handed her a flower and a Bible. Torchy hugged the girl. Then several others standing in the wings. For the first time in her life she felt truly fulfilled.

Torchy was born again.

Sonatina

Holly and Kim were checking every room on the fourth floor psychiatric ward. Kim slowly opened the door to a paranoid schizophrenic's room. At first she thought the schizophrenic was watching a game show on TV. But then she saw Torchy's face on the screen. The show was called *Reverend Jim's Revival Hour* and was being broadcast live.

Kim called the cable channel on her cell phone to find where the telecast was coming from. The address was only a few blocks from the hospital. Holly and Kim rode in the ambulance that was sent to pick her up.

During the short ride back to the hospital, Torchena would not let go of either the Bible or the flower She said she felt better than she'd ever felt in her life. She claimed that Jesus had healed her.

Kim took a pap smear. She couldn't believe the results. The oncologist on staff fully re-examined her. The results came up the same: Torchy's cancer was in complete remission.

"It's an extreme example of the placebo effect," Kim explained to Holly in the hall. "When we test new drugs, we always give a certain percentage of the test subjects a placebo — sugar water or something — and without fail, some of the subjects are actually cured by the placebo. The power of the mind is something science has only just begun to tap."

"But how does the mind know exactly what chemicals to produce to cure a certain ailment?" Holly argued, "There must be a Higher Intelligence that guides the process. If someone can heal themself just by *thinking* they're being healed, is it the thought itself that heals them? Or does the mere act of thinking those kinds of thoughts connect us with a Higher Source? A plane of consciousness where illness doesn't exist?"

"There are so many things we don't know," said Kim. "We're like ants in the Empire State Building. Whatever the ant may think of the building as a whole is based on a very limited viewpoint."

Torchy came out of the room holding a plastic bag filled with her belongings. "I'm ready to go," she announced.

Kim patted her on the head. "Holly tells me you're doing great in school."

"Yeah, I like it a lot," Torchy said, then added: "Kim, when are you coming home?"

Kim was dumbstruck by the word 'home.' It was like an arrow to the heart. Kim looked at Holly, who spoke only with her eyes. Kim looked back at Torchy and finally smiled.

"Soon," she answered.

Holly reached for Kim's hand, "Why don't you come over this Friday for dinner?"

"Depends on what's for desert."

They laughed and embraced. In the fluorescent lighting Kim noticed the dark circles below Holly's pale-blue eyes.

"You're getting way too pregnant to be working the way you've been," Kim advised. "You need somebody around to take good care of you."

"It would be nice to have a doctor in the house," Holly smiled, touching the edge of Kim's lab coat.

"We'll talk about that this Friday," she said, softly caressing her hand.

Torchy's mouth made a whale of a yawn. Stretching her arms — the Bible in one hand, the flower in the other.

"Let's get you home to bed, Young Lady," Holly said, as she led the tired teenager toward the automated hospital door. "You've gotta get up early for school."

Kim stood at the Emergency Room entrance and waved as the Volkswagen Jetta disappeared into the night. She thought of a poem Holly wrote for her on a hand-painted card a few years back. Written while they both were still in grad school:

> *Every melody is lonely at first,*
> *No matter how beautiful, graceful, or sublime,*
> *Until it is joined with its counterpoint*
> *Then the two melodies*
> *become inextricably intertwined.*

*

LUCIUS STEERED THE RENTAL car up to a cheap motel near the Tuscaloosa Regional Airport. The paint-peeling, weather worn sign read:

"Adult Movies in Every Room."

Senator Bane slipped the key into the lock of room number eleven. Lisa May was already there. She was stretched out on the king-size MagicFingers bed, wearing a purple teddy bought from a mail-order catalogue. Sucking on cherry licorice sticks that got softer the more they stayed in her mouth, she was watching pornography on the wall-mounted TV.

"Hi, Doll, I brought you some candy," Bane greeted as he plopped a box of expensive chocolates on her lap.

"Oh, goody!" she replied, as she peeled the clear wrapper.

"And champagne," he added, taking out a bottle of *Dom Perignon*.

"Mmmmm," she hummed after stuffing an amaretto truffle in her red-lipsticked mouth.

Bane popped the cork and began filling two Waterford glasses he brought for the occasion. He knew it was unlawful to give liquor to a minor. Lisa May hadn't even turned eighteen. But he poured the illegal liquid and they toasted "to the future." She downed it. Then he filled up her glass again.

In his coat pocket was a diamond ring that cost thirty-five thousand dollars — money skimmed from his campaign funds. More than anything in the world, he wanted her to say "yes" to the question he intended to ask her.

Lisa May Bane. It had a nice ring to it. How could she possibly turn him down? In four years time she could be living in the White House. What more could a man offer his wife?

Lucius took off his coat, draped it across a chair and reached in the inside pocket for the ring. But a face that flashed briefly on the motel TV screen suddenly derailed him from his train of thought. He closed his eyes and opened them again, hoping it was a hallucination.

On the TV screen was a close-up of a very large penis. A woman's mouth was wrapped around it sucking it for all it was worth. After a minute or two of incessant sucking, stroking and licking, the screen once again showed the face of the man to whom the extra long penis belonged.

"Oh, my God, I don't believe it!" Bane bellowed like a tuba.

"What?" Lisa May asked in her high flutish tone.

"It's him!"

"Him who?"

"H-h-h-h-*him!*" the Senator stuttered, pointing at the well-endowed man on the screen.

"You mean Biff Bone?" asked Lisa May, "the big porn star?"

Biff Bone, the enraged Senator thought to himself, *at least the little bugger had the decency to change his last name.*

"Do you know him?" she asked.

"No," the Senator snorted, denying his own son.

"He's very well hung," Lisa May commented while watching another close-up of the fourteen-inch prick, "I'd like to meet him sometime."

"What for?" Senator Bane barked like a bone-crunching pit bull.

"To get his autograph," she replied, never taking her eyes off the relentless swabbing of the female porn star's throat. "Watch this," she added as Biff's big appendage began picking up speed on the small screen, "This is my favorite part of the movie."

Biff pulled his pecker from the mouth he was muffling and artilleried his semen all over the girl's face. It drained down her forehead and drooled down her cheeks. Then she licked her lips as if she'd just eaten a whole bucket of fried chicken.

"You've seen this movie before?" the Senator queried with a paternal edge to his voice.

"Twice," Lisa May answered as she popped another truffle.

"But you're not even eighteen years old!"

"So?"

"Where d'you see it?"

"On the internet."

Bane stared at his son's penis looming large on the TV screen. Now, not only people in seedy motel rooms could see it. All you needed was a computer and a hook-up to the World Wide Web and you could tap into an endless supply of pornography with the click of a mouse.

Senator Bane recalled the day when his son left home to seek fame and fortune in Hollywood. Lucius told him he would never amount to anything. He thought about what would happen if the media got hold of the fact that his son was a porn star. It could blow his chance at the Presidency once and for all. Bane thought about hiring a hit man to make his son take a walk in concrete shoes at the bottom of the Mariana Trench in the South Pacific.

"Isn't there anything else on we kin watch?" asked the Senator, "Re-runs of *Petticoat Junction* or somethin'?"

"Watchin' this movie makes me *soooo* horny," drawled Lisa, while unfastening the three silver snaps holding her teddy together at the crotch.

She ran her painted fingernails through her light-brown pubic hair. A thin white string protruded from her vagina.

"Too bad I'm on the rag," she sighed, still not taking her eyes off the motel TV: *as Biff plunged his boner up the Porn Actress's Bing-cherry-red rectum as she bent over the side of the tub.*

Lisa May unzipped the Senator's fly and fished out the serpent with the bulging blue veins. Rolling over on her knees, she lifted her tight tender tail in the air and announced: "I like takin' it up the ass!"

Senator Bane wasn't keen on the idea of putting his precious pork-rivet into his bride-to-be's beckoning bung-hole. The anus was the only one of the three main bodily orifices he had not yet pioneered. Like the voyage of the Starship Enterprise, this area of the anatomy was his final, fecal frontier. But seeing his son Biff, in the buff, ramming his piston-like pecker up a *Penthouse* girl's tightly clenched poop-chute seemed repulsive to him. Especially when the camera would go in for extreme close-ups.

But he loved Lisa May. He was willing to go the extra yard for her. Even if that yard included a few inches of the lower intestine.

"C'mon, Arnie," the pert Political Science major purred, wagging her rollicking rump in the air like an alley cat in heat: "Do me. Please *do* me! Do me from behind!"

Her pink sphincter muscles flexed betwixt snow-white hips like lips of a sea Siren serenading a Sailor to come hither. Heeding the call, Senator Bane climbed behind her like an overweight jockey mounting a horse half his size. Lisa May reached in her purse on the nightstand and unscrewed an extra-large jar of *LubriGlide*. Scooping a four-fingered dollop, she coated his erection like the icing on a fresh baked éclair. The Senator paused just before her rear entrance. Then, slowly, he spiraled it — inch by inch — in.

He was way past the portal. Past the point of no return. Like a soldier bringing up the rear, he burrowed deep into enema territory.

"Fuck me! Fuck me!" she howled as he tunneled, "Please *fuck* me!" she pleaded as he plowed her rectal rose.

Bane began pumping like a runaway locomotive. He liked that Lisa May often used the word 'please.' *Please fuck me!* or *Please eat me!* Or *Fuck me harder, please!* At least it showed she was the product of a decent upbringing.

"Harder! Fuck me harder!" she hollered. This particular time she omitted the word 'please.'

She reached one hand under and felt his tube-steak going in her, making mince meat of her appendix and rubbing her anus raw. While her thumb was busy wiggling her increasingly quivering clitoris — her other four fingers were tickling his rapidly slapping balls. She egged him on raucously like a cheerleader — chanting:

"*Fuck* me! Fuck me *harder!* Fuck me, Arnie! Fuck me, *please!*"

The Senator kept pumping like an oil well on overdrive. His heart raced like a hamster running in a treadmill attached to a lathe. Sweat poured off his face. Flew in every direction. Sprinkled her back. Splattered her buns. Trickled and dripped in her hair.

His butt banged like a butter churn. Her cheeks were laden with cheese. As he railroaded her with his golden spike, she yelled:

"Fuck me harder! Fuck me, *please!*"

Gearing toward an orgasm, he hastened the velocity of his ream. But he lost his concentration when something appeared on the motel TV screen:

The camera went in for a close-up. Biff pulled his fudge-rippled ramrod from the centerfold's gruesomely gaping anus. Then he continued to jerk himself off until sneezing his pecker snot all over her pimpled, perspiring tush.

Senator Bane immediately lost his erection. His shrinking wangger slipped out of Lisa May's bum like a dollar bill rejected from a change machine.

"Don't stop. *Please* don't stop," she begged while accelerating the tempo of her thumb. The Senator was glad that she used the word 'please.' But his penis hung its head like a World Series pitcher being sent to the showers before the last out.

"Oh! Oh! *Ohhh!*" Lisa May caterwauled, as her fingers finally finished the inning.

Her clitoris trembled like the San Andreas Fault. Her *derriere* shook like Candlestick Park. As her whole body buckled like a stretch of the Nimitz Freeway in the Earthquake of '89 — Lisa's tampon dislodged from her like a circus man shot out of a cannon to conclude *The Greatest Show On Earth.* A cloudburst of blood poured down on the white bed sheets, forming a red circle that made the bed look like a gigantic Japanese flag.

Lying in a pool of blood, Bane's wet macaroni prick smelled like a stick that was used for latrine duty. All while his son, Biff Bone, was boffing some bimbo on the tube. And little Miss Hartley was spread-eagle beside him, legs in the air, inserting a fresh tampon.

Senator Bane left the ring in the pocket of his coat. He decided to wait for a more romantic occasion to ask Lisa May to marry him.

*

KIM PLACED HER EAR against Holly's pregnant belly. The sound was the same as a seashell she'd heard in her youth. A vulvic-pink conch she'd held to her ear to hear the 'Om' of the ocean inside. Now in the 'Om' of Holly's swollen womb had a faint steady heartbeat of a soon-to-be Being. Someone who would someday have dreams of their own.

Holly felt a jolt. A sharp pain in her abdomen. Seven months along, the fetus practiced placekicking — as if dreaming of future field goals with the Miami Dolphins.

Holly still hadn't gotten used to Kim's haircut. Where there once was a mane was now more like a putting green. As if someone who'd been sleeping with Alanis Morissette for five years suddenly woke up with Sinead O'Connor. As Holly let her fingers glide softly down the ridge of Kim's cheekbones, she felt a sensation she had never felt before.

"Boo Boo?"

"What?"

"You've got stubbles on your face."

"It's these hormone treatments I'm taking," Kim informed.

"Taking for what?"

"A condition I have."

"Boo Boo, are you all right?"

"I'm going to be fine," Kim reassured, stroking Holly's protuberant tummy.

"Thank God," said Holly, pulling Kim's close-cropped head even closer, "I don't know what I'd do if I ever lost you, Boo."

Suddenly there was a second head peering over the flesh hill of Holly's belly. It was Torchy. She had a Bible with her.

"I've come to witness to you," she said with the utmost sincerity. "Both of you."

"Well, witness away," said Kim with a hint of sarcasm. She'd been proselytized to before on several occasions. She felt secure in her perception of Reality, based as it was on logic and scientific reason. Religions to her were mass mind-numbing systems. They soothed people's pain. And eased their sense of insignificance. 'The Opiate of the Masses' as Karl Marx observed.

"Did you know it's a sin to have sex out of wedlock?" Torchy asked.

"Look who's casting the first stone here," Holly countered.

"I have a clean slate now," said Torchena, referring to her new 'born again' status.

"Kim and I would be married now," said Holly, "but the state doesn't recognize same-sex marriages."

"That's because it's an abomination," the ex-child prostitute charged.

"Torchy," Kim smiled, "be careful how you use big words like that."

"It says it right here in the Old Testament," the young girl stated as she thumbed through the thick Judeo-Christian tome. "Here it is. Leviticus 20:13: 'If a man lyeth with a man as a man lyeth with a woman, it shall be an abomination in the eyes of the Lord."

Kim gently returned fire: "It doesn't say anything in there about 'if a woman lyeth with a woman as a woman lyeth with a man', does it?"

Torchy glanced down the page for a few silent moments. After a while she replied: "No, I guess not."

"See," said Kim, "God doesn't seem to have anything against lesbians. At least not on record—"

"Oh, Boo, *shush*," scolded Holly, then she touched the girl's hand and said: "Torchy, Kim and I are very happy that you've found a direction in life that works for you. But you need to understand that everyone has their own path. Everyone has to find their own way through the wilderness."

"But there's only one *right* path — the straight and narrow one," Torchy corrected, "and that's to accept Jesus Christ as your Savior!" Torchy squeezed Holly's hand, then grabbed one of Kim's, saying: "All you have to do is accept Him. Open up your heart and let Him take over your life. Take Jesus into your heart!" Torchena closed her eyes and clenched their hands tightly.

Holly closed her eyes. She thought of her Jewish mother and her Catholic father. She remembered going to Temple on Saturday and Mass on Sunday. She wished all her philosophical questions could be answered in the simple manner that Torchy prescribed. By accepting as her personal Savior a Jew who was fathered by God and nailed to a cross by the Romans almost two thousand years ago.

Holly wanted to accept Him. She wanted to quell the turbulence in her soul. But how could she know if this really was The Truth out of all the truths available on civilization's spiritual smorgasbord? A soul who is searching must maneuver amongst them like a child through a babble of carnival barkers. Each one insisting that their path is the only true path and all the others are imposters.

"The fear of death," said Kim aloud, "is what draws us to religion. We'd like to think there's a purpose for our being here. We can't stand the notion that we're accidents of chemistry on a big ball in the deep void of space. Ultimately, what we do here with our fragile little lives won't mean squat in the infinite realm of things. The only purpose is the purpose we create for ourselves."

"That's what Satan wants you to believe," Torchy admonished. She closed her Bible; got up from the bed. "I'll pray for you both," she said, walking out of the room.

The first snow of winter was beginning to fall outside as a rare mid-October nor'easter began to blow through. Holly liked seeing the snowflakes returning again. Bouncing against the window. Dusting the trees lit by the streetlights outside.

The phone rang. It was Roger. Holly could tell by his slurred speech he was on drugs. He demanded that she drive down to the Chesapeake Bay cottage. Immediately.

Holly said she was busy. Roger told her he had just finished the finale of "the fucking oratorio," as he often called it. But he didn't trust sending it through the mail or Fed-Exing it either. He insisted she drive down and pick it up in person.

The doped-up mediocre musician told her he'd recently had a dream about "Evil People" trying to steal "The Fucking Oratorio." That's why he was demanding that she pick it up in person. He claimed he couldn't trust anyone else.

"Not even Senator Bane," Roger said in his paranoia, "Cuz that fat motherfucker was in the dream, and I'm pretty fucking sure he was evil. He even had horns sticking out of his fucking head!"

Holly tried to talk him into mailing it. Then Roger finally said if she didn't come down he would fire her as his "copy bitch." Not wanting to jeopardize her position in any way, she agreed to drive down and pick up "The Fucking Finale."

"I don't want you going down there alone," Kim intoned.

"I'll be all right," said Holly, pulling her coat on and buttoning it over her belly.

"This is a man who drugged and raped you," Kim said. "If I didn't have to be at the hospital, I'd go there with you. With a *gun.*"

"I'll be all right," Holly sighed as she kissed Kim and walked out the door of their bedroom.

She saw Kim in the window watching her worriedly as she got into her car and drove away. It was Friday the 13th of October, 2ooo in the Year of Our Lord.

As Holly headed south on Interstate 97 toward Annapolis, the clouds in the eastern sky were too thick for her to notice it was also the night of the full moon.

Vivace

The freezing air reminded Holly once again that she should get the heater in her Volkswagen fixed. She wrapped the scarf around her neck while driving. Her pregnant stomach pressed against the steering wheel, making it hard to turn. The first snowflakes of winter were sticking to her windshield until the wipers brushed them away. During her one-hour drive down the western shore of Chesapeake Bay, a train of thought chug-a-lugged along the railway of her mind:

After Jesus passed on, or ascended — if you will — all He left behind were his teachings. His ideas. *"Love thy neighbor as thyself"* and *"Do unto others as you would have others do unto you"* spread like parachuted dandelion spores gliding on the wind — seeking fertile mindsets to settle on. These ideas were the essence of His life. Not His physical form. The ideas are what continued on. Alive today in the human hearts and minds of all who live by them. The idea of altruism: living for others. Loving all things, even your enemies. These are the gentle Christ teachings that prevailed through two thousand years of wars and insufferable human brutality.

So Holly decided to change the title of the *Hosanna's* first movement from "Immaculate Conception" to "Immaculate *Concept*." Rather than celebrate the birth of the flesh and blood Jesus she thought it better to celebrate the inception of His beautiful ideas.

Holly pulled up to the guard gate at the entrance to the cottage. Clarence the guard opened the gate and waved her on in. The gravel driveway was littered with beer cans, tires, motorcycle parts, and even a couple abandoned broken down cars.

The cottage itself was in bad disarray: windows were broken, screens slashed, storm shutters severed, and the front porch was trashed. Roger's Ultimate Party raged all summer long. The last of the survivors left earlier in the week, after Roger — in a drunken frenzy — called them all "a bunch of fucked-up pieces of shit!"

"Yoo-hoo! Anybody home?" Holly called from the rubbish-strewn porch where used condoms mixed in with the multi-colored leaves of autumn.

"Enter!" came Roger's voice from inside.

Holly could barely push the door open, so high was the trash heaped on the floor on the other side. She pushed it open just far enough to squeeze her extended belly through. Once inside, the stench almost bowled her over.

She waded through heaps of garbage of the most vile and despicable variety. Rotted food colored green with mold. Dried vomit caked to the walls and floorboards. Flies buzzing. Vermin rustling. Roaches pissing on three-month-old cheese. Shards of broken glass and dishes. Cigarette butts. Rat shit piled in cannonball array.

The living room was even worse. And there sitting naked atop a huge pile of beer cans piled halfway to the ceiling was Roger. His body was covered with self-inscribed needle and ink-pen tattoos. Mostly dirty words interspersed with infantile drawings of genitalia more befitting a junior high school toilet stall. Across his chest were twelve multi-headed ejaculating penises all aimed at a vagina drawn in detail on his throat. Like some perverse Monarch reigning over his Kingdom of Filth, Roger held out the manuscript as if it were the Holy Grail.

"Here it is," he said with weighted reverence.

Holly reached for it. He pulled it away.

"What's wrong?" she asked. "You're the one who wanted me to come and get it."

"How do I know you're not one of the Evil Ones?" Roger queried in a paranoid tone.

"You're just going to have to trust me," Holly replied, holding out her hand.

He slowly held the manuscript toward her again, keeping a firm grip on it — as if the Secret of the Universe was contained within its folds. Holly reached for it. Carefully. It was like trying to take a rubber ball away from a dog's tightly clenched mouth. She grasped one end of it. Roger held on to the other.

"This is the greatest fucking piece a' music ever written since the beginning of Time," he boasted. "Fucking Bach and that bastard Beethoven never came close to any fucking thing like this!"

He looked Holly straight in the eye. His pupils were dilated from whatever drugs he was on. "Are you one of the Good People?" Roger asked sincerely.

"Yes," Holly answered patiently.

Finally he let go. Holly unrolled the crumpled manuscript. Just as she had expected, the computer printed music was just as horrible as the others he had sent her. It belonged on the floor with the rest of the garbage in the room. But to placate Roger the Unknown Composer, she dealt with the situation diplomatically. She would dispose of it in a roadside litter barrel on her way back home.

"I was really high when I wrote that," he announced.

"I can tell," she replied. Then rolling up the musical score and sliding it into her inside coat pocket, she politely asked: "Is there anything else you need from me?"

"Yeah!" Roger slid down the mountain of beer cans, causing an avalanche of aluminum. "I want you to suck my dick!"

"I'm afraid that wasn't in my job description," Holly said as she started to wade toward the door.

"Wait a minute, Bitch!" Roger grunted, grabbing her arm and twisting it violently.

"Let go or I'll call the police!" Holly screeched, working her way toward the phone.

Roger grabbed the telephone and ripped it from the wall, snapping the cord at the outlet.

"Stop it!" Holly shrieked as the thin naked man pushed her down on her knees. Holly began whacking him with the manuscript, the same way her mother used to beat the dog for pooping on the rug. It only made Roger angrier. He grabbed both her wrists and wrestled her to the floor.

"You're one of the Evil Ones, I knew it!" he bellowed, salivating at the corners of his mouth, "You're out to steal my fucking music!"

"No one wants to steal your fucking music, Roger!" Holly hollered in his ear while struggling to break loose from his grasp. "You're a pig! And you write music like a pig! And smell like a pig and act like a pig and live like a—"

Holly stopped — staring down the barrel of a .38 caliber revolver Roger held to her face.

"Now you listen to me, Bitch," he implored, "Either you suck my dick right now or I'm gonna blow you a new hole an' fuck you right between the eyes!"

All Holly could think of was the child she was carrying. She would gladly risk her own life to thwart Roger's intentions. But she couldn't risk the life of her unborn child.

"Suck!" he said, cocking the gun. The sound of the click echoed eternally in her ears.

Holly moved her head closer to Roger's penis. It hung limp between his legs like an empty stocking. Never in her life had she sucked a man's cock. Her boyfriend Paul, the folksinger, tried to get her to suck his on several occasions. Despite his many metaphysical exhortations about oral sex paralleling "The Infinite Wellspring of Existence," she never let him stuff his penis in her mouth. The mere thought of it made her sick to her stomach.

Now she was being forced at gunpoint. The life of her yet unborn child was at stake. She pressed her lips against the circumcised tip of it. Then wrapped them around it like a tootsie roll pop.

"Yeah, Baby," she heard Roger groan. She kept her eyes closed, not wanting to see. "Take it all," Holly heard him command as he shook her. At her temple she felt the cold steel of the gun.

As his penis slipped all the way in toward her tonsils, she gagged, almost vomiting — but held it for fear of being killed. She thought for a moment about what Kim said earlier about the fear of death being the essence of all religion. *Was this her punishment for not accepting Jesus? Was Roger really one of Satan's minions come to whisk her away into the jaws of Hell? Had she sold her soul to write the*

Hosanna? And for this would she have to suck everlastingly on this putrid cock for all of Eternity?

Then something happened in the dark recesses of her mind. A memory so long repressed it had cobwebs in its corners. Holly saw herself as a young girl of eight. The summer after third grade. She was at her grandparent's house, eating cookies. When her Grandmother left for the beauty parlor she said: "Now, Holly, obey your Grandpa Bibble while I'm gone, all right?"

"Yes, Grandma," the young Holly answered with a cookie crumb chocolate-chip smile on her face.

After Grandma backed out of the driveway, Grandpa Bibble came into the kitchen. He suggested they play a game called "Secret Popsicle." Grandpa took out his pee pee and pushed it in her face. Then asked little Holly to open her mouth like she did for the family dentist. He pushed it inside and told her to suck.

"Just like you do with a popsicle," he said. She did as she was told. Grandpa made some weird noises. She sucked till some icky-stuff squirted out of the end.

Afterwards, while Grandpa was wiping off his weenie, he warned her not to tell anyone about their secret game. "If you do," he threatened, "your Grandma and me will get a divorce and you'll never see either of us ever again."

Holly buried this memory deep in her subconscious. After years, it suddenly had reared its ugly head. Roger's prick was the shovel that unearthed this dark skeleton from the closet of her past: *she had sucked off her Grandfather when she was only eight years old.* That was why Grandpa Bibble gave her his prized clarinet. Not out of love — but out of a profound sense of guilt.

That was the summer that The Holly Bibble of Babble On became Holly the shy, introverted, musical prodigy. Like the Dutch Boy removing his finger from the dyke, the memory of his member going into her mouth came back quickly as a flash flood. Filling her with hatred. Gut-churning hatred. Feeling betrayed and abused.

As Roger was ramming his dick in her mouth, in her mind it turned into her Grandfather's. *How she hated him!* Molester! Robber of youth! His hands at the back of her skull. Pushing and pulling her head like some two-bit Love-Sandwich. Keeping her on course with his bobbing beef-bobsled.

Holly opened her eyes. Her face was forcibly pressed against Roger's blond pubic hair that was beginning to grow strands of gray. Dark intense loathing rose up from her stomach. Swelled in her torso. Tied her in knots. Seething from every pore. *Hatred.* Filling her head with its need for explosion so dire she saw bullfighter's red. *How she abhorred him! Detested him! Despised him!* Everything went black. Blacker than black. Blacker than infinite nothingness. *Black.*

Then there was a scream. A spine-t i n g l i n g scream. A blood-curdling, horror flick chainsaw-up-the-rectum SCREAM! Holly opened her eyes. Roger falling backwards. Screeching like a banshee. Into the heap of beer cans. Scattering them like atoms. Grabbing his gonads. Squirm-ing like a worm. Blood covered tattoos. Blood geyser scrotum.

"FUCKING CUNT! MOTHERFUCKING SHIT FUCK PISS FUCK CUNT!" Roger screamed at the top of his lungs as Holly ran horrified from the cottage to her car leaving footprints in the freshly fallen snow. She jumped in. Started the engine. Then realized she couldn't breathe.

She was choking. Really choking! Her face in the rear view mirror was red as a brand new fire-truck. Her eyes bulged. Bloodshot. Gasping for air. Something was clogging her windpipe! She grabbed her throat. Squeezed upward. Tickling her tongue — out it came. Barely believing her bulging eyes when she saw what bounced on the car seat beside her:

Roger's bloody, dismembered penis.

Cadenza

It was bitter cold all the way home. The early cold snap had put much of the Northeast below freezing. And Holly never did fix the heater in her car.

The snowstorm had stopped. It left only a dusting. The clouds to the east were clearing and the eerie silver glow of the full moon began pouring through the passenger side window.

She turned on the radio. Switching anxiously between stations. She'd listen to a piece of a top forty song. Then switch to country. Rap. Easy listening. New Age. Even classical. Nothing could get her mind off "THE THING" on the bucket seat beside her. Or the long suppressed memory of the molestation by her Grandfather.

When she got to the outskirts of Baltimore she ran into some late night traffic that was slowed by the evening snowfall. As she inched along in the soft parade of dinosaur-shit-guzzlers she would sometimes laugh uncontrollably. Then suddenly sob. Feel anger. Remorse. Guilt. At certain moments even suicidal.

Watching the string of vehicles stretched out on the highway in front of her, she noticed the pattern of red brake lights being applied like dominoes set off in succession. Leading ever toward her till the car in front applied its brakes. Then it was her turn to put her foot on the pedal and push. She played these simple mind games as a diversion until she'd accidentally look down on the passenger car seat and see

THE PENIS THAT WOULD NOT GO AWAY!

staring up at her from its bucket seat lair. The one-eyed monster reminded her of a terrible truth: *she bit a man's dick off!* A penis, just like the one her Grandfather stuck in her mouth that summer. The Grandpa who gave her his prized clarinet. The Grandpa she'd loved so much as a child.

Her heart flipped back and forth like a fish on land trying to get back to water. Love Grandpa. Hate Grandpa. Love—hate. Hate—love. Back and forth until the two became a jumble of emotional fettuccini. Till she couldn't tell the difference between one or the other any more.

The only constant during the one and a half hour drive was the bone numbing cold. So cold she could barely hold the steering wheel. She could barely move her fingers. But the sharp, bitter cold kept her mind off the pain. The pain inside that — like the penis beside her — simply would not go away. She parked her car in the empty driveway. Ran into the house. Called Kim at the hospital.

"I'll be right there," her lover promised when she heard Holly sobbing on the other end of the line.

It was a good thing Torchy was sound asleep in her room and didn't have to see Holly looking like a refugee from a Halloween party gone awry. Her knees and pants were soiled with spilth from crawling around on the cottage floor. Dried blood caked around her mouth. Splatter stained blouse down to her belly. Hair frazzled. Sweater ripped. Skirt torn. Sanity whipped. Shivering from the cold and babbling incoherently. Holly had just stepped out of the shower when Kim came rushing in. She hugged her. Then gave her a sedative and put her to bed.

As the tranquilizer took effect, Holly told Kim about the episode with Roger.

"Where is it now?" Kim asked, motherly tucking Holly under the covers.

"Where's what?" Holly mumbled.

"The penis."

"Car seat," Holly whispered as her eyelids fluttered one last time before gently sliding off into a very deep sleep.

Holly slept for twelve hours straight. When she awoke, she found a box, wrapped with a bow, on the pillow next to her head. The sort of box that long-stemmed roses are delivered in. Unwrapping the pink satin bow and removing the lid, she didn't find roses. What she found instead was Kim's hair. All of it. Clumps of long black tresses. The same ones she used to run her fingers through back when it was attached to Kim's head. Whenever they made love, Holly used to say:

"Oh, Boo Boo, I wish I could have your hair."

A small piece of paper was tucked among the strands. She pulled it out like the inside of a fortune cookie. In Kim's slightly sloppy handwriting (she was, after all, becoming a doctor) were the words:

My Love,

I must go away for a while. I'm not sure how long. But please, be patient. I love you more than anything. Please wait for me. When I come back, it will be forever. Promise.

Your Soul mate,

Boo Boo

Like a dark cloud covering an already overcast sky, an emptiness swept over Holly. *How could she abandon me at a time like this?*

Holly crawled out of bed at a snail's pace. Still groggy, she inched her way to the bathroom. After throwing up, she felt much better. She put on her bathrobe and walked into her studio.

Slowly. Note by note. Nuance by nuance. She composed "Easter and Ascent." The final movement of the *Hosanna Millennia.*

LUCIUS AND DOLORES BANE put their costumes on early. The Halloween party in Annapolis wasn't until eight. But the Senator wanted an early start so they could swing down by the Chesapeake Bay cottage beforehand.

"I can't understand why that nitwit won't answer the dang phone!" Bane huffed as he put on his Norseman's helmet — a bronze cone hat with two upturned horns on the sides.

Bane was dressed as a Viking, replete with fur boots and animal skins tied with leather straps. Bronze armbands squeezed his flabby biceps. They bulged out like bundles of overcooked ricotta cheese.

Dolores was going to the party as Glenda the Good Witch of the North from *The Wizard of Oz*. The two of them were quite a sight leaving their Watergate apartment and stepping into the limo.

During the ride over to Maryland, the Senator turned on the TV in the back of the limo. The evening news was just coming on. Toward the end of the show, Tom Brokaw reported the Senate race in Alabama had become the one to watch:

"Conyers, the Democratic challenger, was nine points ahead of the incumbent, Republican Lucius Bane just a week ago. The most recent poll shows Bane not only closing the gap but surging several points ahead of his opponent."

Bane chuckled and poured himself a glass of *Old Forester*. He knew what was responsible for his resurgence in the polls. True, the publicity about the black Baptist choir helped make a few inroads into the black vote. But what really turned the tide was the barrage of TV ads on the stations that Guy M. Landsworth owned. The Charles Manson spot was getting great response. But the newest ad was even more of a humdinger:

It began by showing a mother and father going out the door, leaving their pre-school age son and daughter in the living room with a seedy looking forty year old man. The man, dressed in dirty, tattered clothes with a five-day stubble beard, looks at the children leeringly. The voice-over reads:

"Would you let a known child molester babysit your children?"

The seedy forty-year-old pulls a couple of lollipops from his pocket and gives them to the youngsters as he smiles, licking his lips. The voice over continues:

"Of course not. But Rupert Conyers thinks it's okay to allow homosexuals to teach in our public schools..."

Then the ad pictures a thin, limp-wristed twenty-something man opening a school restroom door for a six-year-old boy carrying schoolbooks. The voice over continues:

"Since homosexuals can't increase their ranks through the normal means of reproduction, recruitment is their only option."

The boy goes into the restroom, the swishy teacher looks around, shifty-eyed, then slips in behind him. The restroom door closes. The camera zooms in on the word "BOYS" on the door as the voice-over finishes:

"Don't let Rupert Conyers have his way
with our future generations.
Re-elect Lucius Bane to the U.S. Senate.
Lucius Bane—he'll keep Alabama straight on course."

Bane knew 'attack ads' were low underhanded politics. But that was the way elections were won at the turn of the millennium. Politicians who took the high road, more oftentimes than not, found the 'high road' took them right back home.

Election Day was Tuesday, November the 7th — still a week away. Bane would saturate the Alabama airwaves during the final week of campaigning. His barrage of commercials would do to his opponent what napalm did thirty years earlier along the Ho Chi Minh Trail.

After an hour ride, the limo pulled up to the guard gate at the cottage. The Senator rolled his automatic window down to wave to Clarence the guard.

"Eve'nin', Senator," Clarence greeted as the limo eased on down the gravel road.

"What's all this garbage in the yard?" Dolores gasped incredulously when she saw the aftermath of Roger's Ultimate Party, "how could you let him do this to our place, Lucius?"

"For art," he replied. "From now on, no one kin say Lucius Bane wasn't willin' to go the whole nine yards to support the dang arts."

The chauffeur stopped right in front of the cottage. The Senator patted Dolores on the head with her Good Witch of the North magic wand and said: "You'd better wait out here, Dear. It ain't no pretty picture how musicians like to keep house."

"I guess I'll just have to hold it till we get to the party," she said, in reference to her bladder.

The Senator found the front door already ajar, although he did have to push against the garbage a bit to open it wider to accommodate his girth. He was down to a respectable two hundred and forty pounds thanks to his improvised GloptaFast cunnilingus diet.

Once inside, he wished he had brought one of his Scratch-N-Sniff tickets to stick under his nose. The stench was worse than anything he could have imagined. Even worse than the outhouse at his Grandparent's farm.

He switched on the light. The place was a disaster. Worse than any house-of-horrors he'd ever seen on Halloween. He remembered what a quaint little cottage it was before he lent it to the degenerate middle-aged guitarist. A place where he and his secretary could slip away to — so he could slip it to her away from the watchful eyes of Washington. He wanted to get Roger out as soon as possible so he could start bringing Lisa May over. He had planned on sending out a maid to clean the place up. But he now saw the cottage needed much more than a mere maid. It needed the Army Corps of Engineers.

"Roger!" Bane called out, stomping through the knee-high rubbish with his rabbit fur Leif Erickson boots.

The left helmet horn of his Viking cap got caught momentarily in a poster that was peeling away from the wall. Bane tore it the rest of the way off and held it out in front of him. It was a full color poster of a topless teenage girl bending over and licking the seat of a Harley-Davidson. Bane recognized the girl. It was Lisa May Hartley, manager of his Tuscaloosa campaign office and head of his statewide "Get Out The Student Vote" campaign. The girl he was planning to marry.

Angrily, he folded up the sleazy poster and shoved it down his deerskin loincloth. He would see to it that the people responsible for producing it would be arrested for exploiting a minor. Plus, he thought he could gain some points with the women's libbers for clamping down on smut peddlers who make money portraying women in a degrading manner.

Then he saw it. There amongst the beer can pile, a pool of dried blood. A rust-colored line led away from the pool, smeared along the garbage-strewn floor like a snail-trail.

Bane followed the blood trail through the doorway of the bathroom. It led to more blood under the crapper.

On the seat of the toilet sat Roger. At his crotch was a reddish-brown, silver-dollar-sized scab where his prick used to be. He sat leaning back on the toilet. Motionless as a statue by Rodin, with tattoos, smelling like dog-shit left all day in the sun. Deader than a dag-gum doornail.

Bane's entire Congressional career flashed before his eyes like a fast-forward video. If he called the police, the investigation could blow the whole lid on the ghostwritten oratorio. Guy M. Landsworth would pull his free television time. Or worse, make payment due on time already used. All the publicity would annihilate his narrow lead in the polls. With the election a week away, Senator Bane had everything to lose. The Unknown Composer would have to have his whereabouts from this moment forward forever unknown.

Peeling Roger's dead butt off the johnny seat was like uncorking a bottle of bad, cheap wine. Just as Jon LaRue had described in *The Johnside Review*, Roger's bowels had completely emptied after his death. The toilet bowl waters below him were a veritable Whitman's Sampler of droppings. Every size, shape, and color.

It was a fitting finish to the Unknown Composer's life. If the Senator had known why the Polaroid camera was hanging on the wall above the toilet paper roll, he could have snapped the final photo for Roger's *"My Favorite Dumps."* But he didn't, so the posthumous work was sent spinning down to the depths of the white porcelain bowl to the dark septic tank of obscurity.

Even though he'd been dead for two weeks, the body hadn't decomposed much due to the cold mid-Autumn weather that had kept temperatures below freezing most nights. But rigor mortis had well set in, casting Roger's naked body in a perpetual sitting position.

Bane huffed and puffed as he dragged the stiff carcass out into the backyard toward the Bay. The Senator was terribly out of shape. The only exercise he'd gotten lately was banging Lisa May. And occasionally he'd still throw one to Loni for old times sake.

He dragged Roger's body across the dried leaves and garbage to the edge of the water. The Chesapeake was cold. But the air was colder. Bane's breath pluming outward looked just like where his career could go if any of this ever came to light: up in a puff of smoke.

Finally he leveraged the lifeless lowlife into a small wooden dinghy. He slid the small boat with the body into the Bay. Picked up the concrete block it was moored to and put it in next to the corpse. Then he climbed in himself. Set both the oars. Then rowed out nearly a quarter of a mile. The moon was a mere fingernail-sliver in the sky. The night was just a hair shy of total pitch black.

While he was rowing, Bane thought of his wife back in the limo complaining. He knew how badly she had to use the john. The first thing she would ask him was "what took you so long?" He would hear about his lack of consideration throughout the evening. Thirty years of marriage made him well versed in the harangues he would hear from Dolores. But soon they would be over. He would file for divorce right after the election. And a June wedding with lovely Lisa May — future First Lady and former Topless-American-Made-Motorcycle-Seat-Licker.

He would pay Loni off with a couple hundred thousand dollars to keep her mouth shut about their five-year affair. It could easily be skimmed from the coffers of his campaign fund. There would be lots of money left over — thanks to his deal with dead Roger's Dad.

These things percolated in the Senator's mind as he rowed through the dark water with dead, prickless Roger sprawled beneath him on the boat's floor. Bane dropped the oars and looked around. The only lights were the bay-side houses spread far and wide along the distant banks. He untied the rope from the boat and attached it to Roger's ankles. Struggling to lift the foul-smelling corpse into the water, he managed to get the head and arms over first. The Senator was careful not to capsize the dinghy as he got the body bent over the side at the waist. A shaky hand-drawn tattoo on the dead musician's buttock read:

"MURDER THE ORGANIZERS OF YOUR BOREDOM"

Neutered Dead Roger slid into the water. He bobbed up and down like an ice cream scoop float. Bane picked up the mooring block to which the other end of the rope was attached. Heaving like an Olympic weightlifter, he hoisted the concrete rectangle high above his two-horned Viking helmeted head. With one single grunt he tossed the block into the darkness. A waterspout geysered up into the air. Suddenly the rope jerked the unsung guitar hero under the waves — leaving ripples in its wake. The bay by which the erstwhile rock musician partied all summer had now become his watery tomb.

The Tomb of the Unknown Composer.

Rhapsody

Martha Grimson, a retired widow, was walking her dog Shep along the shore of Chesapeake Bay. Normally a well-behaved dog, Shep suddenly went berserk and ran away from Martha, leash and all.

By the time she caught up with the run-amok dog, Shep was sniffing a body that had washed up on the shore. The naked, tattooed, mutilated body of Roger Milford Landsworth. Lying sideways on the sand in sitting position, the scene looked like something Salvadore Dali would paint.

Sound carries well across water. Martha Grimson's scream could be heard at least a couple miles away. Suddenly all of the birds within earshot went silent in the midst of their mid-morning song.

HOLLY TOOK THE AFTERNOON off to celebrate Torchy's fifteenth birthday. As a present she took her horseback riding. There were stables a few miles from the house. None of the horses had wings, of course, so Torchy couldn't fly one like Pegasus. But nonetheless, she was in Seventh Heaven as the horse galloped across the field with her on it.

Torchy gave up cigarettes after she became a born-again Christian. But the handle of her hairbrush was harder to completely let go of. Riding the horse made her horny. So when she got home she went right to her room. Reached for the brush. And got off on its elongated handle.

Afterwards, she felt guilty about it. The teacher of her Bible group said that masturbation was a sin. Torchy wondered how something that felt so good could be so bad. Torchy knew that even thinking a thought like that was a sin. So she prayed to Jesus for forgiveness. He forgave her like He always did. Then she put her hairbrush away and went out into the living room. Holly was composing, so she couldn't watch MTV. Instead, she brought out her Pegasus note-book and wrote a poem before going to bed.

Holly found the Pegasus notebook on the living room sofa chair. She read the poem that Torchy had recently written:

> *Every moment is a miracle,*
> *Every day is a gift from You,*
> *Let me show you my gratitude*
> *By what I think, and say, and do.*

Holly felt like going into Torchy's room and giving her a big hug. But she didn't want to wake her — especially on a school night.

She went to her studio to work on the final movement of the *Hosanna Millennia.* The Finale was proving to be difficult. Holly was beginning to feel the pressure of the deadline. It had to be finished before Thanksgiving for the orchestra and chorus to have time for rehearsals.

Holly worked until three a.m. Before going to bed she turned on TV. She flipped through the channels. Stopped on CNN. There on the screen she saw Roger's dead body washed up on the shore of the bay. She turned up the sound. Her palms were sweating. The coroner was quoted as saying that Roger bled to death from a severe laceration to the groin.

Holly was shaking. She drank several shots of gin to calm down. Climbing into bed she pulled the quilt up over her head — the same way that she and Kim used to play sexual circus. She wished she could be a little girl again and not have to deal with an adulterated world full of Assholes and errant penises.

She tossed and turned. Floundered and fidgeted. The bed became a casket. Then a boat. Then a cave. She drifted in and out of semi-consciousness like a radio halfway tuned between stations. For a moment she thought she saw Roger's ghost taking Polaroids of things in her room. While the bed was a boat, he was using his eleven-foot cock as an oar — splashing yellow water as he rowed.

Just before dawn Holly finally fell asleep as a sliver of red traced the eastern horizon. Unleashed in the sub-conscious mélange of her mind were dragons and demons with nostrils aflame. Scorching her titties. Singeing her crotch. Jabbing the protuberant parts of their bodies deep into her vagina and wide-open mouth. One by one she would bite off their appendages. An arm. A leg. A purple penis with scales. On the kneecap of one of the monsters she chomped off a wart the size of a baseball. Blood spouted like a geyser. Drenching her face. Pouring down her breasts like Niagara. Drowning in a raging red river — her mother on the riverbank admonishing her not to ruin her clothes.

She awoke in a frenzy. Her face in a cold sweat. She thanked God the whole thing had been a bad dream. Slipping on her bathrobe she ran to the front door. Opened it. Looked down on the doorstep. Hoping the rest of it had been a dream too. But the bold lettered headline on the newspaper's front page confirmed the reality of her nightmare:

"COMPOSER SLAIN"

IT WAS SUNDAY afternoon. Two days before the election. Senator Bane had just finished giving a campaign speech in Dothan, Alabama. Amidst the handshaking and baby-kissing that followed, a CNN reporter informed the Senator that Roger Landsworth was found murdered in Chesapeake Bay. Bane did his best to act surprised at first. He feigned repulsion when told Roger's penis had been severed.

While the news cameras rolled, the Senator made his official comment to the Press: "Sounds like the work of homosexuals to me. The same people my opponent Rupert Conyers wants to teach our youngsters in the public schools."

Bane had a ten-point lead in the polls. He didn't want anything to blow it. He called Guy M. Landsworth from the Dothan Airport to personally offer his condolences. Said the Senator to the wealthy businessman: "When we catch this pervert, I will personally guarantee he gets a date with Yellow Mama!"

'Yellow Mama' was the nickname given to the electric chair that Alabama used for executions at Kilby State Prison. It got its yellow color using highway-line paint from the State Transportation Department lab that was located next door.

But what was foremost on the Senator's mind that Sunday was not Yellow Mama or even Roger Landsworth for that matter. It was Lisa May Hartley. He was picking her up at the Tuscaloosa Airport — a quick hop skip and a hump from Dothan. Not by car — driving would have taken three and a half hours. But he still had free use of Guy M. Landsworth's Learjet and by golly he sure as sugar wasn't going to let it go to waste!

The sun had just set when the jet touched down in Tuscaloosa. The Regional was a private airport; its air traffic was minimal. There was fog on the runway — just like the movie *Casablanca*. Lisa May was standing there enshrouded in the fog. A small suitcase was held in one hand. A fake mink coat made of dyed rabbit fur was wrapped around her. She wore nothing underneath, just as "Arnie" had requested.

She ran out to the jet. Climbed the narrow steps. Butterflies were fluttering from her tonsils to her clit. An attendant led her back to where the Senator was seated. He let her sit by the window.

Off the jet roared. North by Northeast. Into the sky that was filling up with stars. In two hours they would be in Washington, D.C. Lisa May had never been there. This was the second time she'd ever been on a plane. The first time was only a couple months before when he flew her to Mobile.

"You stick with me, Kiddo," Bane said while pointing out the lights of Birmingham as the Learjet passed over, "and you'll do lots a' stuff you ain't never done before."

"I can't wait," said the bubbly political science major.

As she leaned against the window to get a better look at the ground, her dyed-rabbit fur coat hiked up high on her legs. Creeping way up just above the small curve of her fanny. The sight of her unwrinkled bare flesh set the Senator's testicles shaking like Brazilian maracas.

A cabin steward poured them champagne. Then left them alone in the back of the aft cabin. Lisa gulped down the bubbly while looking out the window. She felt like a fairy tale princess being rescued from the dumb little hick town in which she was raised.

Senator Bane couldn't take his eyes off her. The peaches-n-cream skin of her lovely long legs. Her soft, tender thighs. And her perfect round hips. He drank the champagne.

And savored every sip.

*

"He pulled a gun on me," Holly explained to Detective Nicosi of the Baltimore Police Department, "and forced me to suck his penis." She had driven to the police station after seeing the headline of the Sunday newspaper on her doorstep.

"I see," said Nicosi, a tall, dark, middle-aged man of Italian descent. Above his lip curled a neatly groomed mustache that arched like a caterpillar when he talked. He grew up in Houston, but budget cuts there forced him to relocate to Baltimore. Homicide was a nasty job. He hated it. But at the time it was the only one available.

"It was horrible," Holly continued, as she wiped the nervous spittle from the side of her mouth, "He kept jamming it in. I thought I was going to throw up. Then everything went black. The next thing I knew, I was sitting in my car. And his penis was there on the seat beside me."

"And where is the alleged penis now?" Nicosi inquired with a slight Texas drawl. Like most men, he had trouble keeping his eyes off her knockers.

"I don't know," Holly answered, "somebody must have broken into my car and stolen it."

"Did they steal anything else?" Nicosi asked, "Your stereo? Your purse? Any other valuables?"

"No. Just the penis."

"I see."

Nicosi was beginning to become perturbed with Holly. He hated coming down to the station on Sunday. He would rather have been home watching NFL football on TV.

"Detective Nicosi," a policewoman with a large posterior interrupted, "we have the gate guard on the videophone at the Annapolis Police Station."

"Thanks, Rachel," Nicosi responded, "Miss Bibble, would you mind stepping over here by the videophone?"

Holly struggled to get up from the chair. In her seventh month of pregnancy it became increasingly harder to maneuver about. She sat in a chair in front of a monitor with a camera on top. On the screen was the face of Clarence Green.

"Mr. Green," the Detective spoke to the African-American man, "you see everyone who comes and goes at Senator Bane's cottage?"

"Yessir," he answered. "Ev'rybody."

Pointing to Holly, Nicosi asked: "Did you see this woman enter the grounds a few weeks ago on the evening of October thirteen?"

"Nossirree," Green replied, "I never saw that lady there before in my life."

"What?" Holly blurted, taken aback.

"You're sure?" the Detective prodded.

"Sure I'm sure," said Green, following Bane's orders, "I'd a' 'membered somebody as pretty as that."

"Thank you, Mr. Green, for your time," said the Detective.

"You're welcome," the elderly guard answered just before the screen went blank.

"I don't know what's going on here," pled Holly.

"I think you know very well what's going on here," the Detective responded, lighting a cigarette, "You told us you were employed as a copyist by Senator Bane's office. But the Senator's office has no record of that. The Senator, himself, claims he's never even heard of you—"

"That's a lie," Holly insisted, "I signed a contract with Senator Bane and his lawyer."

"Do you remember the lawyer's name?"

"Not really. I think it was a Jewish name."

"Great," huffed Nicosi to the police woman next to him, "That'll be easy to narrow down: a lawyer with a Jewish name!"

"Okay," Holly sighed, "I'm going to tell you the whole truth."

"Good," said the detective as he blew out a long billow of blue cigarette smoke that hovered in the air, "I've been waiting for someone to tell me the truth all day now."

"I shouldn't be," said Holly, "there was a confidentiality clause in the contract I signed. But since the Senator isn't even admitting that I signed it—"

"Go on," Nicosi coaxed.

"I wasn't actually employed as a copyist. That was just a ruse. I was hired to compose the entire oratorio from beginning to end because Roger was incompetent. But for some political reason his name had to be on it. So I was paid fifty-thousand dollars to ghostwrite the whole thing."

"Who paid you the money?"

"Charles Russell, the Senator's publicist."

"The guy who runs The Charles Russell Agency?"

"That's him. You know him?" Holly asked.

"Yeah," said Nicosi, "he was arrested earlier this year on a Peeping Tom charge."

"Sounds like Charlie."

"You got any records of this money changing hands?"

"It was all paid in cash. Small bills. There were five payments of ten thousand each. The last one was paid in September."

Detective Nicosi picked up the phone and dialed inter-office:

"Arthur? Nicosi here. Could you check if Charles Russell's still on probation? Yeah, the Peeping Tom with the PR firm on Bastinado Street. Yeah? Thanks. Have him picked up and brought to my office. Pronto. Thanks."

Nicosi hung up the phone and turned to Holly: "Is there anyone else who could corroborate your story?"

"Yes, said Holly, "my roommate Kim."

"Her full name, please?" he prodded, picking up pad and pen.

"Kimberly Louise Jackson," Holly answered, "*Doctor* Kimberly Louise Jackson."

"And the two of you share a domicile?"

"Well, we *did*. We lived together for five years and then we broke up for about six months and then we got back together last month. But she left again a couple weeks ago."

"So, I take it your relationship with Dr. Jackson was a bit more, uh, involved than just two people splitting the rent?"

Holly swallowed, deciding it was better to tell the truth: "Yes, we're lovers. We're in a relationship."

"Then how'd that happen?" he asked, pointing to her pregnant belly.

"From a prior meeting I had with Roger about seven months ago. Going on eight."

"So I take it your relationship with this Dr. Jackson lady isn't exactly what you'd call monogamous, is it?"

"Listen, my relationship with Kim Jackson has nothing to do with what happened to Roger Landsworth—"

"But she can corroborate your version of events?"

"Yes, she can."

"Do you know where we can contact Dr. Jackson now?"

"She was doing her internship at Johns Hopkins."

Nicosi started writing on his pad, but stopped when Holly added: "But she took a leave of absence a week ago and nobody there knows where she went. Or when she'll be back."

Nicosi scratched Kim's name of his short list of witnesses, "You sure got a lotta missing pieces in your puzzle there, Lady. And you better not be jerking us around with Charlie Russell, that's all I've gotta say." He put down his pad and walked out to the Men's Room located just down the hall.

Within half an hour, Charlie Russell was brought into the station. He took a seat next to Holly. Nicosi returned from the men's room having failed in his attempt to empty his bowels. And the accumulation of solid wastes in his body tended to make him more irritable.

"This woman claims Senator Bane paid her fifty thousand dollars to ghostwrite an oratorio," said Nicosi, "Is that true?"

"No," Charlie answered.

"Charlie!" Holly protested.

"You are the Senator's publicist, aren't you?" Nicosi quizzed.

"For national coverage, yes," Mr. Russell replied, "but he has a local firm handle his media relations down in 'Bama."

"Did you ever go over to Ms. Bibble's residence?" the detective asked.

"Yes," Charlie replied, "on several occasions."

"Thank you," said Holly.

"And what was the purpose of your visits?" Nicosi prodded.

Charlie looked at Holly. "You really want me to tell them?" he asked. "I thought we were going to keep this confidential?"

"Charlie, somebody died as a result of an unfortunate accident," Holly said, "it's time we stopped playing games and started telling the truth."

"All right," said Charlie, looking down at his shoes, "if it's the truth you want." Then he looked at Detective Nicosi and the woman officer present and said with the utmost sincerity: "I went to see Ms. Bibble in response to her personal ad."

"That's a lie!"

"Now, now, calm down, Ms. Bibble," Nicosi interceded.

"You asked me to tell the truth," Charlie pleaded.

"What kind of a personal ad was it?" the detective inquired.

Charlie said: "Perhaps Ms. Bibble would rather tell you herself. She's the one who's so adamant about telling the truth."

Nicosi looked at Holly, waiting for an answer.

"An ad for a sperm donor," Holly mumbled looking at Charlie with daggers in her eyes.

"Oh, of course," said the detective, exchanging glances with Rachel, "Charlie The Peeping Tom becomes a Sperm Donor, a profession he's been rehearsing for most of his life."

"But that's not why Charlie Russell came over," Holly explained, "He came over to pay me the money from Senator Bane!"

"Holly," said Charlie, "what's all this malarkey about money? I was bringing you sperm samples like we agreed to."

"Liar!" Holly screamed, holding her large pregnant stomach.

"How can you say something like that to me? The father of your child!"

"So you're the father?" Nicosi asked.

"Yes, I am," Charlie said proudly.

"Charlie is *not* the father," said Holly.

"What do you mean I'm not the father? What did you do with all those sperm samples I gave you?"

"I put them in the freezer."

"Well, if I'm not the father, who *is?*"

Nicosi jumped in: "She claims it was Roger. The deceased."

"So he was sending you sperm samples too," Charlie whimpered, "Is that all we were to you? *Dueling donors?*"

"Roger wasn't a donor! We had sexual intercourse."

"Why would you have sex with him if you're gay," Nicosi queried.

"I was on drugs," she answered, beginning to have doubts as to whether honesty was always the best policy.

"And you led me to believe I was the father," sulked Charlie in the tone of a spurned lover.

"Shut up, Charlie! My personal life is none of your

business!"

Then Holly broke down crying.

Nicosi handed her a tissue and turned to Charlie, "You can go now, Mr. Russell. Thank you for your time."

"Any time," said Charlie, getting up to leave.

"I will never, ever, use any of your sperm samples!" Holly hollered down the hall as Charlie vamoosed. Then she blew her nose into the tissue, sounding like a herd of wild elephants in an old Tarzan movie.

"Ms. Bibble," said the Detective, exhaling smoke through his nose like a dragon in a medieval tale, "we've had fourteen people confess to this crime ever since it got on the news last night. The Annapolis police have had twenty more confessions on top of that. Any time there's a high profile crime like this we get all kinds of weirdoes claiming they did it. I know the psychological reasons: everybody wants to be a star. Everybody wants their fifteen minutes of fame. I have to admit, your story is one of the more creative ones so far — claiming you were the one who wrote the oratorio. And that the deceased is the father of your child. That stuff makes good press. The tabloids would love it. But it's sickos like you who make police work all that much harder! We're out there every day busting our balls trying to catch *real* murderers and thieves. But we've gotta sift through this crap that you people dish out just because you wanna see your names in the papers!"

"I just want to say," Holly said between sniffles, "that everything I've told you is the God's honest truth."

Nicosi's lower extremities rumbled again. He hoped it wasn't another false alarm.

"Rachel!" he said to the policewoman with him, "show Ms. Bibble to the door!" As he hastily headed for the restroom, he muttered to himself: "And I missed the Ravens playing the Packers for *this!*"

THE PRODUCERS OF *America's Funniest Home Videos* watched the clip several times. It was sent in by Gary Gunst who lived on the east bank of Chesapeake Bay. Shot on one of the new SONY infra-red digital camcorders that can videotape images in extremely low light, the ten minute video showed an obese Viking in a rowboat dumping a tattooed rigor mortis stiff naked man's body overboard. Then the Viking tossed in the concrete block that was tied to the stiff dead man's leg. And both rock and failed rock star went plummeting to the icy depths. The Viking then proceeded to row his boat ashore.

The show's producers turned the tape over to the Los Angeles Police Department. The LAPD gave it to the FBI. The FBI showed it to the Annapolis Police Homicide Department who were investigating the Roger Landsworth murder. The tape was then sent to the Video Enhancement Lab.

There, a team of technicians worked diligently to learn the identity of the Viking in the boat.

WHEN HOLLY GOT HOME she went straight for the freezer. There, behind several stacks of microwave dinners, were seven frost-covered vials of semen.

As she tossed them in the garbage bag underneath the sink, Holly thought of all the humans those popsicles could sire. And to what lengths she had gone to acquire them. Each semensicle contained enough sperm to re-populate the earth. But the *last* person she would think of, from then on, when she thought of sperm was that lying son-of-a-bitch Charlie Russell!

Holly sat in a kitchen chair and felt the fetus kicking inside her. The sun was setting outside, sending its rays into the room. All her crystals were hung by strings tied to the top of the large kitchen window. Sunlight streamed through them, making little round rainbows dance on the walls and appliances. One of them settled on her tummy and stayed there. As the sun set outside, she watched the round rainbow fade away. Wishing to God she was an aphid.

THE LEARJET LANDED at Ronald Reagan Airport where Senator Bane's limo was waiting. The Senator had gone over his instructions with the chauffeur from the satellite phone on the plane. Following those instructions, the chauffeur drove them toward Washington. The white alabaster buildings, lit in the distance, jutted up in the sky like carved ivory. They drove past the Arlington Cemetery. A torch was burning on the Kennedy brothers' grave. Then over the Potomac. Past the Lincoln Memorial. The Vietnam Veterans Wall. Around the Mall. Along the Smithsonian. Past the Capitol — lit up so nobly at night.

The Senator could see fireworks in Lisa May's eyes. She had never been out of Alabama before. The grandeur of the nation's Capital had her under its spell. The limo continued up Constitution Avenue to the White House.

"Four years from now," said the Senator as they passed the big mansion with fountains lit up on the south lawn, "I'm gonna be movin' in to that big ol' house right there."

"I hope I can come visit," Lisa May cooed, rubbing his pant leg as if a genie-in-a-bottle was in there — aching to get out. His cock started to stiffen like the sword of an Arabian Knight.

"Visit?" Bane laughed, reaching into his coat pocket and taking out a small jewelry case, "I wantcha to do more than just *visit.*" He opened it. A brilliant diamond ring sparkled magically inside. "I want ya to be the First Lady of this Land."

"Oh, Arnie, do ya really mean it?" the teenager gasped as if she'd just won the grand prize on a TV game show.

"More'n I ever meant anythang in my life," he replied.

She slid the big ring onto her finger. Then kissed him, thrusting her tongue long and deep into his mouth. Their tongues intertwined in between their bicuspids with the ferocity of piranhas devouring a freshly fallen sloth.

"Donald," Bane said to the chauffeur up front, tapping on the glass divider, "The motel on Old U.S. One. *North* U.S. One."

The driver nodded. Veering the limo out of its White House orbit, he headed up Vermont Avenue toward the Land of Mary just a couple miles to the north. He knew why the Senator wanted a motel in Maryland where the age of consent was sixteen. If they were to head south into Virginia, where eighteen years old is the legal age, Bane would be committing a crime if he slipped it into Lisa May on *that* side of the Potomac.

One wrong turn on the Road Of Life and you're screwed, Donald thought to himself as he maneuvered the stretch limo around Logan Circle while the newly engaged couple were making out hot'n'heavy in back. Turning onto Rhode Island Ave, the chauffer saw flashing blue lights in the side view mirror. He put on his blinker. Pulled to the curb. Bane used the very same finger he was applying to Lisa's clit to press the automatic window button.

"Senator Lucius Arnold Bane?" the D.C. Policeman inquired as the faint scent of sardines wafted out of the car as the dark tinted window rolled down.

"Yes?" Bane replied, "Is there a problem, Officer?"

The cop had a hard time looking the Senator in the eye. His high-angle view favored Lisa May's fur coat. Right where it barely touched the tops of her thighs.

"Sir, I have a warrant for your arrest."

Cantabile

It was 10 a.m. Holly stormed past the secretary who insisted Mr. Russell was not in. Pushing open the door to his office, Holly caught him humping a Love-Sandwich he had wedged between two Jackie Collins' books on his bookshelf.

"What the hell?" Charlie bellowed as he withdrew his wet wanker from its double-volumed literary pursuits.

"I told her you weren't in," said his secretary, fearful of losing her job.

"You should be ashamed of yourself, Charlie!" Holly reprimanded.

Said Charlie: "Can't a man masturbate in peace?"

As he tried zipping his pants he caught his shirttail in the zipper.

"I'm not talking about your sex life," said Holly, watching him struggle to free his shirt, "I'm talking about your integrity as a human being."

"Miss Leitchter, could you leave us, please?" Charlie asked of his middle-aged, slightly pudgy secretary.

"Yes, Sir," she replied, quietly closing the door behind her.

Charlie had a lot on his mind. He needed to masturbate to relieve inner tension. He had just found out Senator Bane was arrested during the night. Charlie's job was to make sure his client was favorably portrayed in the media. Since Bane was in Alabama when the forensics experts determined was the time of death, he couldn't be charged with murder — yet. But disposing of a dead body in the Bay brought several charges, most of them felonies. And the election was just one day away.

"You should be thanking me for keeping you out of jail!" Charlie blustered as he finally pulled his shirt loose and pulled up his zipper.

"I'm just sick and tired of all the lies and deceit," Holly said.

"Bullshit! You just want your name on the *Hosanna!* Admit it."

"Well, now that you mention it, I *would* like my name on it. After all, I'm the one who wrote it."

"You made an agreement to write it anonymously," he countered, "and you were paid, and paid damn well, I might add, considering the plight of most composers these days."

"I'd gladly give back all the money to have my name on it. As it rightfully should be."

"Believe me, Lucius Bane has enough problems right now as it is," Charlie sighed, "He's not going to take back the money. That would be admitting complicity. Officially, the money doesn't exist. Officially, *you* don't even exist — except as one of a dozen intern copyists brought on board to prepare all the orchestral parts. All those handwritten scores you so meticulously wrote out were destroyed after the notes were entered into a computer program called *Finale.* As far as the world is concerned, you're nothing more than another Unknown Composer."

"If people started telling the truth," remarked Holly, "maybe I wouldn't have to be unknown."

"Let me tell you what would happen if I corroborated your story with the police yesterday," Charlie went on, "You're right, you wouldn't be 'unknown' any more. The tabloids would lap up your story like death row inmates at a cellblock cunnilingus party. But what would you be known *as?* The composer of the *Hosanna Millennia?* Probably not. Roger may be dead, but his father is a very powerful man. He would see that you're portrayed in the media as a lunatic out to steal his son's glory. The contract you signed has long been destroyed. You can claim anything you like, but Bane will deny it. So will his lawyer. Lawyers always deny everything.

"The media would drag you through the mud, Holly. You'd become known, all right, but not as a composer. You'd be forever known as *The Woman Who Bit Off the Composer's Cock.* And good luck finding a job with that moniker around your neck."

"What about you, Charlie? Why don't *you* tell the truth?"

"Do you think for a minute I would ruin my career for a woman who strung me along for six months letting me believe I was the father of her child?"

"Charlie, I admit there was a lapse of communication."

"Right. Seems you and ol' Roger boy didn't have any lapse of communication the night you two got it on."

"I told you I was raped."

"Yeah. Sure. You got any swampland in Florida you wanna get rid of?"

"Don't tell me you're jealous."

"Damn right I'm jealous!"

"Charlie, there's nothing between us. There never was."

"How can you say that? After all we shared over the phone?"

"An impotent Virgo and a lesbian Libra. There couldn't be a worse mismatch than that," cited Holly.

"There's more to life than just sex, you know," Charlie waxed philosophically, eyeing the empty Love-Sandwich six-pack on his desk.

"I know," she said.

"Holly, my offer of marriage still stands."

"Charlie! We're not talking about marriage or fatherhood here. We're talking about truth!"

"You wanna talk about truth?" Charlie asked as he slipped back into his professional tone, "Truth is whatever people believe is the truth. I'm in the business of making people believe whatever my clients want them to. Whether a certain brand of laundry detergent is the best at getting rid of stains doesn't matter. What matters is that I make people *believe* a particular brand is the best one available. Whether a certain Senator sincerely believes in government funding for the arts, or whether he just wants to get re-elected is not my concern. It's not a matter of who's right or who's wrong. It's a matter of who has the best ad campaign. Because what's considered truth today becomes bullshit tomorrow. As far as I'm concerned, the only time a person is really telling the truth is when they call themselves a liar."

BANE WAS RELEASED ON bail by noon. He and his lawyer were met on the police station steps by a swarm of reporters. News cameras and microphones were thrust in his face. Reporters scuffled for position like a pack of hungry dogs grappling for scraps of meat from the table.

"Senator Bane! Is it true the police have a videotape of you dumping the composer's body in Chesapeake Bay?"

"This whole thing is a big misunderstandin'," the Senator squirmed, trying to appear calm. Then his lawyer leaned over and whispered in his ear.

The salvo of reporter's questions persisted:

"Were you and Roger Landsworth involved in a sado-masochistic homosexual relationship?"

"Was he sacrificed in a Satanic ritual?"

"Were there illegal drugs involved?"

Finally Bane cut them off. "Please, please. My lawyer here's advisin' me not to make any comments. But I will say this: when the people of Alabama go to the polls tomorrow, I want ya'll to remember one thang: here in Amer'ca, a man is innocent till proven guilty. And durin' my twenty-five years a' public service, my integrity has been the foundation a' my career. Integrity, Ladies and Gentlemen, is what my campaign is all about. Fidelity and Integrity."

"Arnie!" came a small voice burrowing its way through the orchard of cameras and microphones. It was Lisa May Hartley. She was still wearing the fake mink coat with nothing on underneath.

"Oh, Arnie!" she sighed as she threw her arms around him, "I was so afraid for you last night. I just want you to know I'll be here by your side through thick'n through thin."

"Please, Lisa May," the Senator said to her in a soft voice, trying not to be picked up by the mics, "let's talk about this later."

"Who's this?" blared a voice that cut through the commotion like a foghorn blaring on a misty night. It was Dolores. She had flown up to Washington that morning as soon as she heard the news.

"Whadda ya mean, 'who's this?'" hissed Lisa May Hartley, "I just happen to be his fiancée!"

The teenage girl held up her ring finger. The clear gem sparkled in the noonday sun. The crowd of reporters oohed and ahhed. But not at the ring. Lisa May's fake-fur coat had fallen open in the front. Her perfectly shaped seventeen-year-old body was unveiled for all the world to see. Newspaper photographers snapped away like a string of firecrackers going off on Chinese New Year.

"Wait a minute!" came another voice, "You said you were going to marry *me!*" It was Loni, pushing her way through the chaotic crowd. The overhead mics and television cameras swung wildly to capture the unscripted melodrama unfolding on the Police Station steps like an overwrought daytime soap opera on steroids:

"Who's this?" Lisa May asked, pointing at Loni, whose breasts were three times the size of her own.

"That's his secretary," Dolores informed the teenage girl, then turned to her husband and accused: "I suppose you've been banging *her* behind my back too!"

"Can we discuss this later?" the Senator pleaded, sweat beading on his brow, "I've had a rough night."

"Have you been screwing your secretary, Lucius?" his wife demanded in the tone of a prosecuting attorney.

"Uh, not really," the Senator replied, looking at Lisa May and throwing her a nervous wink.

"Not really?" Loni shrieked. "What do you call all those times you bent me over your desk at the Capitol? Or out at the cottage or even your apartment when your wife was outta town?" The crowd of reporters and gathering on-lookers gasped in disbelief. Cameras snapped away. Loni turned to the bouquet of microphones clustered around her head and added: "And for the last seven months he's been licking my snatch with a GloptaFast sticker stuck under his nose!"

"You asshole!" yelled Lisa May, accidentally letting her coat fall open again.

"Go to Hell, Arnie," steamed Loni as she slapped him across the face and stomped down the steps in her stiletto-high heels, "I'm gonna sue you for sexual harassment!"

"And you'll be hearing from a divorce lawyer too," sniped Dolores as she followed Loni down the granite steps, "I'm gonna rake you over the coals! I'm gonna take you to the cleaners!"

"Fuck you!" hollered Lisa May as she slid the massive ring from her finger and threw it, hitting Bane in the chest. She may as well have thrown a knife through his heart.

"Please, Lisa May, I can explain everything," Bane begged, his eyes filling up like a cupful of rain. "I love you! I can't live without you."

"Well, do the world a favor and go kill yourself then!" sneered cute little Lisa May as she turned to walk away.

"Please, don't go," the broken Bane meekly called out as he fell to his knees — hands outstretched like Al Jolson. Watching her sweet round ass framed through the fur coat swaying side to side as she strode down the steps — fading further and further out of reach.

Hamelstein, his lawyer, was trying to pull him back up on his feet. But, like a badly beaten boxer, the Senator was down for the count. The crowd suddenly went silent as Bane begged and pleaded for Lisa May to come back.

"You're all I have left," he whimpered like a dog. The cameras kept rolling and the mics were left on. CNN was broadcasting live. Millions of homes were tuned in that day. Watching young Lisa May Hartley turning around. Her fur coat flying open, briefly flashing the crowd. Like the final dagger thrust into his heart, Lisa May yelled loud enough that even the hearing impaired would be able to turn off the closed captioning:

"Last week he took me to a cheap roadside motel, got me drunker'n a skunk and fucked me up the ass while I was on my period!"

LATE THAT NIGHT HOLLY sat in her studio. She looked up at Wolfgang hanging on the wall. He was only thirty-five when he died. Jesus was only thirty-three. Both left an incredible amount of beauty behind. Beauty that is still as alive as the day it was first set forth in the world.

Holly was dissatisfied with the end of "Easter and Ascent," the final movement of the oratorio. It was too overblown. Too traditional. Begging for applause. Jesus' life didn't have a big bombastic ending. No marching band serenaded his ascension. It was a gentle departure. A rose petal on the wind. Showing us these physical bodies are not the only thing defining our existence.

Holly tore up the last page of her score. Closing her eyes, she sat there in silence. Her mind finally settled after a half hour or more. That's when she first heard the rhythm. Faintly. Almost inaudible. She eventually realized that what she was hearing was the incessant beat of her very own heart.

All music has meter in either *twos* or in *threes*. The human heart beats in threes. From Holly's own three-metered heartbeat sprang a melody that perfectly fit with the words Torchy wrote:

EV'RY MOMENT IS A MIRACLE   EV'RY DAY IS A GIFT FROM YOU

LET ME SHOW YOU MY GRATITUDE   BY WHAT I THINK AND SAY AND DO

The melody was within the range of a boy soprano. To Holly, there was no sound as lovely as that. As if hearing through a child's voice the way things appear through their eyes: simple and pure. Holly wished once again she could see through those eyes — the ones that never cease to see wonder in the world.

It was daybreak by the time Holly finished the fine-tuning. She heard Torchy stirring in the kitchen around six. Up early for school, fixing cereal for breakfast.

"Torchy, I'd like to use your poem in the finale of the *Hosanna,*" Holly said as she walked into the kitchen.

"Really?" she answered, genuinely flattered, "You think it's that good?"

"Yes," said Holly, "There's one problem though. The contract I signed says that all words and music, except whatever's in the public domain, must be attributed to Roger."

"Why should that asshole get all the credit?" Torchy blurted, then quickly held her hands up over her mouth. "Oops," she added, "I'm not s'posed to use cuss words any more. Forgive me, Father," she said, looking up at the ceiling with her hands clasped together.

"I know how you feel, Torchy. I feel bad about pouring my soul into something knowing that someone else is getting all the credit."

"You can use my poem, Holly," Torchy said after finishing off a big bowl of cereal." I didn't write it to be famous or anything. I only wrote it to show my love for God. *He* knows who wrote it. That's all that matters."

Holly threw her arms around Torchena and hugged her tightly, saying: "You're right. That *is* all that matters."

Holly confronted her own motivation for creating the *Hosanna Millennia.* Did it matter whether the name Holly Bibble would be up there with Ludwig van Beethoven and Igor Stravinsky? Would Beethoven's *Ninth* be any less great if the composer was named Harvey Nimbelschwartz?

From out of the mouths of babes came a response to all Holly's unanswered questions. Torchy opened the Bible she kept with her at all times. She turned to a page in *Psalms* and read the passage aloud:

"Make a joyful noise unto the Lord, all ye lands."

ELECTION DAY WAS Humpty Dumpty Day for Lucius Bane of Alabama. Conyers won the Senate seat with a landslide ninety-eight percent of the vote. Guy M. Landsworth sent the Bane Campaign Treasurer a bill for over nine million dollars. The open-ended credit came to a screeching halt when he found out his son had been de-pricked and unceremoniously marinated in the bay.

Overnight, the Senator became the whipping boy of every tabloid sold in the supermarket checkout lines. A photo of the Viking dumping Roger from the dinghy was leaked to the press. They gave him colorful names such as "Studmuffin To The Valkyries," or "The Capitol Copulator." After Lisa May went on *Larry King Live* and recounted the vivid details of their menstrual encounter in the Tuscaloosa motel, *The New York Sun* anointed him with the moniker "Lucius The Red." Curbside vendors sprang up around Washington like toadstools after a rain. They sold pin-on buttons with sayings such as: "Boffed by Bane" or "I Sucked the Senator." Bumper stickers read:

"HONK IF YOU HUMPED LUCIUS"

The Press interviewed Bane's son, Ted, at the Atlanta Airport. When asked about his father's current misfortunes, the pony-tail-on-top-of-a-shaved-head Ted intoned: "All his problems would be solved if he would just chant *'Hare Krishna. Rama Rama. Krishna Krishna.'*"

When the media found out Biff Bone — the hung-like-a-horse porn star — was in fact the Senator's son, it only added more dinosaur shit to the fire.

Scores of teenage Tesses from two-bit towns claimed they'd had sex with the Senator. And liked it. It became a national craze — like Elvis sightings. Any time a girl in America got pregnant and didn't know who the father was, she'd claim it was Bane who'd done the deed.

The great irony in all this was that following the election, Lucius Bane, lame duck Senator, wasn't getting laid at all.

AT THE CONCLUSION OF his blockbuster world tour, Jon LaRue announced to the press that he would perform a one time only revival of *Crucifax*, his masterpiece. The show would take place at Madison Square Garden on Saturday,

December 23rd, 10 p.m. The performance would be broadcast live via satellite to sixty-one cities around the globe. Seats would be sold in these cities to watch the extravaganza on large closed circuit screens. Tickets went on sale the day after Thanksgiving. They were sold out in less than two hours. It was estimated that Jon LaRue personally would make over forty million dollars for this one performance.

And with that kind of cash, his dream of building Orlando's first Anal Theme Park would soon be a reality.

HOLLY SLID THE FINAL pages of the master score into the Federal Express envelope, peeled the tape and pressed it shut. Like the Mother sparrow pushing her birdlings from the nest so they may fly on their own — there was a certain sadness. The *Hosanna Millennia* for orchestra, chorus, and Baptist congregation was finally done. It would fly or fall on the strength of its own merits. It would catch the wind by the stretch of its own wings. All Holly could do was wish it well. And hope it will have its day in the sun. The Fed-Ex van pulled up in front of her house. The man took the package and drove away.

Holly was left with an emptiness in her soul unlike anything she had ever experienced in her life. Never before had she been so lonely. Never had she felt so desperately alone. She called Kim's new cell phone. The number was disconnected again. She called Johns Hopkins. They said Kim was still on leave. No one was sure when she would be back.

"Maybe after Christmas," someone said.

Holly hung up the phone. Sat there in silence. Torchy would be gone all day long at school. She heard the clock in the living room ticking. She'd never noticed it ticking before. Idly, she walked through the house. Browsing her bookshelves. Her knick-knacks. Her college degrees. None of it seemed to make any connection. In the museum of her life, Holly seemed like a stranger who wasn't invited. Someone who didn't belong.

She went in her studio. Mozart was there. Staring half-tilted from his place on the wall. She sat at the piano. Started to play. But stopped midway through a Bach fugue she had learned at eleven years old. Closing the piano key cover, she stared out the window. The garden was barren and brown. Hard summer rains had washed the last bit of lipstick from the headstone on top of Toes' tomb.

Holly thought about how everything is transitory. A symphony of notes passing one to the next. Played but once. Then discarded in the great scrapheap called memory. Humans find security in repetition. So they try to create patterns. In relationships. Employment. Habits. Trying to make the same group of notes repeat again. In music this is called 'recapitulation of theme.' But in life, Holly found, when events get recapitulated, rarely are they repeated in quite the same way.

Holly went into the bedroom to lie down on the quilt. She admired the care that went into its making. The various fabrics all hand-stitched together reminded her of farmland as seen from a plane. Tracing the stitching with her fingers, she came to a corner where she found a carefully embroidered name: *Carina.*

Carina had signed her name to her work. Holly had not been allowed to. She envisioned a day when artists are all Rumpelstiltskens locked up in dungeons. Forced to spin straw into gold for mediocre politicians who sign it with their contributor's names. The thought of it made Holly even more depressed. Nauseous, in fact. She went into the bathroom and vomited.

She thought about suicide. There were pills in the cabinet. How simple it would be to just turn off the switch. To enter the void. The infinite abyss. Nothingness.

Holly felt a small kick inside her. With it the fear of aloneness flew right out the window. A new human being would soon be in her care. She closed her eyes and thanked God for all of His blessings.

She laughed and rubbed her basketball stomach. No joy could equal what she was feeling right then. No orgasm. Nothing. Not even great sex. Not even hearing the greatest music ever written.

Over on the dresser was the rose-box containing Kim's hair. Holly had a wild idea. And she went for it. She took the box down to a salon that was noted for its long hair extension weaving. It took three full sessions to braid it all in. But she did it. Holly had Kimberly's hair braided to her own. Snug to her scalp. The hair she'd always envied. Always loved touching and smelling and running her fingers through. Now it was hers. All of it. Hers. All the way down past her waist.

GORDON PARKED HIS CAMARO by the dark pool of water. By day, it was a cesspool for a sewage disposal plant. But at night, it looked like a lake, opalescent and beautiful. There were several cars parked there that evening. It was an infamous Lover's Lane. The ground was covered with beer cans and discarded condoms.

Torchy sat in the passenger seat. Gordon turned up his stereo. The latest CD by *The Hung Mussels* blared but the young man ejected the disc and slipped in another that was softer and more romantic.

Torchy liked Gordon. He was seventeen and good looking. Blond, with a tan and muscular build from working summers in his father's pipefitting business. He draped his well-defined arm along the headrest of the bucket seat.

"It's kinda cold outside," he said, moving closer.

"Yeah, it is," she smiled. "I like this song."

"Me, too," he added, rubbing his hand along her shoulders.

It was a ballad, titled: "When You Do Me" by *The Rimmers.*

Gordon's testicles went into overdrive, spilling testosterone like oil from the Exxon Valdez. It raged through his system, changing his demeanor from mild-mannered nice guy to stark raving stud. Suddenly, all Gordon could think about was pussy. Torchy's pussy to be exact.

In all of God's creation, there is nothing more headstrong than a seventeen-year-old boy with a hard-on.

Gordon pulled her close to him. Pressed his lips against hers. She responded immediately, slipping her tongue into his mouth. It had been eight months since she'd last had intimate contact with anyone except for the handle of her hairbrush.

The young man began unzipping her jeans.

"Gordon, please don't," she pleaded, intercepting his hand with her own and squeezing it.

"Why not?" he asked, his hard cock straining at the bit. He began rubbing the crotch of her jeans, hoping the incessant strokes would break down her resistance.

"I wanna wait till I'm married," said Torchy, letting him rub her just a little bit before pulling his hand away.

"Why?"

"Cuz that's what the Bible says."

"Are you a virgin?"

Torchy paused for a moment.

"Yes."

In her mind, she was telling the truth.   To her, everything she did before becoming born again was done by a different person. The hundreds of men, from Manhattan executives on down to the ten-dollar street tricks, all performed their lascivious acts with someone else. In her newfound faith, Torchy was unsoiled. Untouched. Pure as a snowflake and immaculately virtuous.

"I just wanna finger you a little," Gordon offered as he persistently pushed his hand down the front of her pants, which he had furtively unbuttoned without her knowing it.

"No! Not till I'm married. I mean it!"

Gordon began rubbing her wet crotch again. Softly.

"Will you marry me?" he asked. When a teenage boy is being goaded by his gonads, there is nothing, repeat, *nothing* he won't say or do to entice a girl to let him get into her pants.

"I'd have to get to know you better," said Torchy, "but I really like you a lot."

"How 'bout if we just went steady?" he suggested as she allowed him to keep his hand between her legs.

"Only on one condition," Torchy said.

"Name it."

"That you accept The Lord Jesus Christ as your Savior."

"I do," Gordon said. And he meant it.

They embraced once again, only this time she let him pull her zipper all the way down as he kissed her. She offered no resistance as his hand slipped below the loose elastic rim of her panties. Her vagina was primed from the previous struggle. His finger slid all the way in. The wetness and warmth was all the more pleasurable to Gordon since he believed, like Columbus, he was the first to plant his flag on an unexplored shoreline.

Gazing out at the lake that by day was a cesspool, Torchy undid his zipper and jacked him off dry. He writhed and contorted like a worm on a griddle. Then came like a cannon. Semen flew upward in the air between them, arched down toward the dashboard and splattered against the speedometer.

Never before had Gordon felt so religious.

ON DECEMBER 7th in the year 2000 no bombs were dropped on Pearl Bailey. But a bomb, of sorts, was definitely dropped on Holly Bibble.

It began with an early morning knock at the door. Holly got up, still groggy with sleep. She opened the door. Kim was standing in the cold. But not the Kim she had always known.

"I lost my key," said Kim, her voice husky, wearing a three-piece suit and polished men's shoes. A man's overcoat was draped over her shoulders. Her hair was cut even shorter than before. And there on her face was the start of a beard.

"Kim, what happened?"

"I've gone through some changes," she answered, her voice a good half-octave lower than before.

They both stood staring. Breaths visible in the cold. Till Kim opened her arms, saying: "Dee Dee, don't I get a hug?"

The two embraced, carefully, as Holly was very pregnant. Big belly pregnant. Due in less than three weeks.

Holly felt Kimberly's beard against her face. It felt strange. To feel a sharp beard where there once were smooth cheeks.

"My hair looks good on you," said Kim, letting her fingers run through hair that used to be her own.

"Boo Boo," squeaked Holly, "why are you doing this? Why are you turning yourself into a man?"

"I am a man," said Kim with an air of finality.

"Come inside, I'm getting cold," said Holly, leading her girlfriend-in-drag into the living room and closing the front door. "What do you mean you're a man?"

They sat on the couch. Kim took out a wallet. Opened to a driver's license and showed it to Holly. There was a picture of Kim with short hair and beard. But the name on the license read:

"KENNETH DAVID JACKSON"

"Notice the part where it says: 'sex,'" Kenneth pointed. Holly looked and saw the letter 'M.'

"Come on, Kim, this is a joke, right?"

"It's no joke," he said, taking her hand and pushing it down his trousers. "And my name isn't Kim anymore. It's Ken."

"You're taking this too far, Kim."

"Ken," he corrected.

Holly's hand came to rest on an elongated piece of flesh.

"What is this?" Holly smiled, "a Polish sausage or something?"

Holly unzipped her former female partner's striped pants and pulled down the men's underwear. Then, to her surprise, like a Jack-in-the-box un-sprung — out popped the penis that used to be Roger's.

Holly shrieked and threw her hands over her eyes when she saw how well hung her ex-girlfriend had become.

"Oh, my God, Kim!"

"Ken."

Holly peeked through her fingers, "Oh, my God, it's attached!"

"Of course it is," Ken informed her, "You wouldn't want it to snap off while we're in the middle of something, would you?"

"Kim, this is too weird!"

"Ken."

"Whatever! Why? Why did you do this?"

"Because I love you."

"Bull-*shit!*"

"Because I could never get as close to you as I wanted to."

"But I loved you as a woman," sniffed Holly, "I don't know if I can get used to this."

"Sure you can," said Ken, slowly bringing Holly's hand to rest on his penis. The scepter of his manhood. His joystick. His schlong.

Holly felt it starting to stiffen as she caressed it. "It gets hard and everything?" she asked, marveling at its swelling.

"Receptors in the brain," said Ken, pointing to his head. "It was an experimental procedure. But Dr. Kennesaw is the best. I figured it was worth the risk. So I did it."

"But why'd you have to use Roger's?" asked Holly.

"Because, like Mount Everest, it was *there,*" Ken answered, fondling the new addition to his anatomy. "There it was, on your car seat. Still cold. Still usable. It's a good thing you never got your heater fixed. I tested the blood. Type O+, same as my own. The HIV antibody test came up negative. Besides, cockhunters can't be choosy."

"You're terrible," laughed Holly, slugging him on the arm.

"But you know, my Dear, this dick is the Daddy of your child."

"You know Roger's dead, don't you?"

"How could I *not* know about it, it's been all over the news. Good riddance to bad rubbish. But I must say, I am grateful for his kind organ donation."

"You've changed," said Holly.

"Obviously," Ken replied, shaking his dick.

"No, not just that. I mean, personality-wise."

Ken reached for Holly's hand. Their fingers slowly mingled. Holly looked into his eyes. His eyes were the same as always. The same 'windows of the soul' she had known for six years.

"I'm the same person who fell madly in love with you the first time I saw you," said Ken with a sparkle in his eye, "only now, I come with an attachment."

Holly sighed a lover's sigh and said: "I love you...Ken."

They kissed. Holly's long locks tumbled down in the gap between them — cascading over her tummy where the unborn baby stirred. The tips of her tresses tumbled further. All the way till they touched the tip of Ken's new limb.

Holly touched it with her hand again. Stroked the length of it with her fingers. She kissed the buttons down his shirt till they led her lips below his beltline. Staring the serpent eye to eye in the midst of the pubic garden, she confronted the demon that had lurked undetected for so long in her subconscious mind. She thought of the path her life had taken. Every step and turn had led her to where she is now. If any step had been different, she would be somewhere else. Therefore, she thought, if her Grandpa

Bibble hadn't coerced her into that despicable act, he may never have given her his clarinet and started her taking lessons. She may never have discovered her love of music. And she may never have known the joy of composing her beloved *Hosanna Millennia*. She thought of how Jesus always spoke about forgiveness. *Forgive us our trespasses, as we forgive those who trespass against us.*

And in that moment of quiet realization, Holly forgave her Grandfather — rest his soul — for what he did to her those twenty odd years before. And in the gentle peace that forgiveness often brings, Holly overcame her fear of phalluses. She opened her mouth with a heartfelt smile and engulfed the penis that once was Roger's but now belonged to Ken — who once was Kim — who was still her significant other.

Ken had no balls. So when he came, no trickle of fluid poured down her throat. He caught his breath, slid off the couch and turned to her on bended knee. Clasped her hand between his hands and asked:

"Holly, will you marry me?"

Accelerando

Holly reached for the Bible that she'd left on the bedside table. Opening it, purely by chance, to First Corinthians, she read a passage she had heard before at a friend's wedding:

Love is patient, love is kind.
It does not envy, it does not boast, it is not proud.
It does not dishonor others, it is not self-seeking,
it is not easily angered, it keeps no record of wrongs.

To her, this simple statement expressed the essence of Christianity. Not whether Jesus was born as aphids are born, or rose from the dead to ascend into the sky like a hot air balloon. Those were mere card tricks in the realm of matter and energy. People are too easily distracted by the medium and forget the importance of the message. His was a message of Love. A love beyond the capricious nature of romantic love. A love the ancient Greeks called ἀγάπη, or *agápē*. Unconditional love. A love that gives without expecting anything in return.

Holly thought Kim might be right. Or, rather, *Ken* might be right. Maybe a new type of humanity was evolving. Men were becoming more sensitive. And women were becoming more assertive. Perhaps the new species would be something akin to either earthworms or aphids. Something like the Maryland motto of: *womanly words and manly deeds.* Maybe one day genetic engineering will make binary gender classification totally obsolete.

And when that day comes, advertising firms will have to find whole new ways of selling aftershave, toothpaste, and underarm deodorant sprays.

IT WAS DECEMBER 23rd. Bane sat in his Watergate apartment. Alone. The window shades were drawn. He stared at a blank wall, listening to the incessant babble of the TV behind him. He had not left the building for several days. Things had gotten so bad he didn't even want to go outside. Everywhere he went people would point and make jokes. Women passing in cars would flash their breasts and yell: "Come fuck me!" But they didn't really mean it and would drive on by. Even if they did, he couldn't have been of service. Senator Bane hadn't had a hard-on in almost six weeks.

He couldn't even go out to local restaurants anymore without causing a commotion. People asking for autographs. Practical jokers trying to set him up on phony dates. Men giving him their ex-wife's email addresses and phone numbers and saying: "Give her a call." Some people would just come up and spit in his face.

He started sending out for food. Mostly pizza — it was the easiest to deliver. In less than six weeks, Bane gained back all the weight he had lost on his eight-month GloptaFast diet. He tried going back on the Scratch-N-Sniff plan, but it just wasn't the same without his big-breasted deep-dish former secretary.

He hired a call girl to come over one night but couldn't sustain an erection. She had cold sores on her mouth so a blowjob was out of the question. He paid her anyway, even though he did not partake of her orifices. Then he ordered a pizza and stuffed it down one of his own.

One afternoon he walked down to the dildo machine in the Watergate lobby. He put in three dollars and bought a Love-Sandwich. Brunette — super deluxe. The dark hair around the fake clitoris subtly reminded him of Lisa May. But the Love-Sandwich retained its virtue that night despite numerous attempts at penetration. The Senator's penis just hung like a wet noodle. And all the King's horses and all the King's men couldn't make it stand at attention again.

Every day a messenger would bring a big gunny sack of mail over from the office. Along with the usual death threats and such, more and more mail contained photos and love letters from women. Most were from middle-aged housewives in the Midwest offering access to their three main bodily valves.

A New York publisher gave the Senator a million dollar advance for exclusive rights to his biography. They'd already chosen a title: *Stud On The Hill.* But the courts attached every penny of his advance to pay off his creditors. Debts were piling up around Bane like a New Jersey landfill. The campaign debt, including twenty million dollars owed to Guy M. Landsworth's Lapp City Industries. Loni's lawsuit. The divorce. Criminal lawyer's fees for the various felonies stemming from dumping a dead body in the bay.

Luckily, Lisa May dropped her suit against the Senator after getting seventy thousand dollars to pose nude for *Penthouse.* She also received a hundred thousand dollar advance for modeling a new line of women's lingerie. In numerous interviews in all the magazines, she frequently cited how Senator Bane always asked her to wear crotch-less panties. "Either that or no panties at all," she told the reporters.

Senator Bane turned around when he heard a familiar voice. It was Jon LaRue on the forty-inch television screen in the living room of his apartment. The bearded performance artist was being interviewed by Barbara Walters.

"Jon," Barbara asked, "tonight at Madison Square Garden here in New York, you are going to be nailed to an outhouse door. Millions of people will be watching all over the world. Is this an act of sensationalism — as your detractors claim — or is it, in fact, a work of art?"

"A work of art has to be judged by the level of com-mitment by the artist," LaRue explained, "I would like to see some of my critics drive a nail through a part of their anatomy. Until they experience that, how can they criticize it? But critics are by nature cowards, so they would never do anything even approaching that level of commitment. Their idea of commitment is meeting someone for lunch at Elaine's.

"Come on, Jon," Walters interjected, "isn't the money a big part of your motivation?"

"Barbara, I performed *Crucifax* almost two years ago and didn't get a dime for it."

"But the publicity you got from that single performance and the trial afterward launched your career, did it not?"

"Personally, I don't think about money," said LaRue, checking the time on his Rolex watch, "I have accountants who worry about that. I only concern myself with the aesthetics of a particular piece. 'Beauty is Truth, and truth;

beauty,' isn't that what Keats wrote? And as I said before, an artist has to be willing to suffer — to nail himself to an outhouse, a barn door, a cross, whatever — if that's what's necessary to get his message across. The consummate commitment for an artist is to die for their art. Like Diane Arbus. Or Hemingway. Or Kurt Cobain. I would even go so far to say that suicide is the ultimate performance art. The quintessential statement about life."

Bane pushed the remote control, turning off the TV. He rang his chauffeur on the phone:

"Donald, meet me downstairs in five minutes."

Getting up from the chair, he put on an overcoat —the largest size made. He unscrewed the vacuum cleaner hose and put it in a large duffle bag that said 'Sports' on the side. Opening his double-barrel shotgun, he loaded two twenty-gauge shells in the slightly rusted chambers. He'd last used it skeet shooting at a Republican picnic two summers before.

He slid the shotgun into the bag with the vacuum hose, zipped it, then took the elevator down to the garage. Donald, his chauffeur, was waiting there with the black limo.

"I'll get that for you, Senator," Donald said, reaching for the duffel bag.

"No, I got it," said Bane, climbing in the backseat. He plopped the long bag down on the floor beside his legs.

The chauffeur closed the doors and got behind the wheel. "Where to?" he asked, putting the limousine into gear.

"New Yawk City," Bane replied as the limo spiraled out from the underground garage beneath the Watergate building.

Twilight was just descending on the Capital. The white alabaster marble of the many monuments reflected the golden glow of the setting sun. A few bright stars were already breaking through in the east, dotting the darkening Navy blue sky that surrounded the Capitol dome. The cherry trees were bare, forming stark silhouettes. A few patches of snow still lingered on the ground from the prior week's snowfall. Buildings turned from gold to ruby-red to lavender-pink. Like a color television with its hue knob turned all the way down, everything finally faded into a dreary tombstone gray.

The limo crossed the bridge across the icy Potomac to get on the northbound George Washington Memorial Parkway. Through the tinted rear window, Bane took one last look at the city he had come to conquer. Instead, it conquered him. He could never come back. His life lay in ruins. Vanquished. Shattered beyond repair. Like Humpty Dumpty.

THE DAY BEFORE THEIR wedding, Holly received an invitation in the mail to the 'Fremont Elementary School Christmas Pageant.' Holly had a lot of things to do that night. But she couldn't resist seeing some of her old students.

Holly was going to go by herself, but she found she was too pregnant to drive. So Ken drove in the Fiat. In the elementary school parking lot, they saw Mr. and Mrs. McConnahee. But the couple didn't recognize Holly because of her newly added long black hair. And, of course, they never would have recognized Ken. As they walked into the school auditorium they ran into Mr. Adajian, the Principal.

"I'd like you to met Dr. Ken Jackson, my fiancé," Holly said to her former employer.

"A pleasure," said the principal as the two men shook hands.

"How's your wife?" Holly asked.

"We're going through a divorce," Mr. Adajian answered with a look ripe with anguish. "I guess nothing is forever."

"Except herpes," quipped Ken.

Holly elbowed her husband-to-be in the rib cage.

"Funny you should mention that," Mr. Adajian said to Ken, "but the reason we're getting a divorce is because my wife gave me herpes. She told me she was a virgin when I met her. But after I got herpes I hired a private investigator to check into her past. He found out she was a bar girl for three years in the Philippines. Somewhere near the Naval Base until it closed in '91. I figured she had sex with at least two men every night times three-hundred sixty-five days in a year times three. That's over two thousand men. Mostly sailors."

"That's a lot of seamen," said Ken. Holly elbowed him again, this time harder.

"I'm sure there were a lot of Air Force pilots, too," Mr. Adajian amended, his brow heavy with stress. "Clark was right next to Subic back then." As the auditorium lights blinked twice the uncomfortable exchange was abandoned as everyone hurried to their seats after hasty goodbyes.

"That was awful what you said back there," Holly scolded Ken in a hushed voice before the program began, "Those girls in countries like that become prostitutes only because we live in a male dominated society that oppresses women. You, of all people, should know better."

"I'm sorry," said Ken, "it must be the testosterone I'm taking. It's making me say all sorts of things I would have never said before."

"Well," Holly whispered as the house lights faded down, "just because you've got a prick now doesn't mean you have to act like one."

The curtain opened. Schoolchildren dressed up as reindeer and elves sang 'Silent Night' softly and beautifully. They performed a few skits and sang more Christmas carols.

But what captured Holly's heart, and Ken could feel it from the way she squeezed his hand, was 'The Little Drummer Boy.' As the children's choir sang: 'bar-RUM-pum-pum-PUM' there stood Matt, center stage, tapping out his perfect paradiddles on a marching snare drum strapped over his shoulder. Holly remembered his first obnoxious trumpet blares. And his steady improvement during subsequent lessons. Now the redheaded youngster was well on his way.

The audience applauded at the end of 'The Little Drummer Boy.' Matt bowed awkwardly over the marching band drum. He dropped one of his sticks. Then picked it up embarrassedly. But the audience loved it and applauded even more.

At that moment Holly decided she would one day return to teaching. She saw it in a perspective she had never seen before. Education was no longer "something to fall back on." It was something much more. Much, much more. It was planting seeds and watering them. And watching them grow. She finally understood what Professor Bormstern was saying in the letter he wrote to her before he died.

Life is a process of learning. Teaching is a way of sharing what we have learned. Sharing is an expression of love. And love is an energy in constant need of expression.

But love, unexpressed, is a painting never seen — a song that's forever unheard.

Teaching is a way of making God's love more audible and visible in the world.

THE BLACK LIMO EMERGED from Lincoln Tunnel like a giant turd from an under-river rectum. The bulletproof car with government plates slid southward along Seventh Avenue, passing hurried hordes of last minute shoppers until it reached West 34th Street. The long, black limo with dark tinted windows swung into the VIP entrance of Madison Square Garden.

Everyone recognized Senator Bane as he stepped out of the car. For the past month his face was on the cover of every sleazy magazine and tabloid in North America. Even though no one at The Garden knew he was coming, an usher pinned a VIP badge to his coat. He was escorted into the huge indoor arena.

The security guards formed a phalanx to lead him through a standing room only crowd. The people appeared as worms to the Senator, constantly squirming toward him. Their faces contorted like monsters as they tried to get near him and ask for his autograph. One girl wearing a tight miniskirt who looked about Lisa May's age grabbed his crotch as he went by. Then she flashed her "I Boned Bane" button before she was pushed back by Security.

As he was led closer and closer to the stage, the music coming through the stacks of speaker cabinets grew louder and louder. LaRue had come a long way in production design since his early days at the New York Museum of Modern Art. Everything was first class, state of the art: the lights, sound, sets, and props. There were even lasers. On the stage was an outhouse. Not a cheap plywood job like the one for his government-funded show. The outhouse on the Madison Square Garden stage was crafted of the finest mahogany with inlaid mother-of-pearl.

A hologram of a barren desert panorama at sunset was projected on the stage. And there was LaRue, nailed to the door with a handgun sticking out of his anus. The ever-present nun was pulling people up on stage to read the fax messages. Several cameramen had taken up positions around the stage to beam this momentous occasion to ticket-holders in every time zone. The sold-out crowd in Madison Square Garden would cheer every time a fax message was read — as if cheering their team in the NCAA basketball play-offs.

Bane was led to the VIP section directly in front of the stage. Several movie stars and other celebrities he had never met waved to him as if he were one of their own. For a moment, he liked rubbing elbows with the rich and famous, until he overheard some of them talking behind his back:

"I'm surprised the Senator doesn't have a date with him," mentioned one.

"Maybe he came to hump the nun," snickered another. It was followed by laughter.

Bane heard the joke circulating through the VIP section like a game of Pac-Man. The fake nun on the stage tore off a sheet of fresh fax paper from inside the outhouse. She passed by LaRue who was looking rather pained. Walking to the edge of the stage, she reached down and grabbed hold of the Senator's arm.

"We have a famous lame duck Senator with us tonight," the nun said into the microphone. Her voice blasted out of the tall stacks of speakers and bounced off a satellite that was broadcasting the images to all parts of the globe. She coaxed the fat lawmaker up on the stage, continuing to the audience:

"It's too bad I didn't wear my crotchless panties tonight!"

This set off uproarious laughter in the arena that upset Senator Bane greatly. A few VIP's started chanting:

"Hump the Nun! Hump the Nun!"

"Senator Bane is going to read our next fax message," the pseudo-nun announced over the mic and echoed through the arena, "This message came all the way from Nairobi."

The chant quickly spread through the audience like wildfire. Within seconds, large numbers were chanting:

"HUMP THE NUN! HUMP THE NUN!"

Bane held the fax paper in his hand. It read: "Peace on Earth, Goodwill Toward Men." The Senator looked up at the impaled performance artist. LaRue smiled down at him from the mahogany outhouse door. Blood from his palms and feet slowly trickled down the wood like a Jackson Pollock painting.

"What does it say?" asked the nun, then turning the microphone toward the Senator's anxiety-ridden face.

The chanting of the crowd grew louder and louder, booming, echoing, shaking the stadium. Fifty thousand people began clapping and stomping in unison like a gargantuan war drum. Chanting:

"HUMP THE NUN! HUMP THE NUN! HUMP THE NUN!"

The Senator started to read the fax: "Peace on Earth—"

"Go on," coaxed the nun, "read the rest of it."

The roar of the crowd rose to an ear-piercing pitch:

"HUMP THE NUN! HUMP THE NUN! HUMP THE NUN!"

Then Senator Bane pulled his twelve-gauge shotgun from under his overcoat and emptied both barrels into LaRue. The outhouse door swung to and fro on its hinges. The .357 Magnum popped out of LaRue's ass. The naked man's body was blasted wide open. Blood and flesh splattered the door and surrounding scenery.

Globs of muscle and sinew hung from LaRue's ribcage. His stomach, liver and spleen intertwined with his bowels. The whole mess dangled like selections from a delicatessen pinned to a swinging outhouse door.

The nun began screaming but could not be heard above the crowd that was whipped into a frenzy. They were cheering as if Bane had just sunk a three-pointer to win a championship game for the Knicks. He threw the spent shotgun right below LaRue's feet where some of the dead performance artist's guts had fallen.

The crowd at Madison Square Garden gave Bane a standing ovation as he walked off the stage. Even the guards who helped usher him out were saying, "Good show!" and slapping him on the back to congratulate him. The tumultuous applause kept on and on as the Senator made his way toward the exit. No one but the nun knew LaRue was really dead.

They all thought it was part of the act.

Finale

"Where to?" Donald asked.

Bane answered: "I'm hungry."

The chauffeur drove north on Avenue of the Americas, which New Yorkers still refer to as 6th Avenue. Bane swigged *Old Forester* bourbon straight out of the bottle as he looked out the window as if watching TV. They passed by a dildo boutique called Lucille's Insertibles. A sign in the window read:

"SPECIAL CHRISTMAS SALE"

A banner across the window below the sign read:

"Yes! We have the new Bane Banger in stock!"

Eventually the limo stopped at a Nantucket Fried Chicken. Bane went in and ordered a family-size bucket. While waiting for his order to be filled, he asked to use the restroom. But like most Manhattan businesses, they had no public restrooms. This was a policy meant to discourage the homeless from frequenting their facility and driving away business. So Bane walked around to an adjacent alley and emptied his bladder on the side of a wall. Just like the homeless do.

Back in the limo, Bane pulled the lid on the bucket of chicken. Inside were the mutilated remains of a flightless bird, dipped in flour, and boiled in oil. Bane devoured the fried body parts and tossed the greasy bones on the limousine floor. Before long, the bucket was empty. Bane farted and wanted more. He told Donald to stop at McDonald's.

He ordered three Big Macs, a large shake, French fries, two hot apple pies and a fish sandwich. It took him less than five minutes to wolf it all down. Then he belched like the MGM Lion.

"Where to now?" Donald asked from the driver's seat.

"Make a right up here on 42nd Street," Bane urged, slurping the last of the chocolate shake through a straw. The gurgling sounded like someone with severe nasal congestion. Then he tossed the empty cup out the window. If one of New York's Finest had seen him do it, he could have had 'Littering' tacked on to his ever-expanding criminal record.

Cruising along with the late Saturday night traffic, Bane eyed the bevy of prostitutes lining the curb.

"Slow down," Bane said to his chauffeur, "I wanna get a good look."

Walking the street like a decadent fashion show of hot pants and crotch-high mini-skirts, were an array of young women of varied ethnic origins. Bane pulled a wad of hundred-dollar bills from his pockets. It was the last of his cash. Six portraits of Benjamin Franklin stared back at him. Each with an identical smirk on his face. *What was he smirking about?* the drunken soon-to-be ex-Legislator thought to himself. *The fact that I'm thinkin' about spendin' the last of my hard-earned money on a hooker in hot pants?* But Bane changed his mind at the very last minute and instead pulled out his pecker and began masturbating. His right palm was still greasy from the fried chicken. Still holding the stack of money with his left hand, Lucius looked at the six faces of Ben Franklin staring back at him while he choked the proverbial chicken. He recalled as a young boy in church being told that if he played with himself he'd be struck dead by lightning.

Maybe that was how Ben Franklin discovered electricity, the Senator thought as he continued stroking his penis while perusing the parade of rentable orifices displayed outside. *Ben Franklin's pants had no pockets, so he held his house key in one hand. While flying a kite he held the kite string in the other. Deciding to jerk off, Ben hung the house key on the kite string — to free up one hand to pull on his pecker.*

Ker-BLAM! Lightning struck the kite and came down the kite-string, lighting up the house key. And the rest, as they say, is history.

Bane shot his load high into the air and it landed in the empty fried chicken bucket that was now rolling around on the limousine floor every time Donald made a turn.

Lucius slipped his spent penis back in his pants and yelled toward the front: "Pull over." When Bane got out of the car, Donald instinctively jumped out to assist him. But the Senator instead handed him the bankroll of smirking green Bens.

"Merry Christmas," he said to his chauffeur.

"What's this for?" asked Donald, taking the money.

"Go paint the town red," uttered Bane as he climbed in the driver's seat, "I'll take it from here."

"But Senator, you're in no condition to drive!" Donald protested.

Bane put the long stretch limo in gear, then rolled down the window just enough to give Donald these drunken-slurred words of advice:

"One a' my favorite sayin's by Benjamin Franklin is: 'One today is worth two tomorrows.'"

"Right," Donald answered, "that's one of my favorites, too. But, Senator, you might not have any more tomorrows if you try driving as drunk as you are. So here, give me the keys."

"You're dang right," he replied, "But I got one for ol' Ben there," Bane added, pointing at the wad of bills in Donald's hand: "If one today really is worth two tomorrows, then if there ain't gonna be no more tomorrows then tonight's gotta be worth at least a hundred-million years!"

And with that the sotted Senator stepped on the gas and the limo roared off into the cold, city night, screeching its tires at every turn.

Bane steered the Cadillac limo across the 59th Street Bridge into Queens. He turned down an alley and parked behind an Army Surplus Store, leaving the engine running. He pulled the vacuum cleaner hose from the duffle bag and stumbled out of the car. One end he placed over the exhaust pipe. The other end he fit through the half-opened window. Then climbing into the back of the limo, he rolled up the window as far as it would go, squeezing the vacuum hose in place. He poured a tall glass of Scotch and sat back in the seat. It was well upholstered and muffled his fart.

The paint-peeling sign "ARMY SURPLUS" was visible through the windshield. Long suppressed memories of his tour of duty in Vietnam roared through his head like a Huey helicopter. Nineteen years old. Knee-deep in a Mekong River rice paddy. Scared shitless. The face of the first Viet Cong soldier he killed.

Dogs barked in the distance. An occasional police siren rose and fell. Far off gunshots could be heard. Somewhere, someone was screaming. The Senator kept sucking down liquor like it was going out of style.

He looked at the vacuum hose protruding through the slightly opened window. Through it, the sound of the engine could be heard. A low, steady hum. It was calming to the nerves. Like an ocean. Like a river. His mind became drowsy as he sipped some more Scotch. Things started to spin. And vibrate. They changed. The vacuum cleaner hose became red and started pulsing. It suddenly grew veins and became the Dick Of The Devil. Ejaculating invisible poisons into the limo. The leather-upholstered womb was becoming his coffin.

Then, like a caterpillar turning into a butterfly, the round end of the hose became soft, pink, and furry. The Senator smiled as it transformed before his eyes. Little by little, the Devil's Dick slowly metamorphosed into the Vagina of an Angel. Beckoning him home.

He poured more Scotch down his throat and stared at his reflection in the back seat window. Little vignettes from his lifetime waltzed through his mind. Things he hadn't thought of for a long, long, time. The summers of his youth. Catfishing. Quail-hunting. Inner-tubing butt-naked down a lolling lazy river. The peanut oil he'd rub on his scrotum so the minnows would nibble at his balls as he floated along jerking off and then watch as the fishies fought over his jism.

He remembered the first girl he ever kissed. Cory. It was behind the gym in junior high. He wasn't quite sure of what he was supposed to do, but he pressed his lips against hers and she taught him the rest. How surprised he was when she pushed her tongue into his mouth. Fireworks went off under his skin!

Winning the soapbox derby in Cub Scouts. The blue ribbon he pinned on his wall. The first time he managed to get his finger past the underwear of a girl that sat next to him in Science class in seventh grade. The first time he got drunk. The first time he got laid. His valedictorian speech after high school. The whorehouses in Saigon, Bangkok, and Subic Bay.

Being sworn into the House of Representatives. Fucking a sixteen-year-old Congressional page. He savored each memory like a pearl on a necklace. Each strung on the unbroken strand of his life. Where once was a flame now ebbed a few embers. His cells cried for oxygen. The strand became frayed.

His eyelids got heavier. He drank some more Scotch. Like a shopkeeper closing the shades on his windows the Senator's eyes closed for the very last time. His mind kept on cranking the memory Moviola. Dolores. Their wedding. Having their first child. Seeing his firstborn, Ted, for the first time in the nurse's warm, loving arms. Getting the same nurse's phone number and fucking her at her apartment later on in the week. Getting his first bill passed through Congress. His first breakfast with the President at the White House. The time his name came up at the Republican convention as a possible Vice-Presidential running mate.

He remembered a time when he was twelve years old and his parents left him alone in the house. After cutting off the end of a banana, he scooped out the fruit with a long slender spoon. He poured hot water into the hollowed-out banana peel to warm it, then emptied out the water. Placing it between his box springs and mattress, he slid his prick in the banana peel as far as it would go. It was warm, soft and gooshy, the way his twelve-year-old mind thought a real pussy would be. While on his knees humping the mattress, he spanked his bare bottom with one of his Mom's leather sandals until his buns were beet-red.

Fucking the banana peel was the very last thing that passed through his mind before slipping into unconsciousness. Bane's grip went limp. His Scotch fell to the floor with the chicken bones, hamburger wrappers, Styrofoam containers and the cum-splattered cardboard bucket that was no longer rolling around on the carpeting. The Senator's fat body slumped over like a thick tree being felled in a solipsistic forest. His face pressed against the dark-tinted glass. A circle of fog like a cartoon-balloon spread out from his lips every time he exhaled. The fog then contracted, receding back into the nothingness of the window framed night. Expanding and contracting with each dying breath, the wordless cartoon-balloons grew ever smaller. Smaller and smaller.

Till the window was fogged no more.

The solids, liquids, and gases that comprised the Senator's obese anatomy began the long, slow process of converting back into a wave.

As final punctuation to the end of his life, the Senator's bowels emptied into his trousers like the jackpot of a Las Vegas slot machine. Only in death did he find relief from irregularity. Only in death was his colon set free. The 'tube of toothpaste technique' from the mind control video was nothing compared with ceasing to be.

And thanks to the Hotchkins Amendment tacked on to House Resolution 581, during Bane's autopsy the following day — no foul language was heard.

Coda

"Do you, Holly, take Ken to be your lawfully wedded husband? To have and to hold, to love and cherish, for richer or for poorer, in sickness and in health, till death do you part?"

"I do."

"I now pronounce you man and wife."

Ken lifted the veil from Holly's face. She was radiant in spite of the overcast day. Leaning toward her, he turned his head slightly. Holly met him halfway. Their lips firmly pressed, sealing the vow of a lifetime.

The musicians played the *String Quartet in G Minor* by Debussy. The newlyweds turned toward their family and friends. Holly's parents were there. So were her brothers. Their wives and her nieces and nephews. Her Jewish grandparents, Lulah and Gramps.

Torchy and her new boyfriend, Gordon, were there. And some of Ken's friends from the hospital. Doctors and nurses and even some patients. And old Grandma Bibble, in the Italian tradition, was drenching her hanky with teardrops of joy.

They walked down the cherry-brick aisle in the park. Ken in his tux. Holly in her gown. She wore white in spite of being nine months pregnant.

After the vows, everyone walked across the street from the park to a restaurant where the reception was held. It was Sunday, December 24th. The day before Christmas. But Holly's horoscope said it was the best possible day for a joining of Leo and Libra.

"Just in the nick of time," Holly's father whispered to Ken in the reception line, eyeing his daughter's gargantuan stomach. Then he slipped Ken a thousand in cash and said: "Have yourselves one hell of a honeymoon tonight."

The cake was shaped like a grand piano with a stethoscope perched on the lily-white icing. They cut it and Holly smeared a piece in Ken's face. Icing got stuck in his beard.

"It's not a pie hole anymore!" Ken humorously announced to the crowd, "Now it's a cake hole!"

Some people laughed as Ken excused himself to go to the washroom.

"What nationality is Ken?" Holly's Mom asked as soon as he was out of earshot.

"He's Hawaiian," fibbed Holly.

"At least he's American," her older brother commented.

"At least he's a *he*," Holly's Dad added on.

"He may look like a *schvartzeh*," observed Lulah, Holly's Jewish Grandmother, invoking the Yiddish word for Negro, "but at least he's a doctor."

"A brain surgeon," Gramps chimed in.

"All the better!" Lulah cheered, and everyone laughed.

Lulah then said to her daughter Deborah, Holly's Mom: "And the best *you* could do was a fabric salesman?"

"To my eternal shame," Deborah feigned, hugging her husband of thirty-four years.

Ed Bibble smiled as he kissed his wife just as Ken was coming back from the men's room. The groom's beard was free of icing. He looked dashing in his black tuxedo, a white corsage pinned to his lapel. He kissed his lovely longhaired bride on the cheek.

"See, I told you," Holly's Mom said to her husband, Ed, as they watched the newlyweds kissing for the photos, "that whole lesbian thing was just a passing fad."

Some of their wedding gifts were on display, including several pairs of crotchless panties. Among them was a pair of the new *Lisa May* line — which were flying off the shelves during the Holiday Season.

Everyone got drunk, except Holly and Ken. The Jon LaRue assassination and Senator Bane's suicide the night before were the two hot topics of the day. An assortment of Bane jokes were circulating around the party. Some of the older ones that were now passé were still making the rounds:

"You know how the Government can pay off the national debt? Start charging stud fees for Lucius Bane."

But there were a few freshly minted ones going around:

"Why did Senator Bane die in a limo? He was too fat to fit in a Volkswagen."

"Did you hear how did Lucius Bane killed himself? He overdosed on GloptaFast while going down on the 60-Foot Centerfold.

("Attack of the 60-Foot Centerfold" was a B-movie that was popular in video stores that year.)

The person who started the jokes was none other than Bane'se ex-publicist, Charlie Russell. Holly hadn't invited him to the wedding. She still harbored a grudge about the police station incident. But he showed up invitationless just the same.

She watched the chronic masturbator stuff food in his face as if he'd just spent a month in Ethiopia.   As she watched his mouth bite and chew and swallow she remembered what he'd said about truth.

Holly realized how different people are from computers. A computer's reality is either 'on' or 'off,' 'yes' or 'no,' 'right' or 'wrong,' 'one' or 'zero.' Human beings, on the other hand, operate mostly in the gray area in between the two polar opposites.

When computer programmers want to make machines more human they use a principle called 'fuzzy logic.' Fuzzy logic helps computers function in situations that are anything but logical. Neither on nor off. Between yes and no. Humans are quite adept at operating in this mercurial zone. They do it all the time, especially in matters of the heart.

Holly remembered Jesus and His example of forgiveness. If she could forgive her Grandfather for coming in her mouth, she could certainly forgive Charlie for being a liar.

But maybe he's right, she thought as she watched him stuff three or four egg rolls in his mouth at one time, *Maybe we all are just a bunch of liars.*   Who was she to cast the first stone? She told everyone Ken was Hawaiian instead of half black and half Vietnamese. And no one but herself and a few doctors there knew Ken had been a woman just a few months before.

Like Leos and Libras, Truth and Love are predestined to be incompatible. Holly found that as long as she lied — or at least hid the truth — everyone was happy. Holly kept the truth about Ken from her parents. In the realm of fuzzy logic it made perfect sense. She lied only because she loved them dearly. Could it be that truth is merely a booby prize when there's no love left to lose?

Holly looked across the room at Grandma Bibble. The lines on the old woman's face showed her years like the multiple rings in a large silver oak. She walked with a cane. Her knees were quite wobbly. Her body was frail as a twig used for kindling.

Holly thought about telling her what Grandfather did. But she feared that the truth might cut like an axe. And topple the tree that was beginning to teeter.

She knew Grandma still put flowers on his grave as she had every Sunday for the past fifteen years. Her memory of him was all she had left in the world. It was the water that kept her alive. Holly thought: *Who am I to dump my personal trash in her garden?*

So she kept her mouth shut. And let Grandma's memory of her deceased husband remain immaculate and pure. The late Senator Bane was right when he said: "There are certain things in life you're better off not knowing."

"Charlie, I'd like you to meet my husband, Dr. Ken Jackson," Holly introduced.

"So you're the lucky man," Charlie said as they shook hands. Ken had actually met him before one time when Charlie brought a sack full of money. But Ken was Kim back then. It was no wonder Charlie didn't recognize him.

"You must be the infamous sperm donor," smiled Ken as he shook Charlie's hand, "I'm sorry to hear all your hard work has so far been for naught."

Charlie looked at Holly, surprised at what she must have told her new husband.

"But in the future," Ken smiled, "if we ever decide to have another baby, we just might be calling you to lend us a hand."

Charlie looked surprised. Holly leaned over and whispered: "Ken can't have any children." Then she added: "He was injured in the Gulf War." (If she was going to lie, she may as well make it colorful.)

"Oh," Charlie said, "I'm sorry to hear that. But I would be honored to help out in any way I can."

Charlie was heartbroken that Holly got married. Many a Love-Sandwich he'd sullied in her name. But he still held the hope of becoming a father someday.

"Just remember," Charlie said with a gleam in his eye and a comatose cock in his pants, "when you think of making babies—"

"I know," Holly jumped in, beating him to the punch, "we'll think of Charlie Russell."

The string quartet was done. Now another band started to play. A Greek band with dueling mandolins and a Benzedrine freak on balalaika. Everyone, including Grandma Bibble, danced.

Beer cans were strung to the back bumper of Ken's car. Paper flowers were pasted on the windows and doors. On the hood was scrawled in white shoe polish:

"JUST MARRIED"

On the trunk was written:

"HOT SPRINGS TONIGHT"

Holly recognized the handwriting as Charlie Russell's from a letter he'd sent her last spring. It came with a small vial of semen included. "Spunk Mail" she called it back then.

They drove home, beer cans jangling behind the car. Ran in and changed and grabbed suitcases. But they decided to take Holly's Jetta instead of taking the time to clean the graffiti off the Fiat.

Ken drove the Jetta. It still had no heater. He promised he'd get it fixed by the first of the year. It was, after all, the manly thing to do.

Holly wondered where Ken was taking her on their honeymoon. She was due any time, so a hospital had to be near. That ruled out desolate tropical islands, a mountain chateaux, or country inns or cabins. They checked into a hotel in Silver Spring, Maryland, just north of Washington D.C. From the north-facing window of their room they could see a cold front rolling in.

Ken pulled an envelope from his pocket and handed it to his newlywed bride. She opened it. Inside were two tickets to the midnight performance of the *Hosanna Millennia* at the Kennedy Center. The concert had been sold out for months. The demand for tickets got even higher after Roger Landsworth's death. Ken paid a ticket scalper two hundred dollars apiece for them. But Ken was glad he bought the tickets from the scalper when he did. In recent weeks they'd been fetching over a thousand.

"I heard the Senator's suicide last night made the ticket price more than double," he explained to his wife while straightening his tie.

They drove down to the Center. Parked in the multilevel garage. It was an hour before curtain when they both took their seats. Holly opened the program booklet and read:

The Senate Committee for the Arts,

Senator Lucius A. Bane, Chairman,

presents

HOSANNA MILLENNIA

an oratorio by

Roger Milford Landsworth

It pained Holly to see Roger's name as the composer. She felt it was so unjust. But then she thought that she wouldn't have traded the opportunity to write it for anything. And now, to be able to hear it performed by orchestra and chorus! A composer's dream.

The movements were listed on the program in order:

> **Immaculate Concept**
>
> **Virgin Birth**
>
> **Good Young Carpenter**
>
> **Essene at Work**
>
> **Song of Beatitude**
>
> **Fishers of Men**
>
> **Pontius and Punishment**
>
> **Easter and Ascent**

Like an hourglass filling a few grains at a time, the people dribbled into their seats. So many thoughts passed through Holly's mind. Trains of Thought through Grand Central Station at rush hour:

This was the night she'd been working toward for eight months in a row. Through her break-up with Kim. The trauma with Roger. Her pregnancy. Mr. McConnahee. Torchy's cancer. Her Grandfather. Kim's sex change. All of her dramas and triumphs and sorrows are so interwoven in the notes about to be played. But a hundred years from now all her personal problems will be a pimple on the ass of a yak in Afghanistan. All that will remain is the music. God willing.

No one now cares whether Mozart was happy. What he ate. Where he slept. Or when he got laid. All that matters is the beauty he left in his music. Music that lived on long after he was gone like ripples from a stone cast into the water touching future generations who would come there to drink.

The house lights dimmed. The oboe held *A-440*. The orchestra tuned as the robed Tabernacle Choir filed into their positions behind the brass and percussion. On the far stage right the Baptist Congregation sat in neat wooden pews — courtesy of *Al's Lumber,* according to the program.

The conductor walked out. The audience applauded. He bowed and stepped up to the podium. His long silver mane curled down to his shoulders. As he raised his baton there was suddenly a hush. Alongside the baby in Holly's stomach were the thousands of butterflies fluttering through the long pregnant pause.

The downbeat came with the conductor's smooth ictus. The "Immaculate Concept" was impeccably performed. Better than Holly had expected back in the spring when it was composed.

When the Mormon Tabernacle Choir made its entrance during "Virgin Birth," it sent shivers through the audience. Those glorious human voices resonating from the stage. Filling the hall.

But "Good Young Carpenter" was a real showstopper. The Baptist Congregation rose to their feet and wailed with those full unthrottled voices, singing:

"Good Young Carpenter workin' in wood

Workin' in wood, workin' in wood

Build me a house with a strong foundation

Build me a house with a good steady frame

Build me a house with a long duration

Build me a house in the Lord's Mighty Name

Good Young Carpenter workin' in wood

Workin' in wood, workin' in wood

Make all the walls with a great big window

So I can see all there is to see

Raise me a roof made of one big rainbow

So I can never lose sight of Thee"

Holly held Ken's hand like a vice grip. She was so overwhelmed with emotion she thought she might explode like a potato left in the microwave too long. The rapturous singing of the Baptist Congregation segued into the Tabernacle choir intoning "Essene at Work."

"Song of Beatitude" was Holly's favorite movement. It was a slow Adagio in a minor key. The Beatitudes from the Bible were set to canonic melodies — different voices entered one after the other, weaving a multi-layered harmonic tapestry:

"Blessed are the pure in heart for they shall see God."

The sound of the orchestra and the *pianissimo* voices gave her goose bumps right down to the bone.

Then Holly went into labor.

D.C. al Fine

Ken helped Holly to the aisle and quickly to the exit as the orchestra began playing "Fishers of Men." The two left the huge concert hall in a hurry. Got to the parking structure. Found the car.

"Breathe deep," said Ken as he helped Holly into the passenger seat, the same seat where the manhood that now hung from him was found. He ran around, opened the driver's side door and got in. Put the Volkswagen Jetta in gear and roared down the spiraling exit ramp. Smack dab out into the middle of a raging winter blizzard.

Visibility was zero. Ken couldn't see a thing. He knew the way to George Washington University Hospital. The bar where he and Holly met was near there. But he couldn't see the road. Everything was white. Even the wipers at top speed couldn't keep the windshield clear of snow. Holly began to moan from increasing pain.

"Breathe deep," Ken reminded. He turned on the radio. It was tuned to the Washington NPR station. They were broadcasting the *Hosanna* live.

"Listen to what's on, Dee Dee!" said Ken as he struggled to drive through the turbulent snowstorm.

From the car speakers the "Pontius and Punishment" movement started off with a strident chord. The penultimate movement was more dissonant than the movements preceding it. Sounding more like the soundtrack of a horror film. Violent and unsettling.

Ken thought he was heading northwest on New Hampshire Ave. But he wasn't. And it was snowing too hard to read the signs. Holly kept moaning in a rising crescendo. The music from the radio kept surging to a peak. Tempestuously.

Suddenly they crashed into the side of a building — smashing clear through a thin plywood wall. The car came to rest underneath a wood roof that was just large enough to shelter them from the snow. Luckily they both had their seat belts on.

"Are you all right, Dee Dee?" Ken asked, his head still reeling from the impact.

"Yes," Holly said between moans, "I think so."

"How regular are the contractions?"

"Very, very," Holly grimaced, tears cascading from her eyes.

Ken unfastened Holly's seat beat. Lifted her dress. Peeled her underwear down off her legs. "Put your feet up on the dash," he said, helping her to do so.

Once her knees were in the air he put his hand on her vulva and felt inside. The top of the baby's head was in reach. "Push," he said.

Holly pushed. First came the peach-fuzz head. Then the torso. Ken guided the slippery new being into the world. Two tiny feet with toes like little berries. The placenta dragging slackly after him.

"It's a boy," said Ken to his newly betrothed wife. She heard him. Her eyes were still closed from enduring the pain. Not having any scissors, Ken held the child up to his black bearded face and severed the umbilical cord with his teeth. The baby began crying. Then he clamped the fresh wound with a paper clip. He took off his own coat to wrap the infant to warm him from the cold.

Holly opened her eyes as Ken was placing the wrapped infant in her arms. Only his tiny face was visible through the swaddled coat. Holly held him close and smiled as she had never smiled before.

The music on the radio was playing the final movement of the *Hosanna*, The "Easter and Ascent." The Tabernacle Choir sang:

"He is risen for all to see today
Know the Truth — Watch and pray."

The woodwinds and strings played slow legato melodies that kept rising upward into the higher registers. Holding on notes as other ones passed them. Tonal terraces climbing higher and higher and higher.

Holly stretched her sweater down below her milk-filled breast. The newborn partook of her nipple. It quieted his desperate cry. The pink little pilgrim with eyes still closed had his whole life ahead of him. To grow and to dream. Holly hoped he would be healthy and find the world full of wonder. And maybe someday aspire to do great things.

The sound of a lone boy soprano came lilting from the small car radio speaker, singing:

"Every moment is a miracle
Every day is a gift from You
Let me show you my gratitude
By what I think and say and do."

The handclaps began as a trickle. Then, like a dam collapsing, the Kennedy Center was filled with a torrent of tumultuous applause. Shouts of "Bravo!" came from every corner. It continued as the voice of a radio commentator gushed: "A standing ovation for the *Hosanna Millennia.* In spite of all the scandal that surrounded its being brought into the world, it stands on its own as a magnificent work." A second commentator added: "Timeless, I think. It's too bad the composer isn't here to see how the audience is responding."

"The name Roger Milford Landsworth will certainly be remembered," the first commentator said. "I think this *Hosanna* will be performed at Christmases for a long time to come."

"Maybe Roger Landsworth *is* watching all of this from somewhere."

"Maybe you're right," the first commentator replied, "I guess we'll all find that out sooner or later."

The applause continued from the car radio speaker. Ken looked through the windshield — surprised by what he saw: Three Wise Men bearing gifts. A few Shepherds. Two cows and a donkey. All motionless. Surrounding them. Staring into the car.

There was hay on the ground all around the crashed Jetta. The car itself was sheltered from the storm that swirled outside. They had come to a stop in the middle of a manger. Where their child was born.

Ken realized all the Wise Men and Shepherds were statues, housed in a makeshift Nativity scene. It was on the lawn of a church barely seen through the blizzard. Mary and Joseph were knocked over like bowling pins and the lambs were all scattered in between.

The sound of applause kept pouring from the car speakers. Ken wrapped his arms like wings around his wife and son to keep them warm.

"What shall we name him?" Holly asked with the baby nursing on her uncovered bosom.

"Christian," Ken whispered, half-heard above the howl of the wind against the windows outside.

And Christian it was.

About The Author

When not on the road with a traveling circus,
Michael Paul Girard lives in Los Angeles
where he sometimes finds work as a
filmmaker and composer. His films include
Operation Dalmatian, The Perfect Gift, Getting Lucky,
and the cult classic
Oversexed Rugsuckers From Mars.

www.michaelpaulgirard.com